WAS I EVER HERE

NAOMI LOUD

FIRST EDITION

Cover Design: Mallory Parsons (TikTok: @mal_reads)

Editing: Louise Johnson, Literary Maiden Editing

www.naomiloud.com

CONTENT WARNING

This is a dark romance and may contain triggering situations such as active suicidal ideation (this is a major theme), mentions of a suicide attempt, mentions of self-harm, the concept of death and dying, stalking, graphic violence, graphic murder, depression and anxiety, near-death situations, grief, alcohol & drug abuse and explicit sexual situations for 18+. There are also particular kinks such as degradation and praise.

To my sister,
Because without you I wouldn't be here.
And for those who once wished the same,
I'm so happy you're still here too...

PROLOGUE

Byzantine

Blood.

So much of it. It gurgles deep inside my throat as I rasp in a struggling breath. It seeps into my shirt, sticking sickly to my chest while I lay limp against the wall. I can't tell where the bleeding is coming from against the slow delirium of my body dying. I hear screaming.

Close, yet so far.

Like sounds traveling through water. Where are the voices coming from? Hot breaths yelling close to my face, my ear, my cheek. Harried hands cupping my blood into their palms, holding it like a chalice to my body, believing it could somehow protect me from slipping away.

The hands. Are they mine? No. Mine are laying limply on either side of me, a distant weight, feeling barely attached to my body. But they're there. Must be someone else's then. But I can't tell who.

Nor does it matter.

Not when I can hardly make out my own existence from the person trying to cradle me into their arms. Or are they laying me down? I cough, choking on the blood trickling into the back of my throat. My lips part on a breath. Am I trying to speak? My eyes are heavy-lidded, unfocused. With every slow dragging blink I take, the darkness calls to me.

Maybe I should just keep them closed. I can't remember why I'm even fighting this.

Or am I even trying?

My body shakes as if someone is trying to wake me up. But I'm not sleeping—don't they get that? The voice screams a name—my name—but I'm in far too deep now. The sound barely travels to the depth where I've sunk. Visions—or memories, I can't tell—dance behind my eyelids but I can't discern what I'm seeing.

There's another voice here...drifting through my consciousness, I can hear them cry, hear them scream. "Don't do this to me. Don't leave me here. You promised. You fucking promised me..." the voice pleads. My confusion muddles my senses even further when I realize it's happening inside my head, like a faint echo.

But my focus is waning, drifting and straining on yet another sensation.

Of being pulled out of my body.

Disembodied.

Is this how it feels to die? I slip further into the distance. Such a strange feeling, like sinking and being lifted up simultaneously. Floating. Up and up and up. I can no longer fight the current. I'm too tired anyway. Finally, I take one last tender breath and let go. I let go of the tether keeping me tied to my wasting body as the void envelops me.

At long last.

"Don't touch me!" Gabriel seethed through clenched teeth.

The blond curls of his hair fell over his hazel eyes as he stood up from the table, nearly knocking the whole thing over, garnering curious looks from the patrons around us.

"Gabriel, sit back down. You're making a scene," I replied, my stern tone having no effect on his dramatic outburst.

To any onlooker we were merely business partners having a spat. And that was exactly why he resented me. We had met during the gold rush down in Sacramento Valley and a friendship had bloomed easily between us.

But now...we were so much more than just partners.

He was my best kept secret. And I was his.

Although he wished I was not.

Gabriel's love for me was all encompassing. So bright. Although, like the sun, I couldn't bear to look straight into the light from fear of going blind.

I loved him, I truly did. But I was a coward, and I was hurting what I held dearest. I was watching him wilt like a flower ripped from the roots.

He was breathtaking, and he was all mine. And yet, I had made him what he was today. I couldn't blame his anger. Even his anguish. I could never.

He reached over and swiped the bottle of gin from the table and took a large swig.

"Don't you dare follow me out Anthony," he hissed, promptly turning on his heels and stomping out.

I sat on the wooden bench for a little while longer trying to give him the distance he needed. I finished my ale, the bread and cheese on the table half-eaten and discarded.

But I would never truly let him walk away. I could never let him go.

Finally, when enough time had passed, I rose from the chair, smoothed out my frock coat and left through the front door.

It had rained that morning and the roads were muddy as I looked up to the gray skies, wet spongy clouds still threatening to release another torrent of water on our heads.

The inn we were staying at bordered a small coastal village, the air humid and salty from the rough seas nearby. My eyes roved the countryside trying to find Gabriel. He mustn't have gone very far. Then I found him. Trekking his way towards the large cliff in the distance.

He'd always been drawn to the water but in this instance, my heart squeezed, hoping he wasn't as reckless as I thought him to be. Hastily, I followed behind him. At a safe distance, of course, as to make him believe I had honored his earlier request.

He pushed through the small copse of trees at the bottom of the hill, his body swaying from the alcohol as he took large gulps from the gin bottle. The branches snagged on his trousers but he didn't seem to care.

Up ahead, the cliff was so high it seemed perched on the heavy clouds surrounding it. And Gabriel was heading straight for it.

I began to worry.

Surely he wouldn't be so foolish.

Then, he stopped mid-track, seemingly entranced. His shoulders began to shake and although he was facing away from me, I knew then he was crying. I yearned to reach him and pull him into my embrace. To never let him go and lick the tears off his beautiful face.

But I kept my distance. I knew he'd blame me for those very tears. But I couldn't resist following him. As always. My aching need to take care of him even when I was the cause of his pain.

Finally, with the bottle still held limply in his hand, Gabriel started up the slanting muddy hill, panting. I hurried along my shoes sinking in the muddy tracks with every step I took. He reached the cliff and I was now close behind. I didn't bother to hide my presence any longer. There was nowhere to escape but back towards me.

He stalked towards the edge of the cliff and my heart leapt into my throat. I couldn't guess his intention and with his inebriation I could no longer trust his actions.

I watched as Gabriel stared down at his boots for the briefest of moments and then leaned down and haggardly tugged them off his feet. One foot and then the other. He threw them over the cliff and into the water with a small grunt. He closed his eyes, digging his toes into the muddy earth, and raised the bottle to his mouth. I could almost taste the salty mist on his parted lips.

Gabriel grew suddenly still as he peered over the edge. The hairs on my arms rose and I could no longer stay quiet as a sudden fear burrowed into my chest.

"Gabriel!" I yelled, trying to keep my voice steady so as not to alarm him.

He swiveled around at the sound of my voice, finding me standing there behind him, his hazel eyes glassy and bloodshot.

"I told you not to follow me Anthony," he muttered, his voice trembling and the pain I found in his gaze was suddenly unbearable.

"My love. You've proven your point. Please step away from the edge. Come back to the room with me," I pleaded.

"Don't call me that," he said, choking through sobs. "What is the point of this love if it is only to leave me so hollow? I am nothing without your love but I am also nothing with it. Can't you see?"

"Forgive me Gabriel. Just please. Take my hand. Come down from there. Don't you understand? I am nothing without you either. Who am I without you? You are the very breath in my lungs."

I was still a few steps away, my hand reaching for his when a large gust of wind blew through. I watched on in horror as his body swayed backwards, knocked off balance from the gin in his blood. His eyes went wide, taking an unexpected step back, grasping at the air in vain.

But it was too late.

My name slipped through his lips in dismay, "Anthony?"

It happened all so fast. Time slipped through my hands as I watched him topple over.

"Gabriel!" I screamed as I ran to the edge.

No. No. No.

This wasn't happening. Not my Gabriel. My life.

I peered over, terrified. Beyond terrified. There was no one word able to describe the agony I felt.

I bellowed his name once more, watching his body bounce off the jutting rocks and into the crashing waves.

But this time I knew speaking his name was pointless. He was gone. Swallowed up by the water.

And I had done nothing but watch him die.

"Byzantine?"

My eyes shutter open, peering over to the voice coming from the corner of the room. The man sitting in the chair scoots to the edge, relief written all over his face. His straight black hair hangs disheveled over the shaved sides, his tattooed hand swiping over his tight square jaw, black eyes creased with worry despite the relief.

I blink once. And then again. I know him. His presence is familiar but my brain is slow in coughing up the important pieces of his identity.

Instead, my thoughts are full of Gabriel. His name still a whisper on my parched tongue. The memory of his death still so fresh at the edge of my mind.

What the fuck is going on?

These recollections feel like prayers, spoken in tongues only my soul can recognize. Faces from long ago—lifetimes even—flash in my head in quick succession. So many faces. So many names. But somehow...they all belong to the same soul.

Why is this so confusing?

What the hell am I doing back here?

I was far away from here only moments ago. At least that's how it feels. But now, nothing is making sense.

I squeeze my eyelids shut, my chest hurting, while I try to sort out my current reality. All these memories are baffling but they *feel* real. As real as the face staring down at me when I find his gaze again.

He paces near the foot of the hospital bed, then stops, fingers curled in tight fists, staring at me. "Can you hear me, brother? It's me, Connor."

Connor? I latch on to the sound of his voice. It anchors me while everything else in my head is making me feel fucking crazy. His name brings back hazy impressions of our friendship and years spent working side by side.

I steady my breath and realize in sudden clarity how much it burns to fill up my lungs. I try to swallow through the pain and nearly choke on the agony. My lips part to speak, but Connor cuts me off. "The doctors say you shouldn't try speaking, your wound is too fresh. You've been out for a few days..."

Wound? I lick my chapped lips, hardly able to swivel my head towards him. I cough but it comes out more like a throaty whine. I pull my trembling hand up to my neck, feeling the thick gauze tight around my throat. Questions lodged in my unsteady gaze.

"Your throat was slit," Connor explains, turning away from the bed, looking ready to punch through the hospital wall, his body wound tight. "It was Davis. The piece of shit ran with the money from the job, leaving you to die...you were near unconscious when I found you. You bled out in my hands Byzantine..." Connor trails off, glaring down like he can still see my blood painting his palms red. I hear the fear in the lilt of his words although he tries to hide it. All the while, I struggle to process what the hell happened to me. "You fucking *died* in my arms," he adds, his icy stare holding back the pain he seems unwilling to speak out loud.

I'm trying to keep my expression blank but his words are digging into me like a shovel into soft dirt. They're threatening to uncover a memory I'm not prepared to face.

Of how I looked death in the face and said *show me*.

Show me what I have forgotten. Show me what I've unknowingly been searching for all these years.

"I don't know how you survived. The doctors had to jumpstart your heart. You were fucking *gone*."

I'm overwhelmed. I can't make out one thing from the other, his voice grating at my senses. Like a tidal wave, memories, faces and places continue to pound over me and I can't catch my breath.

I fucking died?

Chapter 1

SUNNY

Five years later

I wake up crying. Gasping. Hand to my neck, my throat convulsing like I was suffocating only moments before. My body's drenched in sweat, wavy hair matted down my back, the loose shirt I wore to bed sticking to my rising chest. The sheets are tangled around my legs, and I wrestle with them in haste, kicking them off my heated body. I sit up, still heaving, my head resting heavily in my palms.

That damn dream again.

I was near the roaring sea. On the edge of a cliff so high I could hardly see the water below. I remember the wind whipping into my eyes, angry and cold.

But oddly, it also felt very still. A dream on mute.

My fingers drag down my face, my thumb finding my mouth, gnawing at a loose thumbnail. I can taste the cheap black nail polish chipping off on my tongue.

My heart is still beating too fast, my eyes shifty and erratic, struggling to focus. I'm desperate to mend the broken pieces of the dream I just flailed out of.

Was I alone?

The vision is quickly evaporating like mist in my hand the more I dig. But what I still remember perfectly is the ocean whispering my name. A melodic murmur with every crashing wave.

Why did it all feel so familiar?

If I allow the feeling I'm suppressing to rise to the surface it felt more like a memory than just a dream. A déjà vu from long, long ago. The near desperate squeeze behind my rib cage seems to agree with me. As if a piece of myself was stitched back up and given back to me.

I glance at the time on my phone. It's still early morning. I pull the covers back over my shoulders and roll onto my side, staring at the wall in an unfocused gaze. I continue to scratch at the edge of my memories, needing to recollect every detail.

But why? Why does it feel urgent to do so? I must be delirious if I think I'll discover this magical, life-changing answer to why my life feels so fucked up. Yeah...that will be the day.

Suddenly, I suck in a breath, my heart dropping into my stomach.

There was someone else there.

Or more like the sensation of someone. An off-focused presence near me. My body chose that precise moment to convulse back to life. My skin is still pulsing with the image of it, my anxiety sitting heavy in my stomach like wet cement.

Finally, I pull myself out of bed and tug my still damp shirt over my head. The air from the open window near the bed cools my burning skin. It's the only window in this place but at least it's large and airy.

I live in a ground floor studio apartment—the only thing I can afford on my bartending wage. It faces Grand Boulevard and I often find myself sitting on the large window ledge, smoking the occasional joint, lost in thought. I'm not allowed to paint over the off-white walls so I've covered most of the surfaces with tapestries or colorful pictures ripped out of magazines. It's small but cozy.

I stagger down the short hall to the bathroom. My shoulder bouncing off the wall, trying to find my balance. Maybe a shower will help. The dream has left my senses with a feeling close to a hangover.

In the bathroom, I lean over the small sink to stare at my reflection. I peer at my own face like I'm studying a stranger. Long auburn hair, freckles spattered across my upturned nose, my skin white but sun-kissed, hazel almond eyes, my cheeks a little hollow.

I know something isn't right with me. And I hate it. But I can't seem to control it. I'm untethered. This recurring dream always seems to worsen the feeling. Every time, it rockets me back into consciousness, making me land in my body at an awkward angle.

Breaking out of my self-induced trance I turn on the shower, letting the steam rise before getting in. I sit down in the tub, too weak to stand any longer and close my eyes, the mist of the water washing over my face as I lean back and let out a heavy sigh.

It's not the first time I've felt this disconnected. Won't be the last. Even my life feels foreign to me sometimes. Like this too is all but a dream. A sick joke on repeat. And I wonder if I'll ever feel at home here—wherever *here* is.

For the past year it's been Noxport, California, specifically chosen for its proximity to the ocean. It's also conveniently far away from my hometown back in Vermont. It's a bustling metropolis with the beaches well-kept and beautiful—and where I spend most of my time.

But even Noxport will eventually run its course. I'll grow bored and move on. A hopeless attempt to distract myself from the widening hole in my chest for just a little while longer.

I sink even deeper into the tub, letting the water trickle down my skin, a heavy groan trapped in my lungs.

It's times like these I miss River the most. She'd know what to do. How to pull me out of the depth that I can't ever seem to escape.

In a final attempt to recenter myself, I focus on how the spray feels on my body, like raindrops on the skin. It's not helping much but at least it's preventing me from slipping further into the nothingness of not feeling.

Even now, I'm an outsider looking in, often feeling like I'm locked outside of my own body. A sob ripples through me as salty tears mix with the water trailing down my face.

Fuck. I feel...homesick?

Maybe.

But ironically, I haven't had a home worth the feeling in a long time. If ever. Still, I feel lost. Like a ghost haunting the walls of my own body.

Unwilling to look at my confusing emotions for even a second longer, I force myself to snap out of it and stand up, turning off the shower.

I need a fucking distraction.

And by the time I wrap a towel around my body I know exactly where to find it.

Chapter 2

Sunny

I eye-fuck Hunter from across the bar while he plays indie rock covers for the crowd, preening on stage. It's a small unimpressive platform, the type you find in every Irish bar designed with cover bands in mind. Still, it's a stage and I can't look away.

In the past month, he's become my favorite pastime. It's becoming a *thing*, this game between him and I. And oftentimes between sets, he comes and leans next to me at the bar. While I pretend to be casual—cool.

We flirt, clinking our shot glasses together, lust dripping like honey from our lips. A shot of whiskey as foreplay. A promise of more.

And something about the look in his blue eyes tonight tells me he's finally ready to take the dive. I can sense it in the air, like an electric charge rippling across the empty space between us.

When he finishes his final set, he saunters over and orders a beer next to me, his leg brushing against mine. His thin lips pull into a smirk while looking at me sideways, dirty blond curls falling on his forehead. The lights are low. The candles lined all around the bar are the only real source of light in this place, creating shadows along his features. I play coy, pretending like I can't see how his gaze is telling me he's dying to fuck me.

After a few more shots elbow to elbow, he leans even closer and stares straight into my eyes.

"Do you like me?"

I laugh. Cute. Bashful. "Maybe," I reply simply.

He grins at me, his smile now a devious curl of his lip that makes my mouth water in anticipation. "Wanna follow me?"

I lick my lips and swallow hard, my heart skipping a beat inside my chest. *Fuck, this is it.*

"Lead the way," I say, my tone laced with seduction.

The excitement rises quickly through my chest and into my lungs as he takes my hand in his. I follow him down into the musty pub basement, leading me through a small, winding corridor lined high with kegs and empty cardboard boxes on either side. It's a tight fit, but we squeeze through like two crooks in the night, high on the very act of sneaking around.

When we reach the bathroom he was leading us too, I slip in, followed by Hunter locking the door behind us.

God, I crave this. Always have.

The thrill of the chase, men or women—I don't care—as long as it leaves me high and sated.

I'm addicted to the crackling static before the first kiss. The first touch of our parting lips. Where lust and fantasy meets reality like a moth to a flame.

Hunter hastily takes my shirt off before our lips even touch, his fingers traveling up my waist and then down to my hips. He lifts me up and sits me on the sink behind me.

I lean over and catch his lips with my own. His mouth parts open for my hungry tongue as I hurriedly unbutton his shirt. I'll yield under his hands as long as he continues to touch me.

He pulls away then, lips wet and wanting. With a jerk he brings me back down on my feet and flips me over to bend me over the sink. I hear the sound of his zipper as he pulls my leggings and thong down my legs. The tell-tale crinkle of a condom foil triggers a low kind of adrenaline to course through my body.

"You ready for me, baby?" he asks, and with barely a graze of his fingers to see if I *am* ready, he unceremoniously pushes into me. I gasp as he growls, kneading my ass with his hands. My cheek presses against the mirror, my breath staining the glass with his every thrust.

"Fuck you feel so good. You like that?" he groans.

I swallow hard and roll my eyes but don't answer. The anticipation is gone and now I feel...nothing.

I half-heartedly let out a small moan so as not to bruise his fragile ego. But he's clearly unbothered, continuing to grunt behind me, the fantasy of him that I've so eagerly perfected evaporating with every throaty sound.

Now I'm just *bored*. So—while he pounds into me—I take stock of my surroundings.

A dirty bathroom in an even dirtier bar. The once white wall tiles now grimy and cracked. A single lightbulb buzzing above us. I hate to admit it but this is definitely *not* the first time I've been bent over a dirty bathroom sink.

I feel myself drift while his hips slap against my ass, almost like I'm watching myself get railed from above. Having half a mind not to dissociate completely, I focus my attention on Hunter through the mirror instead. A lone curly lock of hair bounces up and down on his forehead as he slaps my ass and I pretend to like it.

I roll my eyes again. Does he think I'm into it? Why did I even like this guy in the first place?

No reason really.

He isn't even particularly attractive except for his blue eyes. And I'm pretty sure he's shorter than my 5'11". But anytime he's on stage, I romanticize everything about him and become mesmerized.

I'm such an idiot. It was all part of the fantasy though wasn't it? But this, *this* is real life. Shitty fucks to make the time go by. But I'm addicted to every part of the thrill except the actual sex itself.

When he finally comes with a throaty sigh, I'm just glad it's over. Glad I don't have to touch or look at him ever again.

As soon as he pulls his limp dick out, I quickly tug my leggings back up, fling my shirt over my chest and run out the door before he can catch his breath.

When I reach the top floor, I squeeze myself through the crowd hoping no one can pick up the scent of the mediocre sex I just had. By the time I stumble outside, I'm already actively trying to forget this whole hook-up ever even happened.

I walk home under the drizzle of a rainy night sky, attempting to escape my gloomy thoughts with every soggy step I take.

I can't do this anymore. I'm so sick of this. My twenties are chock full of one-night stands I can barely remember. And for what? For once in a while orgasms and empty promises? Now that I'm twenty-seven, it's getting real old, real fast.

"Aren't you tired of this?" River's voice echoes in my ear, so clear it feels like she's standing right next to me. I squeeze my eyes shut trying to chase away the gnawing feelings her words evoke and remind myself I'm alone. It's only a figment of my imagination.

It's not real. She isn't here.

When I arrive home, I fling myself into the shower, barely removing my clothes in time before the hot water scolds my skin. I scrub myself clean from Hunter's touch, the monumental let down of tonight only heightening the shame of what I just did.

When I finally crawl into bed, my eyes droop immediately, the alcohol still coursing through my veins wrapping itself nice and warm around me, lulling me into what is thankfully a dreamless sleep.

"I fucked that guitarist last night," I admit reluctantly.

Lenix rolls over on her beach towel, her golden brown skin glimmering with suntan oil, and almost launches herself at me. "You did not!" she squawks, her face fixed into a half shocked and half curious expression. "Spill, right this second," she says, poking me in the shoulder.

The public beach is crowded this time of day and the couple camped out beside us glances curiously our way while Lenix makes an unnecessary raucous.

I lay my arm over my face and groan into my elbow. "Be quiet, will you?" I whine. Why did I even bring it up? I would rather forget that I've even added Hunter to my body count. "It was...disappointing, to say the least," I finally say, hiding behind my sunglasses trying to evade Lenix's inquisitive stare.

"Let me guess," she says, playfully tapping her finger on her chin, lips in a pout seemingly deep in thought. "You made him into something he wasn't and you were crushed when he didn't meet the romanticized version of himself you spent weeks perfecting?"

Ouch.

"I wouldn't say crushed..." I grumble.

"Classic Sunny," she replies, giving me a small patronizing pat on the thigh.

"Wow. I really hate you, did you know that?" I say, glaring back at her, raising myself on my elbows to better give her the stink eye.

Lenix snickers and sends me a kiss with her glossy lips. "It's actually the exact reason why you love me babes," she answers as she finds the bottle of suntan oil and gives herself another generous lather, her black hair almost blue under the sun's rays.

Lenix is one of the first friends I made when I moved to Noxport over a year ago. We both work at Sammies, me as a bartender and her as a waitress.

Our relationship might have started as a flirty fling but it didn't take us long to realize we were better off as friends. Minus the benefits.

Besides, she is notoriously single and avoids commitment like the plague. We have that in common unfortunately.

Our past history has created a comfortable intimacy between us and she's become the most important person in my life and the only one I trust in Noxport—or anywhere else really.

"So, are we going to have to find a new bar to drink at now that you'll start avoiding yet another lackluster hookup?" she teases, smirking at me and I resist the urge to pinch her.

I hate how she knows me so well.

I roll my eyes. "I mean...maybe just for a few months. What's the big deal?" I mumble, yet smiling at how ridiculous I sound and Lenix laughs, settling on her back, her knees raised up.

The afternoon sun is beating hard on us as I lay back down, sweat trickling down my stomach. I consider going in for a dip but lack the energy and decide to continue getting roasted by the rays like a heat-seeking lizard instead.

We fall silent after a while, taking in the relaxing afternoon until I feel my phone vibrate near my shoulder. I turn my head to take a peek at who's bothering to text me.

"Gary just texted me," I sigh dramatically.

"What does he want?"

"He needs me to cover for Julie tonight." I lay back down with a huff, my mood souring, having planned to do absolutely nothing this evening.

"I mean, you don't need to say yes. You can just say you're busy," she adds.

"I know...but I need the money anyway."

"Plus—" Lenix reaches over, her eyes still closed behind her giant sunglasses and squeezes my arm. "You'll be working with yours truly."

"Thank god for that," I say. She's the only reason I haven't quit yet. I've been sick of Gary's shit for months now. He doesn't know how to run a bar to save his life. "That place is such a shitshow."

Lenix sits up, her nose slightly pink from the sun and pulls her sunglasses up on her head, revealing her deep brown eyes.

"I don't know, I kind of like the chaos," she says with a mischievous smile tugging at her lips.

I laugh. "I know you do."

Lenix starts to gather her stuff and stands up, pulling her summer dress over her light pink bikini.

"Come on, let's go then. We can get ready at my place and have a few sneaky drinks before our shift later tonight," she says as she brandishes her hand for me to take. I place my hand in hers and she pulls me to my feet.

After stuffing our beach bags in the trunk, we climb into Lenix's car. Pop music blares through the speakers as she drives us to her place while I mentally prepare for yet another boring night at Sammies.

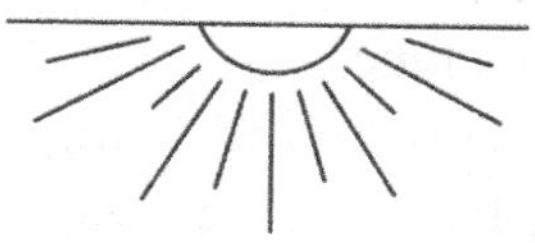

Chapter 3

Byzantine

"And then I came so hard, I forgot my own name, I swear to god!" Connor barks out a laugh and takes a sip of his beer, raking a hand through his slicked back hair. We're hanging by the pool at his place like usual, sprawled on the long chairs, my eyes squinting behind my shades against the sun.

I don't even bother acknowledging what he says. He's been giving me a play by play of his night—against my will—for the last twenty fucking minutes. And I'd rather tear my own fingernails off than to listen to any more of it.

"You finished?" I ask.

"Oh, I definitely finished," he replies, giving me one of his quintessential cocky looks before laying back down in his chair, pleased with himself.

"You're so boring to talk to sometimes," he complains.

"Maybe you just tell boring stories," I retort, running my hand over my shaved head and then taking a long swig of my beer.

"Fucker," he mutters. "Remind me why I keep you around?"

He flashes a smile and I grin back at him. Our banter is cut short when Bastian storms out from the kitchen with a victorious look on his face.

"We got him!" he says, brandishing a stack of crumpled papers in his hand, heading our way. "I finally found the motherfucker."

Bastian doesn't need to elaborate who the motherfucker in question is—I know it's Davis. The traitor who slashed my throat and left me to die in a dark alley. The scar on my neck itches with the promise of revenge at the thought. We've been looking for the fucker for the past five years, nothing but cold leads and empty results leaving us hungry for retribution. Especially me.

I spent weeks in the hospital after the assault, learning to reuse my vocal cords, nerves so damaged it made my smile permanently lop-sided. Days spent trying to speak, when I couldn't even find the words to explain my near-death experience even if I wanted to. I was left uncomfortable in my own skin. My body feeling almost too heavy, awkward even, after the weightlessness of what I had undergone.

And what about Gabriel? How could I make sense of the visceral knowledge that I had been Anthony in another life and in love?

And it didn't end there. I had seen a multitude of faces—and lovers. Deaths. Secrets. Love. An innumerable amount of lives. Different bodies. Different genders, personalities. But always the same soul.

It was so vivid when I first woke up and still is now five years later, the feelings lingering like a nostalgic perfume.

I never told anyone, even Connor, but it didn't stop me from wondering. The question with no answer.

Was I destined to find them in this lifetime?

Him? Her?

Considering my current sexual orientation, I was hoping for the latter.

Hell I didn't fucking know.

It's not as if I had instructions given to me when I came back from the dead. I've been trying to make sense of it ever since. When I was finally released from the hospital I even bought a book about reincarnation.

I must have looked so out of place in the small crystal shop, grunting about past lives and looking like a thug with my scowl, scars, and tattoos. I got the fuck out of there as soon as the clerk handed me back my change. Half embarrassed, and the other half secretly hoping I could finally find some goddamn answers.

I didn't.

Not for the questions I had anyway. All this metaphysical bullshit was confusing. All I knew is what I had seen and what my gut was telling me.

Bastian's voice pulls me back from my drifting thoughts. "He did a fine fucking job erasing his identity, I'll give him that much. But he's not as good as me," he boasts, rare for him, his eyes twinkling. "Goes by Gary now."

"Gary?" I repeat, pinching my lips as if the name tastes as foul as the man himself.

"Yeah," Bastian continues, looking smug. "He made one crucial mistake though. He came back to Noxport. Owns a hole in the wall near the water now."

Connor sits up from the long chair, his muscles corded with anger. "The fucking rat was dead the second his fat fucking toe crossed the city limits," he growls, his lip curling in disgust while he looks over to me, his eyes almost as black as his hair. "So what's the plan?"

He wouldn't typically give me free reign on something like this. But this is different. It's personal.

He inherited The Sin Eaters when his father was gunned down near the docks while brokering a drug deal worth millions. Connor was only twenty-one at the time, but he stepped up fearlessly. Eleven years later, he's become one the most respected drug and arms dealers on the west coast. I've been his second-in-command for as long as I can remember, primarily responsible for laundering money through the bars and clubs we own around Noxport.

Bastian is Connor's cousin and our resident hacker. The family resemblance runs deep between the two, both having broad shoulders, dark features, square jaws and roman noses. However, Bastian keeps his hair bleached almost white, a stark contrast to his black eyebrows and dark eyes. And as loud and boisterous Connor is, Bastian is quiet and observant. They're more family than my own blood.

I look over to my brother-in-arms, a thirst in my throat that won't be quenched until I get my hands on *Gary.* I run my hand over my throat, the scar still thick and raised even after five years. I've considered covering it up with a tattoo but something always stops me. Maybe it's the subconscious need to keep the reminder of why I'm still here.

"I want to make him bleed," I sneer, baring my teeth.

A sadistic smile creeps across Connor's face. If I didn't know him my whole life, his way of slipping from casual jokester to ruthless killer would unnerve me. But I smile back instead, knowing exactly what he's thinking behind his cruel stare. And I am right there with him.

"I think it's about time we gave dear ol' Gary a visit, don't you think?" he says.

"I think you're right," I respond, standing up, my muscles buzzing for what's to come. "Our reunion is long overdue."

Chapter 4

Sunny

I walk into Sammies from the back door with Lenix following right behind. I'm greeted by the same odor as yesterday. And the day before that...and the day before that. A mixture of sweat and yeasty stale beer that wafts up from the decades old carpet lining the front of house.

Sammies is a run-down pub close to Old Town. It's a popular hangout for the locals but far from a tourist attraction. The proximity to the water makes the rats fat and not the least bit shy. They mostly come out after hours when the bar is quiet, staying close to the dumpsters and making me yelp anytime I catch one sprinting across the kitchen floor.

I inhale deeply—despite the smell—and swallow my rising anxiety back down into the pit of my stomach where it belongs. I don't exactly hate my job, it's more like a general dislike of my entire existence. A low throb that follows me around anywhere I go. I never want to be here—wherever here is—at any given moment.

We cut through the kitchen, waving a quick hi to the cooks. Stifling a yawn, I push my way into the employee room.

The thought of pouring pints for the next eight hours is making my stomach lurch but I change into my work shirt anyway, pulling my shorts over my tired legs. The leftover shame from last night still coursing through my veins, I internally wince at the memory of Hunter grunting into me. Steadying my shaky hands, I gather my hair into a loose top bun.

"I'm like, already over it and I haven't even started," I whine.

"Such a gloomy baby," Lenix teases, winking at me before she pulls her shirt over her head, her pink lacy bra on full display.

I roll my eyes. "You know I hate it when you call me that," I shoot back.

"It's funny 'cause it's true," she says, chuckling through her shirt.

I do a final check of my outfit in the dirty staff room mirror, then lean on one of the lockers as I wait for Lenix to change into her work shoes. Then, begrudgingly, we head for the door and clock in.

I'm cleaning the bar with a dirty rag when I hear the bell over the door clang. We're only minutes away from closing and I stifle a groan from the thought of pouring another pint for *another* lousy tip.

I'm the last one here aside from Gary hiding somewhere in his office, and I'm itching to clock out. I huff out a long exhale and mentally prepare myself for the night to drag on even longer. I look up, trying my hardest to slap on my best fake customer service smile but it quickly falters when I see three guys standing near the door.

An ominous chill snakes down my spine as my eyes skip to the one stepping closer to me, his black hair slicked back, his dark eyes staring straight at me. My smile might have been fake but his is eery, mischievous even, as if he's in on a joke that I'm not privy to.

I somehow manage to rip my stare away from him and survey the other two behind him. One has bleached blond hair and a bored look on his face. The other has shaved brown hair, his eyes on his waist, busy unclipping his gun from his holster in slow, deliberate movements.

Terror freezes me to the spot, the rag I'm holding falling with a splat at my feet. Suddenly, I do the first thing that springs to mind—I duck behind the bar, a feeble attempt to protect myself from the danger buzzing in the room.

The silence is deafening, when I hear footsteps coming from the back.

"Have you started cleaning yet? I want to lock up soon," Gary asks, popping out of the hallway near the bar area. His eyes are fixed on his phone, but his steps falter when he sees me cowering near the sink. "Sunny, what are you doing ther—" A menacing laugh pierces the room, making Gary stop short.

"Hello *Gary*, long time no see."

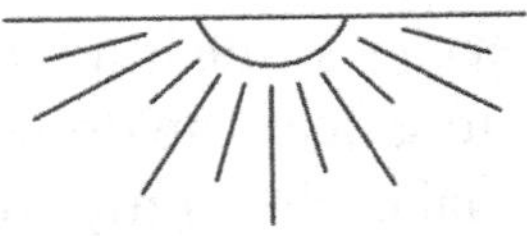

Chapter 5

Byzantine

It takes Davis—Gary now—only a second to register who's in the bar. He locks eyes with Connor first and blanches, his phone clutched tightly in his hands. There's a slight tremor to his lips as he stares at him, then Bastian and finally, me. When his gaze lands on the scar on my neck, he turns a sick shade of gray. I can't help but smile.

Surprise, motherfucker.

How does it feel to know you're about to die?

"I...I...can explain."

Gary chokes on his words, sounding as befuddled as he looks. An idiot frozen in place. Shifty eyes swiveling left and right.

I let out a dry laugh as I stalk towards him, pulling my gun from my holster and shoving the cold barrel under his chin. Gary chokes out a shriek but says nothing more.

He's dumber than I remember if he thinks he can explain how he *happened* to slit my throat while out on a job together. The shitstain thought he could just take the money and disappear.

I came back from the dead so I could send him in my place instead. Looming over him, I dig my gun even deeper into his jaw.

"Now listen to me carefully, *Gary*," I spit his stupid name out like venom. "Let's make one thing very clear. Your death is *mine* and it won't be quick. I'll make you suffer for what you did to me. Maybe torture you for a day or two. Who knows? I haven't decided yet. The inspiration will come to me—I'm sure. So now you have two options. You either be a good little boy," I taunt, tapping my Ruger twice on his cheek and he whimpers in response. "And walk out with Bastian right now, or I can happily drag you out by your ball sack instead. Your choice."

The fear in Gary's eyes is almost laughable, he sputters to answer, knowing that death is his only option tonight.

"I—I'll go. I'll go," he finally stutters out.

"Good choice," I reply, giving my gun a final shove before dropping it to my side, the pungent scent of ammonia filling the room. I take a step back from Gary's petrified body and cover my nose, realizing he just pissed himself.

"Jesus fucking Christ, Gary, have some fucking decorum," Connor says as he gestures to Bastian to drag him out into the SUV waiting outside. "We have a lady present after all."

An almost inaudible gasp finally tears my attention from Gary but I see no one until Connor leans over the bar and drags a girl up by her arm. She doesn't fight him, only clasping her trembling hands over her mouth.

Her eyes swivel around the bar until they slam into mine.

Suddenly, time slows down, then speeds back up.

I take a step back, feeling like I've been knocked off my feet. I swallow hard, unable to move. I'm transfixed as she continues to stare at me, her hand still firmly covering her mouth. I can't tear my gaze away from hers.

Her eyes. Hazel brown and terrified.

This can't be fucking happening. This can't be...*her*. The one whose possible existence has been haunting me for the past five fucking years.

I can hear Gary's feet drag against the carpeted floor as Bastian pushes him out the door, but I still can't move.

I can't fucking *move*.

"Brother, the fuck are you doing just standing there?" Connor asks.

I look back at him, back at her, then back at Connor again. He must see the shock slapped across my face because he cocks his eyebrow with a questioning look. But says nothing, jerking his head towards the door instead.

I desperately try to swallow the words back down, but the question tumbles out of me before I can stop it. "What about the girl?"

Shit. Shit. Shit.

Connor's cruel smile slithers into place. "The girl?" he drawls, a low cackle leaving his lips that would make my skin crawl if I wasn't so used to hearing it.

"Oh, she's going to keep her pretty little mouth shut if she knows what's good for her," he says mockingly.

She flinches when he steps towards the bar. Something buried deep inside me cracks as I watch the fear seep out of her pores. Connor stops and cocks his head.

"Isn't that right, *Sunny*?"

Sunny? How does he know her name?

Her eyes are wide as she stares at him, her body now trembling uncontrollably. But she doesn't answer.

"It's Sunny, isn't it? That's what our dear friend Gary called you when he walked in," he says.

Oh. Right.

I can tell his patience is dwindling so I clear my throat. Sunny jerks, the sound knocking her out of her stunned daze. Her eyes lock with mine for a split second before shifting quickly back to Connor.

My heart lurches out of my chest. The *fuck* is happening to me? I will myself not to step towards her while I ignore the tethered string wrapped around my ribcage pulling me to her. I ball my hands into tight fists, fighting the urge to protect her. Even if the current threat is my oldest friend. All I want is to touch her.

Just once.

Just to confirm I'm not hallucinating her standing there after all this time.

She clears her throat and finally speaks with a soft quivering voice,"Y—yes, my name is Sunny." Her tongue darts out and quickly licks her lips, before clamping her mouth shut again.

Amused, Connor starts back towards her, with every step he takes, her breath grows more and more frantic. It's taking everything in me not to stop him.

But who am I to her but the man who just threatened to torture and kill her boss? Anger slices through my chest. This is so fucked. If it *is* her then why did she have to be witness to this?

I watch in horror as Connor now looms over her. His fucking smile still sprawled across his face. It doesn't take an expert to tell she's absolutely terrified.

"So," he starts, taking a strand of her hair that's fallen out of her bun and gently tucks it behind her ear before grazing her cheek with the back of his fingers. He then grabs her face and jerks it up towards him, his fingers hollowing out her pale cheeks.

I'm aching to do something. *Anything*. But I try my best to ignore it and gulp down the anger, crossing my arms over my chest just so I have something to do other than pounce on Connor. He needs to get his fucking hands off her before I do something I regret.

Because this is batshit crazy, right? Sunny doesn't even know who I am. And am I absolutely certain I even know who she is to me? Deep down I know though. I just fucking know. How can I forget those eyes when I've been searching for them for the past five years? How can I forget when I've stared back at those same eyes for lifetimes now?

This is insane. *I'm* fucking insane.

I try to snap out of it as I hear Connor prattle on.

"Like I said before, *Sunny*, you're going to keep your sweet little mouth shut, and not tell a fucking soul about what you saw here." He squeezes her cheeks harder as if to drive in his point. She lets out a small whimper, her eyes glued to his in terror.

"Do I make myself clear?" Her head strains to nod. "Good girl," he says, leaning in and giving her a quick teasing kiss on her forehead. "Because if you do say something, it will take me half a fucking second to learn who you are and where you live. And we wouldn't want that, now would we?"

She looks like she might fucking piss herself. But instead, she gives another slow nod. Connor's eyes trail down to her parted lips for half a beat before finally letting her go. Sunny staggers back, rubbing her chin but says nothing, tears welling in her rounded eyes.

"Let's get the fuck out of here," Connor orders and without a second glance he stalks to the door leaving a trembling Sunny in his wake.

I'm fighting every cell in my body not to approach her and take her into my arms. Instead, I steel my expression while her eyes travel back to mine. Her hand falls to her neck as she notices the scar around my own. She continues to stare, a sudden blaze igniting in her eyes, while I'm still rooted in place.

I can't tell if the fear in her eyes is directed at me or a lingering effect from her cozy encounter with Connor but it kills me all the same. I don't want her to fear me. But there's nothing I can say that will assuage the fact that she just witnessed her boss get dragged out of the bar, pissed-soaked and whimpering. I take a deep breath and close my eyes for half a second, trying to break the spell I'm in. Then, I look at her one final time, turn, and walk out the bar.

Chapter 6

Sunny

I close my apartment door with a soft snick. I can still feel the tremor in the tips of my cold fingers as I lock the door. And then the deadbolt just to be extra safe.

I watched the sun rise from the dirty slatted windows of Sammies while the cops interrogated me about Gary. I had to call them...how else would I explain his disappearance to the rest of the staff? Lenix especially.

They tried to access the cameras installed throughout the place, only to discover that the footage had been wiped clean. It made it that much easier to lie. What else could I say but half-truths anyway?

No, I couldn't remember their faces. No, I didn't remember any distinct features. No, I hadn't known Gary was hiding from dangerous criminals.

The last one was the truth at least. What the hell had Gary been running from for these men to find him and threaten him like that? A deep shudder wracks my shoulders.

I'm exhausted.

My body can't stop shivering and I keep getting annoyed by it like this is all an overreaction. As if I didn't just witness a man deliver cold promises of a painful death to my boss. I mean, Gary wasn't the best of dudes, but he didn't deserve to die. Not like this.

I choke out a sob, heavy tears falling over my cheeks and down my neck. I need a shower. If only to wash away the memories of last night. I slink over to my small kitchen first and grab a half empty bottle of wine from the fridge. It's not even seven in the morning but I currently don't give a fuck. I take a large swig straight from the bottle, making a left into the hallway before closing the bathroom door behind me.

I peel off my clothes and chuck them straight into the trash. I don't want a reminder of last night anywhere near me ever again. I turn on the water, the steam from the shower billowing out as I tuck the bottle of wine under my arm and climb in. I stand under the scorching water, breathing the humid air into my lungs. My head hangs limp as I watch the water spill over my body, before lying down at the bottom of the tub, the wine at my lips and my eyes closed.

While in the company of the cops, I was unwilling to let my mind wander but now, in the somewhat safety of the shower, it's hard not to. I don't want to think about the *other* thing.

I can't help but to conjure up the memory of his face. If I could have told the truth without the fear of being found and killed, I would have answered *yes*. Yes, one of the kidnappers did have a distinct feature.

The one with the shaved head. The one who looked like he'd seen a ghost when his light green eyes had finally bothered to land on me. *After* he had promised Gary a slow painful death that sounded like revenge.

My body shudders again at the thought and I let out a long sigh. He had a dapper elegance to his gait, a strange contrast to the sharp edges of his tattoos peeking out of his black hoodie and onto his hands.

His blazing stare had both made my blood boil and freeze over again. Had peeled off my skin and stitched me back up in the span of half a glance. He seemed almost desperate to speak up when his friend held my face in his hand, but said nothing instead.

Yeah. That one.

Even here under the hard spray of the water, I can remember that distinct feature clearly. A scar slashed across his neck, as if his throat had been slit—and somehow survived.

But I didn't need the scar to remember him. I'd easily make him out in a crowd—if I ever had the misfortune of coming across him again, that is.

Now that the shock has worn off, my brain has gone fuzzy. But the image of him hasn't. Even his friend, who clutched my face in his hands and spoke words so cold it froze my spine, feels hazy compared to him. No, his face haunts me, even now.

I shake away the thought, standing up and stepping out of the shower. I wrap a towel around myself, the bottle of wine tucked under my arm as I pad towards my bed. After changing into the coziest clothes I can find, I fall into the covers. My wet hair splays around me, soaking into the pillowcase.

Like I care. I polish off the wine, wrap myself tight under the covers and fall into a fitful sleep full of threats and menace.

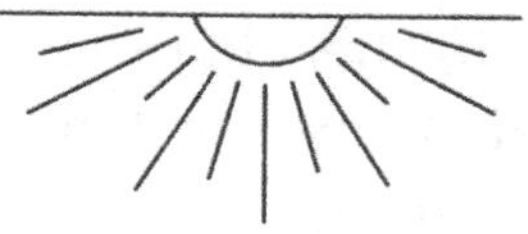

Chapter 7

Byzantine

The brass knuckles I'm wearing collide with Gary's face. He whimpers, his split lip dripping blood onto the plastic tarp, a mumble of words pouring out of his mouth, and his cheekbone most likely broken.

After dragging him out from Sammies, we brought him back to Connor's. His house—an architect's dream—sits right in the middle of one the most affluent neighborhoods in Noxport, near the water. His yacht club neighbors willfully ignorant of the less than legal business we conduct behind the thick cement walls of the basement. I own a condo downtown but I practically live here, Bastian too.

The corner of the room is draped in blue plastic while dear ol' Gary hangs from a hook in the ceiling by his bound wrists. I drag a chair across the floor and sit down facing his drooping body. He's blubbering something about forgiveness but I can barely focus. I've waited so long to exact my revenge.

But the feeling in my chest now is anti-climatic at best. I can't stop thinking about *her*.

Sunny.

I guess in an ironic way I've spent five years searching for her too. Ever since I woke up confused in a hospital bed. Not to mention the bizarre coincidence of this asshole leading me straight to her. I can't help but wonder if she recognized me like I did her. But I know she didn't. Why would she?

I had to die to remember.

But her eyes can't lie. Sunny was Gabriel once...just like I was Anthony.

She's mine—she's been mine for lifetimes.

I know, I don't make sense. Doesn't change the fact that it's true. And now I'm sitting in front of the asshole who wasn't only responsible for me nearly dying and ultimately remembering lives before this one. But he's also the fucker who led me straight to her. How could this insignificant piece of shit be such a catalyst?

Nothing makes any fucking sense.

I refuse to think about it any further. I originally wanted this little tête à tête with Gary to last a while. Torture him for as long as he could be conscious to feel. But now, I can't bear to even look at him.

Fuck it.

I stand from the wooden chair that's barely holding up my weight and head over to the small display of knives I laid out near his suspended body. I pick up the meanest looking one and stalk towards him.

There will be no last words for Gary, no final important end to his miserable fucking life. I need out of this room and out of the lingering questions attached to this worthless waste of breath. But he sees me coming and starts to whimper all over again, mangled pleading words barely exiting his mouth. I don't even let him finish.

I grab him by the hair, lift his chin up and unceremoniously slit his throat from ear to ear. The blood seeps through his shirt in seconds. I don't even bother to stay to watch him die. I just throw the knife back onto the table with a clang and walk out. My skin itches as I climb the stairs two by two.

I need a fucking drink.

Chapter 8

Sunny

It feels like I've been sleeping for days. I don't even know what time of the day it is and I don't care. I can't afford so much time off in a row but Mike, the manager at Sammies, has been gracious enough not to schedule me while I get my bearings straight. I'm going to have to face the world eventually. But for now I keep the curtains drawn closed and drink myself to sleep.

I'm burrowed deep into my duvet, my finger hovering over the saved voicemail on my phone. I've been unable to decide whether to listen to it for the past hour. Finally, I press play and settle even deeper into the pillows, closing my eyes to better listen. River's voice echoes through my small studio apartment, taking up so much space I can hardly breathe.

"Sunny, pick up! Why aren't you answering my texts? Can't believe you're making me call you. Gross. Anyway, I'm heading to Derek's with Amanda, are you coming? Of course you're coming." River's dorky laugh rises through the speakers and it hurts. It fucking hurts. "I'll see you there, okay? Love you!"

The sound of her message ending is jarring, even if this is the hundredth time I've listened to it. It never makes me feel like I hope it will. It only makes me sink deeper into the morose web of feelings I'm currently caught in. I fall back asleep hoping to see her face. But I never do.

The coffee shop is always quiet this time of day. It's why I've agreed to meet Lenix here. It's been nearly a week and I'm trying to avoid crowds for as long as possible until I'm forced back to work.

Any loud noise can set me off. It doesn't matter where I am or who I'm with. It only takes me a split second to fall back into the memories of the night that still sticks to me like cellophane. Like slipping into familiar waters. Except the water is ice cold and rips my breath right out of my chest, leaving me gasping for air.

Nothing seems to help. Well...it's not like I have many healthy coping mechanisms to begin with. I've relied mostly on weed and booze to fight off the dread that promises to latch onto my heart like a blood sucking leech.

Certainly coffee is not helping my crippling anxiety either, but here I sit nonetheless. My drink lukewarm in front of me while I stare at the sticky rings lingering on the table. I wonder if I should say something to the waiter but decide against it. I don't want to be a bother.

"Hiya babes!"

My eyes snap up to find Lenix heading my way. Her long pin straight hair is flipped over one side of her shoulders, and her big doe eyes are sparkling in the midday sun as she squeezes herself beside me into the booth. She leans in for a long hug. My body softens into her embrace while I mutter a half-ass response into her hair, inhaling her familiar vanilla scent. It grounds me back down to earth and away from the memories nipping at my heels.

She hugs me for longer than usual and I let her until she finally pulls back. Keeping a hold of my upper arms, she pushes me away so she can give me a serious once-over.

"You look like shit," she deadpans, her eyes twinkling and her dimpled smirk infuriates me but it's also exactly what I need and she knows it. I scoff, shrugging out of her hold and crossing my arms, leaning back in my seat.

"You're such a bitch." I roll my eyes while trying to conceal my smile.

Lenix just laughs and waves the waiter to our table. After ordering her usual mocha half white whatever, she turns back to me, her knees brushing against mine under the table.

Any sign of amusement falls from her face as she studies me further. I squirm under her stare and snatch my coffee off the table so I have something to hold.

"So you've heard the news?" she prompts.

"Yeah..." I answer, my voice meek.

They found Gary's body in an alley in Old Town last night. A vicious attack. That's what the media is describing it as. He was badly beaten but the cause of death was a knife wound to the neck. They have no leads.

But I know.

I nearly spiraled into a panic attack when I heard.

What if I'm next?

"What's happening to the bar now that Gary's gone?" I wonder, taking a sip of my lukewarm coffee.

"The bar was only closed for a day. I hear there's already a new owner, no one has seen them around yet though...so for now Mike is keeping everything afloat while they sign the papers or whatever," Lenix responds, carefully assessing me with her caring eyes, then finally, "Most importantly, how are you holding up?"

I just shrug my shoulders not knowing what to say. I'm not fine and we both know it. I'm sure even our waiter knows it. But denial is a safer friend than the words trying to clamber out of my cracked lips.

"Have you been eating?" she pushes, her voice laced with worry. My mouth opens with a response but she cuts me off. "And no, Sunny, I don't mean a bag of chips for dinner and some wine to wash it down." I snap my mouth closed again.

"Give me a break will you?" I whine, lowering my gaze and staring at my hands while I shred a soggy napkin between my fingers.

She sighs but says nothing. I swallow hard, knowing she's waiting for me to talk, but doesn't want to pressure me into it.

"I just don't get it..." I trail off, my voice trembling. "My mind keeps focusing on the strangest details of that night. The most mundane shit, anything other than what really happened. Like how there was a bucket full of dirty water near my feet that I needed to empty before I closed up, or how the floor smelled like lysol but was still sticky from bar grime."

I refuse to look up at Lenix but I can feel her body tense beside me as I continue, "My life feels changed somehow. As if those guys stole something from me when they dragged Gary out of the bar." I take a sip of coffee trying to make sense of my feelings. "It's like somehow I know I'll never be the same and I resent them for it. I *hate* them. But the hate is nothing compared to the fear of wondering if one day they'll decide I'm not worth the risk and come back for me."

I look up to find her eyes brimming with tears. She reaches over to squeeze my hand in hers and I let out a heavy sigh.

"You're not alone in this, babes. You know I'll always be here for you. I hope you know that. I hate seeing you this way knowing there's nothing I can really do about it. I feel helpless," she says.

I squeeze her hand back, a way to acknowledge what she just told me. Her presence soothes me but her words fall between us and into the chasm I've perfected between me and everyone else. A part of me doesn't even understand why I'm reacting so strongly to any of this. It's not as if I've ever felt safe before this. Before them.

My childhood certainly never felt safe, often neglected. I spent my most formative years berated by my mother and ignored by a passive father who spent most of his time in the basement, building model trains away from the cacophony of raising a family. Nothing I did was ever good enough for my mother, and she made sure to remind me of it daily. I've lost count of the amount of times I was sent to my room for what felt like merely existing.

At least I had River, we had each other.

But now she's gone and nothing has made sense since.

The final nail in the coffin was hearing the news about Gary. It solidified what I already knew in my heart—*I will never feel safe*.

And now I'm left with an overwhelming need to disappear so that no one can ever find me and hurt me ever again.

Whether the need to disappear is figurative or literal I don't really give a fuck. As long as I disappear.

But for now, I hold on to Lenix's hand, our interlaced fingers promising a comfort I desperately crave but can never quite reach, and hope that one day the answers will come. That one day I'll finally experience what it really means to feel secure.

We sit in silence while I try to keep the darker thoughts at bay. But they bubble up anyway. They crackle at the edge of my eyesight while I pretend not to notice. Especially the thought I try to avoid as often as possible.

That maybe, just maybe, death is the only time I'll truly feel safe.

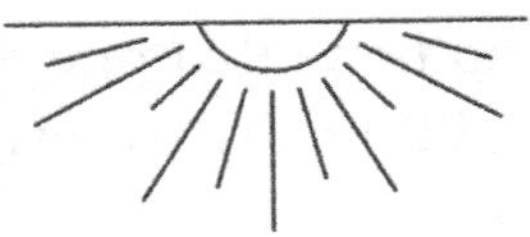

Chapter 9

Byzantine

The sun is high in the sky as I watch Sunny walk out of the coffee shop, hugging her friend goodbye. They've been meeting every other day for over a week now.

I'm sure it isn't a coincidence. Witnessing a kidnapping would rattle anybody with a conscience. Lucky for me, I lost mine a long time ago.

She turns the corner towards Turner Avenue, heading down towards Old Town. I push myself off the brick wall I was leaning on and trail behind her.

I pull my black hoodie over my head and shove my hands into the pockets, careful to stay well behind her. But does it matter? Would she even remember me even if she did catch a glimpse of me?

Does she dream of me as I do her?

Stupid. That's just stupid.

I watch her pull her tangled earphones out of her bag, not even bothering to unravel them before plugging them into her phone and popping them into her ears.

Jesus, really? Who does that?

She continues down the street, her face facing the rays of the afternoon sun while tilting her cheeks towards the sky, as if chasing the warmth. It would have looked like a serene moment if she didn't seem so haunted. Tight-lipped, eyebrows knitted, and eyes closed as she continues to walk towards the beach.

She's gonna walk into a fucking pole if she doesn't open up her eyes soon. I have to force myself not to yelp at her from afar. She eventually snaps them open, unbothered, as if she knows exactly where her feet are guiding her.

I also happen to know where she's headed.

This isn't my first time following her. Won't be my last. Some might call it stalking—I call it getting acquainted. I follow her because I have no fucking clue what my next move is. I crave to be close to her, but I'm also painfully aware that the current haunted look on her face is partially my fault.

I'm surprised Connor even let her live. Deep down, I know he saw something in my eyes that night, even if he didn't let on or even mention it. I might have not said the words out loud but he knows me all too well for it to matter. Sunny was to be spared, no questions asked. Which is why he threatened her life instead.

The threat was equally effective. Hell, Connor looks like he has the grim reaper on speed dial. Only an idiot would go against one of his threats.

Later, he had only mentioned one thing about it—*keep tabs on the girl.*

And I was more than happy to oblige.

According to the police reports that Bastian hacked into, she kept her word and kept her mouth shut.

Finally, Sunny reaches the waterfront. She's been doing this almost daily. Eventually, she finds a spot to her liking surrounded by other beachgoers and drops her bag on the sand.

She pulls her black tank top over her hair, dropping it next to her things and wiggles out of her jean shorts, revealing a yellow bikini underneath. Her auburn hair gleams almost red in the sunlight, her toes sinking into the sand as she struts into the water like she owns the place.

Fuck me.

I'm burning to touch her. My feet fight against the urge to walk straight into the ocean and just run my fingers against her cheek. To ask—no plead—her to remember me as I do her. To run my tongue across her parted lips and taste her for the first time. Or like the countless times before this.

My phone rings and I snap back to reality. I groan when I see Connor calling.

"Yeah?" I keep my eyes on Sunny as I half listen to his answer.

"I need you to take care of something for me," he barks, and I know he won't tell me any more details over the phone. Knowing Connor he probably needs me to take care of *someone* so I grunt my response and tell him I'm on my way. Sparing Sunny one last look, I turn away and walk back up the hill.

This better be fucking good.

Chapter 10

Sunny

I reach for the back door and swing it open, the distinct scent of the pub hitting my senses like a brick wall. I stand frozen in place while still holding onto the door handle. I waver in between wanting to run away as far as possible and walking inside to finally face the terrible memories still clinging to me.

It's my first shift back since Gary's kidnapping—and subsequent murder. I couldn't avoid it forever. Alas, I have bills to pay. Only the rich can mourn the dead.

Eventually, I yank myself out of the stupor I've inadvertently fallen into and walk inside, readying myself for my shift. I made sure to schedule my first night back with Lenix. I'm desperate for moral support, but try to pretend I'm not dead inside while I pour drinks all night for faceless customers.

As usual, Lenix works the floor while I tend the bar. Eventually, I fall into a workflow, attempting to concentrate on the repeated movements of making drinks and stashing bills into the till. I try to keep my head down as much as possible while the bar fills up with the rowdy evening crowd.

When the rush finally slows down, I slink towards my best friend, who's leaning against the service bar pouring us shots for moral support. She takes hers with a smile but keeps her eyes over my shoulder as she drinks it down. I bring the glass to my lips, swallowing the gin in one gulp. I hold the back of my hand to my mouth as the familiar burn trails down my throat.

"Dude, who's the hottie in the corner?" Lenix asks with a crooked smile, still peering over my shoulder. I watch her tilt her chin over to the corner of the bar, prompting me to follow her gaze and swivel around, curious.

I find piercing green eyes staring back at me. My heart crashes into my ribcage and I duck down on instinct, adrenaline shooting up my spine.

"Sunny?" Lenix laughs peering over the bar only to find me trying to hide and failing. With the way the bar is designed—an oval area with a large space in the middle for the bartenders to work in—and his current vantage point, I'm not hiding for shit. And he's staring straight at me. I look at him in defeat, knowing all to well it's pure terror he sees splashed across my face.

It's the one with the scar coiled around his neck. The one who I still remember in perfect detail even if I've tried very hard not to.

Unbothered, he continues to watch me, an amused look in his eyes. I turn my attention to Lenix, my body beginning to shake. *Am I going into shock?* Her smile suddenly drops when she sees the expression on my face.

"Babes, what's wrong?" She looks over to him and then back down to me, confusion dragging her eyebrows down. I'm once again paralyzed, unable to sound out any words, let alone move.

Lenix finally grabs my arm from over the service bar and shoves me out and into the hallway near the kitchen. "Sunny what the fuck is going on? You're scaring me." Her worry rises as I tremble in place, barely able to push the words out of my mouth.

"I...I need some air," I manage to mutter out. Lenix is clearly confused by my sudden reaction but says nothing more, she makes sure Jack is covering the bar and follows me out back.

As soon as we're outside near the dumpsters, she finally speaks, "Bitch, you better tell me what the hell is going on right this fucking second!"

I'm barely keeping it together as I glance at her, wishing I could be anywhere else but here. Her arms are crossed looking worried, waiting for me to start explaining. I wrap my arms around myself, trying to gather my thoughts.

"It's him, Len." I feel small and defeated like an animal waiting to be slaughtered, while Lenix's expression goes from slightly annoyed to confused to sudden realization in under five seconds. Her mouth falls open, her eyes growing wide. "Well, it's one of them at least," I add.

"What the *fuck*," she whisper-yells. "What is he doing here?"

"I don't know," my voice rising in panic. "I didn't tell anyone anything...what if they think I did? Why else would he be here?" I splutter, swallowing hard and looking at Lenix with defeat. "I'm fucked aren't I?" I finally say, my voice trembling, eyes watering.

For once, Lenix is at a loss for words and simply stares at me with what I can only assume is pity. She looks up to the night sky as if waiting for an answer from the heavens and then glances back at me. Instead of answering, she snakes her arms around me and burrows her head into the crook of my neck.

Her warm breath on my skin grounds me and I wrap my arms around her waist, squeezing hard. There's nothing she can say to make this situation any better. She knows it. I know it, too.

I'm screwed. Pure and simple. Eventually, I take a deep breath and unravel myself from Lenix's embrace. I'm desperately trying to convince myself I can do this while I eye the door with dread.

"I need to go back in. There's no way out of this," I murmur, turning to Lenix. "No one can *ever* know, you hear me? I shouldn't even be telling you this." My bottom lip trembles, so I bite it hard to make it stop.

"Don't worry about me, babes," she sighs with a sad smile. "I'm a pro at faking it." She winks and struts back inside, ready for the best performance of her life while I ready myself not to implode in the middle of Sammies.

I turn the corner and walk back behind the bar, finding him sitting exactly where I left him, his eyes boring into mine. I quickly look away, my mouth turning as dry as sand. I thank Jack for covering for me and peer around the bar, trying to see who needs a drink.

Fuck.

He's the only one who seems to be missing a drink. I grab a hold of Jack before he walks away. "Has he ordered anything yet?" I ask, covertly pointing to the threat at hand.

Jack glances over and shrugs. "He said he was waiting for you."

Great. Of course he is.

Jack walks away and I'm left alone with no choice but to step toward him like a sinner walking the narrow plank to their death. Or hope the void hovering above me can swallow me up whole instead.

Anytime now.

Since the void seems to be ignoring my urgent request, I continue towards him, back straight, head held high. His sly grin hasn't moved from his face as I approach him, and I fight the sudden urge to punch it clean off his stupid fucking face.

"You ready to order?" I sing-song but my voice cracks and I cringe internally.

He just sits there with his smug look, observing me for far too long. His eyes rove over my face and then down my body while I try not to spontaneously combust.

Finally, he speaks, "I'll have a Talisker on ice."

Quickly, I turn around, desperate to escape his penetrating perusal. My hands shake as I grab the ice pail and prepare his drink. Unfortunately, the task takes me less than a fucking minute to accomplish. I walk back to him on unsteady legs and slide his drink and napkin across to him.

"Thank you, Sunny," he drawls.

I wince, my name on his lips jarring to my ears. His jade eyes never leave me. Never waning in intensity. His stupid grin still in place. My entire body is buzzing, desperate to walk away. But something equally powerful roots me in place.

I finally make up my mind.

I clear my throat and lean closer, false bravado written clear across my face.

"So are we just going to pretend nothing is going on here?" I give him my most provocative smile, the one I usually reserve for wealthy patrons with fat wallets.

He chuckles. Fucking *chuckles* as he wraps his lips around his glass and takes a sip.

"Which is?" he says.

Even with the anxiety pulsing through me, I try my very best not to roll my eyes. The fucking gall on this guy. Scoffing, I cross my arms, feeling rattled. Or more rattled than I already was, his unrelenting eyes demanding respect. Respect and something else I can't quite pinpoint as I gulp back the fear crawling like a spider up my throat.

Making sure no one is in ear-shot, I lean a little closer. "Did you kill Gary?" I whisper.

He takes another sip of his drink. His stare assessing me before finally responding.

"Yes."

I suck in a breath. The edge of my vision grows dark, a tell-tale sign that I'm about to spiral into a panic attack if I can't manage to control it. My hands grow clammy while I fight the urge to unravel.

Carefully, he sprawls his tattooed hands flat against the bar on either side of his drink. Condensation drips from the glass and onto the napkin underneath. He clears his throat and my eyes fly up to his as I watch something flit across them but it disappears as fast as it came. He leans closer.

"Look, I'm not trying to scare you. I'm just here to..." He trails off, his hand waving around in a lazy circle. "Make sure everything is as it should be." He flashes a toothy smile, the left side of his lip dipping lower than the right and winks. I blink rapidly in disbelief.

Wait a second. Is he flirting with me?

I'm shocked into silence, trying my best to quickly process his demeanor. Hell, I might have even considered flirting back if the circumstances were different.

If he was literally anyone else.

Instead, I'm terrified but—I hate to admit—equally enraptured. I lean over and rest my hands on the bar in front of him, determined not to feel squashed by his aura or whatever.

"I haven't said anything I wasn't supposed to if that's what you're implying," I retort, glaring at him from over his half-drunk scotch glass.

He leans back in his seat, glass in hand, and takes another sip. His eyes continue to burn a path down my skin, and I try not to shake under his stare.

Oddly, I'm also fighting with the conflicting need for him not to stop his slow peruse of my body. Taking a final swig of his scotch, he crunches an ice cube between his molars.

Shit, why does him breaking ice with his teeth feel like a power move?

Standing up, he fishes out some money from his jean pocket, drops the bills onto the bar and flashes his infuriating grin at me one final time.

"Good," he growls, his voice coming out an octave lower than before. I can't help but flinch at his tone. From fear...or something else?

Just as he's turning to leave I stop him halfway.

"Wait," I say, the word slipping out of me, my shaky hand reaching out towards him.

He looks back over his shoulder, and says nothing, cocking an eyebrow instead.

Fuck. Why did I just do that?

I swallow hard and say the first thing that comes to mind.

"What's your name?"

His lips twitch slightly, a dimple appearing on his right cheek while he gives me one last searing gaze.

"Byzantine."

He doesn't wait for my response before walking out of the bar. It's only when the door slams shut again that I let out a shaky breath, unclench my jaw and allow myself to relax. I grab the money he left on the bar, realizing he left me two crisp hundred dollar bills.

"Gee, thanks for the tip and not killing me, I guess?" I mumble under my breath. My sarcasm sounds flat even to my own ears. I reluctantly finish my shift on unsteady limbs. Lenix shooting me worried looks every half hour while I continue to tell her that I'm fine.

But I'm far from fine, and my torment now has a name.

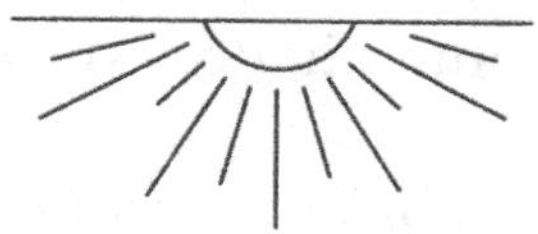

Chapter 11

Byzantine

She'll be the end of me.

Just like I've been her demise before. Long ago. Somewhere else.

I stand across the street from Sammies, waiting and scowling at the air, trying to shake off the sticky memories of lives lived long ago. Before her name was Sunny. Before tonight, when I sat in front of her trembling body in a busy bar. The fear in her eyes scratched at a bleeding wound I didn't remember having so deep inside.

I'm a stranger to Sunny. Worse—I'm a killer. She might have not witnessed it but I have blood on my hands, nonetheless. The same hands that yearn to wrap around her neck and squeeze while I chase the gasp from her lips. That crave to undress her, and slowly part her naked thighs, watching her cunt unfurl beneath me.

I knew I couldn't stay away. Or won't. At least I have an excuse to visit her. Little does she know I'll be doing much more than just visiting Sammies in the very near future.

Following her this week has only left me hungry for more. I'm ravenous for her attention. For her eyes to be on me and only me. Even if her gaze is laced with disgust, I can smell the shame like perfume on her skin. She's attracted to me, nonetheless. And oh, do I know that feeling quite intimately.

I once looked at Gabriel the same way. Before I was Byzantine. Before I watched him fall to his death. Before, when Sunny was Gabriel and I was Anthony.

Before. Before. Before.

I fall back into the shadows of the building behind me, hearing Sunny's voice pierce the night. It's only been a few hours since I left her dumbstruck behind the bar. She's changed into a pair of tight jeans shorts that make me groan aloud. Her loose black t-shirt trailing across her ass and my fingers flex, the hot need to touch her squeezing my chest tight.

I continue to study her when I notice a man trailing behind her. He catches up to Sunny on the sidewalk and wraps his arm around her shoulders, prompting her to look up at him with a smile.

What the fuck? Who the hell is this guy?

His hand hangs loose on the edge of her shoulder, like a stranger masquerading as a lover. Was he inside the bar this whole time? Watching her work just like I was? I've never seen him with Sunny before tonight.

I would've noticed. Stepping out of the shadows, I peer over to take a better look. Where are they heading? This leaves me no choice but to trail behind them. Partly because I care for Sunny's safety, but mostly to further stoke the raging jealousy barrelling through my veins.

Ten minutes later, they finally come to a stop in front of Cloakroom, a busy nightclub in the heart of Old Town. They take a spot in the winding queue full of party-goers eager to get in. This doesn't quench my curiosity one fucking bit.

It only fuels it further.

Pulling my hoodie over my head, I cross my arms, shoulders hunched while I wait.

Opposite desires curl up inside while I watch Sunny dish out coy smiles to the man she's with. The desire for her to notice me watching her. And the desire to stay invisible, free to steal small sips from her life unencumbered. I clench my jaw, unwilling to walk away.

Unable to let her live a life without me in it.

Chapter 12

Sunny

I know this is a mistake.

I knew this was a mistake when he asked what I was doing after my shift and I gave him my best fuck me eyes, telling him exactly what he wanted to hear. I knew it was a mistake when he slipped his arm over my shoulder and I felt myself tense up under his touch.

And I especially know it now as we wait our turn in line, exchanging pleasantries as if we both don't know how this night will end. How most of my nights with near-strangers end—recent memories of dirty bathrooms and foggy mirrors still lingering at the forefront of my mind.

While I pretend to listen, a cold chill trails down my spine. An awareness that makes my skin sing. I spin around, my eyes wild as I scan the street behind us. The area is crowded but I see nothing out of the ordinary.

And I refuse to admit who I thought might be staring back.

"Are you okay?" Mark asks. Or was it Mike? *Ugh.* Let's just call him Mark.

I plaster on my fakest smile and face him. Mark has been a regular at the pub for a while now. Always flirty, always cheeky. He can never tell when I'm feigning kindness for tips or when I'm genuinely interested. Tonight is no different.

Or maybe he doesn't care to tell the difference as long as he gets to fuck me by the end of the night.

"Um, yeah I'm okay..." I force out a tight laugh. "I thought I saw someone I knew across the street. No biggie."

I shrug my shoulders in an attempt to appear casual, relieved he can't see my heart pounding in my chest. He looks puzzled for a moment but quickly shakes it away, taking my hand and dragging me inside when the bouncer finally waves us in.

Cloakroom is packed with writhing sweaty bodies. It's a multi-level bar, with numerous dance floors peppered around the place and a rooftop patio. There's no dress code and caters to the early twenties crowd. The decor is non-descript. It's the blaring music and patrons that makes this place attractive and popular. Perfect for the kind of night I need.

Deciding to stay on the first floor we take a few shots at the cramped bar before I take my date by the hand and lead him to the dance floor. I weave around dancing limbs and find a small opening for us to share. The room is in a state of drunken osmosis, skin on skin heat from total strangers yearning for the same release as us.

My chest vibrates along with the bass bouncing off the walls and I can feel Mark's hands slowly slide across my hips, pulling me closer. I give in, eager to forget the feeling of Byzantine's eyes on my body as I lean into his touch and wrap my arms around his neck.

Mark's gaze locks with mine. A slow, sensual smirk forming on his face. We grind our bodies together in time with the beat, swaying back and forth. I allow myself a moment of surrender, letting his hands travel down to my ass, his fingers digging into my shorts. Shivers snake down my arms, head rolling back on my shoulders as I lose myself in the moment.

Suddenly, the same chill as before tunnels its way through the hazy bubble I've created on the dance floor. I straighten abruptly, my arms dropping from his embrace, nearly pushing him off of me.

His eyebrows raise up and he cocks his head as if to say *is everything okay?* I try to shake the feeling and salvage the moment, waving away his concern and laughing, my voice barely audible over the music.

I point to the women's bathroom and give him a quick kiss on the cheek before leaving him on the dance floor, hoping he won't read into my sudden change in behavior. Maybe I'll sneak in a shot or two before finding him again.

Pushing through the crowd, I stumble to the bathroom. Luckily there's no lineup and I walk right in. I face the mirror, trying to catch my breath. Noticing my flushed cheeks and my mascara a little smudged, I turn on the faucet and splash some water over my face and neck. After fixing my makeup, I inhale deeply and try to re-center.

I have no proof that Byzantine has followed me here but somehow I know he's here. What would I do if I did find him staring back?

I don't let myself answer that thought and make my way back to the dance floor instead, only to find Mark missing. Thinking he might have gone to the bathroom as well, I dance on my own, easily slipping into the gentle sway of other peoples bodies, sweat trickling down my spine.

He never comes back.

After fifteen minutes, I roll my eyes, slightly miffed and decide to see if he's held up at the bar, thinking maybe he's busy buying us another round. But I can't find him anywhere. I scan the club trying to make out any glimpse of his hair or shirt, but nothing.

Wow.

Did he just ditch me? What a douchebag. I mean, I know I was acting a little strange and distant but does it justify him leaving me like this?

With my ego a little bruised, I now feel even lonelier than before. Unwilling to stay at the club by myself, I reluctantly make my way to the exit, defeated and a little hurt. I thank the bouncer on my way out, and head down the block, rifling through my purse to find my phone and call a taxi.

I've only managed half a block when a hand curls around my elbow and yanks me into the alley.

I yelp, stumbling and attempting to regain my footing. My blood runs cold when I find smoldering green eyes staring at me, the street lights overhead reflecting his fiery gaze, his lips curled and taunting.

"Y—you..." I stutter. My brain screams at me to run while my body ignores the warning, pulled by his incandescent stare instead. I find myself taking a small step forward, the pull as strong as the tide.

Byzantine seems to respond to the same force and steps forward at the same time.

When I finally realize what my body is doing, I jump and scurry against the brick wall. Unfazed, Byzantine advances on me. Silent. Hunger radiating from his stare as he slowly peruses my body, devouring me from the inside out.

I've seen this look on others before. But seeing it on him alights my cold skin with fire. Heat pools low in my stomach as I continue to press against the wall.

He raises his left hand close to the column of my neck. Slowly. So fucking slowly, until finally his fingers curl around my throat and I gulp against his palm. His hand squeezes, his touch firm yet gentle. Then, he leans closer, his breath a feather across my jaw. My ear. My neck.

"Miss me?" he taunts darkly.

The sound of his voice makes me squeeze my eyes shut. How can two words feel so potent? Every cell in my body has awoken to the low timbre of his voice.

But then, my head nods as if acquiescing to his question, and I'm shocked, not knowing where that reaction even came from—feeling like I've lost all sense of agency yet again. His pull is so strong it feels like being sucked into a black hole.

He gives my throat a quick squeeze as if pleased with my answer and my eyes fly open again, his grasp a constant reminder of him having me trapped against the wall. Of having me so close to his intoxicating—albeit confusing—presence.

He turns his face just an inch, his lips a whisper against my cheek and down to the corner of my lips. I let out a quiet gasp. And with it, his body stills. As if paralyzed by the small sound that escaped my lips.

We stay like this—motionless—for what feels like an eternity. A pocket of time where our two hearts beat with the same aching cadence. The moment feels infinite like a galaxy full of stars, always expanding.

I couldn't move if I wanted to. My body is heeding to his silent command, staying perfectly still until he chooses to release me. Like a firefly trapped inside a clasped hand.

Finally, he takes a long breath and lets me go. My palms nervously grasp at the wall behind me, scared I'll just slip to the ground if I don't find something to hold on to.

He takes a step back, taking a long look at me. His eyes, rimmed by long dark eyelashes peer from under his black hoodie, his full lips parted, chest heaving. If I wasn't so wrought with conflicting feelings of my own, I could almost discern longing in his burning stare.

He then raises his hand to his mouth, the same fingers that were curled around my neck now brushing across his lips as if remembering the ghost of his graze on my cheek.

"I'll be seeing you, my little sun." And without waiting for an answer, he walks out of the alley and disappears around the corner.

Stunned, I blink. Once. Twice.

Then, I burst into heavy sobs, sliding down the wall, the rough bricks chafing my skin on the way down. But these tears aren't born out of distress. Or even fear. I hiccup, my eyes continuing to spill over.

These are tears of release. Of *relief.* But how? Why? What the fuck just happened?

I'm a mess of complicated feelings that I myself can't even decipher. Eventually, I manage to calm down and stumble back onto the sidewalk. My cheeks are still wet as I hail a cab, my mind full of questions but no logical answers

Chapter 13

Sunny

"Byzantine."

I lay in bed, my lips wrapping around the vowels as I sound out his name. The languid *woosh* of the ceiling fan pushing the same vowels into the dark corners of my room.

His name is heavy on my tongue, as if I've already spent hundreds of years speaking his name. Carved into my memory like the deep curves of an engraved tombstone.

"Ugh." I shake my head like an etch-a-sketch. "I need to get out of here," I mumble aloud.

I refuse to think about him for another second. His behavior makes no sense. As little sense as my reaction to him.

I leave the house in a huff and jog down the stairs of my apartment building two at the time, eager to clear my head.

The sun's barely peeking out from the horizon, the city still dormant so early in the morning. I haven't really gone to bed yet. Just laid there wondering what the fuck is happening to me.

My body feels electric, the anxiety ramped up so high, I can feel it like a subtle tremor rattling my bones. My mind has been fried in the process and I can barely focus. Well, I can only focus on one thing it seems. His name is like an entity of its own, determined to block out everything else like an eclipse blocking out the sun.

It takes me about fifteen minutes to end up at the beach. I undress slowly, grateful for having at least the presence of mind to have popped on a bathing suit before leaving the house. I dig my toes in the sand, trying to take as deep a breath as I can but my chest is so tight I can barely suck in any air. The sun glimmers atop the waves and I try to bask in the simple pleasure of the peace I feel when near the water.

The ocean's cold embrace sends shivers down my spine as I slowly wade in, my skin tingling with goosebumps. I let loose a heavy breath, trying to contain my reaction to the chill but continue my way in nonetheless. I need this. When I get deep enough, I bite the bullet and dive in head first. I swim underwater until my lungs grow tight, the water grounding me back into my body—my mind.

Finally, my nerves settle as I swim with no goal or purpose. I pop back up with a gasp, pleased and smiling, out of breath.

Fuck I love the water.

A place that never disappoints, a place I can always count on. They say the earth vibrates at the same frequency as the human body. It calibrates us. Centers us. But with the industrial revolution and the mass migration to cities we've become disconnected. Untethered. Nature being the only thing able to provide us with that frequency.

I like to think that when I sink under the waves I'm actually chasing that subconscious need to recalibrate. A deep instinctual urge for a mother's embrace. Just long enough so I can feel alive. Or feel something at least.

But these moments are fleeting. The groundedness I chase evaporates as soon as the water dries off my skin.

But hey, I take what I can get and try not to think about it that much. Try not to focus on where this feeling comes from. Or this *un*-feeling more like. This...disengagement. I am a collection of moments. Moments, I wish I could forget.

So here I am, floating on my back doing silly little breathing exercises I once saw on YouTube, thinking it might help fix the monumental gaping hole I have lodged in my chest. But fuck, at least I'm here. At least I'm alive, when the thought of death is at times more soothing than fearsome. Do I really have a death wish? Or am I just mentally exhausted?

I don't allow myself the chance to mull it over.

I dunk my head under the water one last time and sidestroke back to shore. The sun is warmer now. The awakened city rumbling in the distance.

Quickly drying and lathering an extra layer of sunscreen for good measure, I sprawl on the towel and let my arms fall wide beside me, my chest slightly heaving from the exertion of swimming to shore. My skin is cool to the touch, and I love the way it feels under the pads of my fingertips.

I close my eyes and allow myself just a few more moments of peace, pushing all thoughts and feelings as far away as I possibly can. This is my moment and no one else's. I need it. Staying like this for another half-hour, I slip in and out of sleep, my yellow bikini drying under the morning sun.

The sound of my phone buzzing in my bag forces me out of my reverie. I roll to my side and dig it out, my heart sinking when I see who's calling.

My mother.

There's no way I'm answering that landmine. I've been avoiding her calls for over a year now. I'm not even sure she knows I'm in Noxport. And I prefer it that way. River was the only thing keeping me tied to her—and my father for that matter. But he would have to have been less of a ghost for that to even count.

To say that my mother never understood me is an understatement. She called me too sensitive, too melancholic, too emotional—just too much and not enough. Answering her call would be like having to admit I'm depressed. That something is *truly* wrong with me. A crack I can never seem to fix.

I'd rather avoid it, sweep it under the rug and file it away for future me to deal with. To be forgotten until the next time I'm forced to face my demons. Instead, I let them rattle in their cages and push myself up from my beach towel. Throwing my shorts and hoodie on, I trudge home. Back to a room full of dark swirling thoughts and heavy with Byzantine's name.

The skies are dark and gray tonight, the rain feels like it's coming at me sideways as I walk with my shoulders up to my ears, my eyes squinting through the misery. I had the bright idea to walk to work and now I'm drenched, the cold wind burrowing into my bones.

Just great.

This is not how I wanted to start my shift. Cold and miserable. Well, at least it's an accurate depiction of how I feel inside too.

It's been a few weeks since the incident. The night that shall not be named. Everyone at work seems to tiptoe around the subject and I'm exhausted trying to pretend I'm not thinking about it all the time.

Then there's the touchy subject of Byzantine himself.

I bristle at the thought. I haven't seen him since he accosted me in the alley. I mean, why would we see each other? I ignore the eager part of me who's waiting for him to reappear. But the sane part of me—the rational and fearful part of me—wishes I would never set eyes on him again.

He's trouble.

He's more than trouble, he's death incarnate for fuck sakes. My bizarre attraction to his searching eyes and perfect lips will not and can not change the fact that he literally killed Gary.

My anxiety spikes when I open the back door of Sammies, a mishmash of uncomfortable emotions fighting for the spotlight. It leaves me with shaky hands and my teeth nervously biting my bottom lip.

I need a fucking drink.

I have about half an hour before my shift starts so I slink towards the staff room, crossing the bustling kitchen as my sneakers squelch across the floor. I give a grumpy wave to the cooks before pushing through the swiveling door. Luckily I'm a pack rat and practically live here, so I head to my locker to scrounge out something dry to wear for tonight.

I take off my wet t-shirt and drop it on the bench beside me before rummaging through the locker on my humble quest for dry clothes.

I don't bother covering up. Finding someone in a state of undress is pretty common around here. We're a tight-knit staff and besides, I've lost count of who's slept with who. Myself included.

So when I hear the staff door open, I'm unbothered, and don't even glance up. My back is turned to the door while I'm still on the search for a decent pair of pants when the back of my neck tingles. My limbs lock, my hand hovering mid-air. My body knows who I'll find if I turn around and look.

Impossible.

My head's obviously playing tricks on me. I'm losing my fucking mind. There's no other explanation. I swivel in place and face the door before I convince myself otherwise. I lock eyes with a stunned Byzantine. My breath hitches and I gulp back down my heart into my chest while Byzantine continues to pulverize me with his heated stare.

"What are you doing?" he asks through clenched teeth, his hand gesturing toward my half naked state.

I'm about to answer, the words almost out of my mouth when I realize the absurdity of the situation. I scoff out a laugh.

"What am *I* doing? What are *you* doing here? This is employee only." I point to the door and glare at him, hoping he doesn't notice the small tremble in my voice.

I'm also painfully aware that I'm far less intimidating than I'd like to be, standing there in a yellow cotton bra and wet jean shorts. But I refuse to break eye contact, even if my skin itches with the desire to cover up.

His silver rings catch the light as he drags his hand through the scruff of his day old beard, looking at me almost pensively. He unnerves me and he knows it. I swallow loudly, my arm still stretched out, signaling him to get out. But he doesn't move an inch.

"Employees only, yeah?" he says smoothly, a barely there grin sliding across his lips. "Well." He rakes his eyes across the length of my body as he stuffs his hands into his pockets and leans on the wall near the door, one foot crossing over the other. His posture is casual but predatory. "Lucky for me, I now own this bar."

His words slam into me as soon as they leave his lips, and I'm unable to form a single coherent thought. I stare at him in shock. Did I just hear him correctly?

"I think that gives me access to this room, don't you think?" He winks—fucking winks at me. "And if I ever catch you like *this*," he hisses with a flick of a wrist. "Where anyone can just walk in and see you, there will be consequences. Do you understand me?"

His upper lip curls, seemingly appalled.

"Now, if you'll excuse me, I have business to attend to and I believe you have a shift to punch in for. *Chop, chop*." he says, clapping his hands condescendingly. He pushes off the wall and turns on his heels, walking out of the staff room and taking all of the oxygen in the room with him.

I try to suck in a breath but fail. The signs of an anxiety attack clawing at my throat and chest. This can't be happening. This isn't real. I stand there—half-naked—for several minutes in shock until I force myself not to unravel. Finally, I pull a dry shirt over my head, my head still spinning.

Byzantine is now the owner of Sammies?

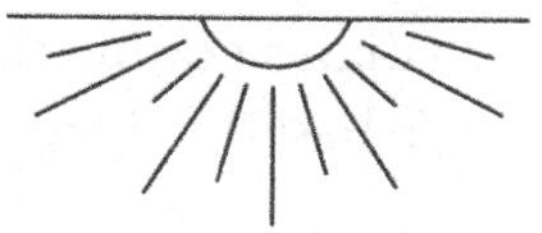

Chapter 14

Byzantine

The door slams behind me as I tramp inside the small dingy office that used to belong to Gary. The desk sits close to the back, two couches lining the opposite walls in front of it. The place is crammed with old files and invoices and smells like grease.

I dive towards the bottom drawer where I know I'll find a bottle of whiskey. Taking it out, I ignore the small tremor in my hand and twist the cap off, lifting the bottle to my lips.

I take two—okay, maybe three or four—large gulps and wince as the cheap alcohol burns down my throat and lights my stomach on fire. I slump down behind the desk and try to catch my breath.

Fuck. Maybe this wasn't a good idea after all. I needed to be close to Sunny and buying this run down bar seemed more logical than stalking her forever. Connor rolled his eyes when I told him of my plan. He knows this is more than just me keeping tabs on Sunny—a kindling obsession, he must think. But still he let me have it, we're always looking for nondescript businesses to launder our money through, so he conceded.

First, Gary had to turn up dead. You can't buy property from a missing person. The red-tape should have taken much longer, luckily Bastian's connections reach the highest places in Noxport. We had the deed turned over to us in mere days.

Funny how that works.

But now, while trying to regain my senses like a fucking schoolboy with a crush, things don't feel so cut and dry. It feels more like being tied up, lying across the tracks while I wait for the train to run me over. I can feel the rumble of disaster in the distance.

How did I ever think this was a good idea?

And then—*then*—I find Sunny half naked in the employee room and nearly fucking lost it.

Years of hiding my facial expressions barely helped as I watched her body flush at the sight of me.

Was it anger? Lust? Both?

Either way, I just wanted to see it happen again. I wanted to watch her skin paint a story her lips refused to tell. My pull to her is unbearable. Undeniable.

How can I remember lifetimes between us and fucking pretend?

Pretend I don't know her. Pretend I don't know how it feels to watch her fall apart as she comes underneath me. Maybe there are parts of Sunny I no longer know, but her soul—I know inside and out. No matter what, I will make her mine again.

This time it will work. *We* will work. There will be no heartbreak, or inexcusable deaths. Or anything of that fucking tragic bullshit.

The door slams open, the handle burrowing itself into the already existent hole in the wall. I flinch but keep my features neutral as Sunny storms her way into the office.

"What do you mean you *own* the bar?" she says, glaring at me, her arms crossed against her chest, trying to look as angry as possible. But I can tell she still fears me. Not as if I've done much to quell her fears.

Collaring her neck in a dark alley wasn't my best move, I must admit. But what else was I supposed to do? Let her fuck another guy? Over my dead fucking body. I scared the loser half to death instead, before telling him to stay the fuck away from her.

She shifts her weight from one foot to the other and continues, "You can't just drop a bomb like that, *leave*, and expect me to be all like, *yes boss, okay boss!* What's even going on here?"

Her voice cracks, an obvious tell that fear lies just beneath the surface. Instead, she tries to hide it by letting out an exaggerated breath and glaring her hazel eyes at me. *Cute.* I could stare at her all day. And I do just that, taking the time to truly take her in while she waits for me to reply.

She's tall, lithe, and with legs any man would pay to worship. I haven't seen her wear anything other than cut off shorts since the day she came barrelling into my life. Or I barrelled into hers...either way, I'm fucked.

I can't tell if this is a simple case of instant attraction or lifetimes worth of longing, but all I know is that the light dusting of freckles across her nose makes my dick twitch and my skin fucking itch.

Still, I keep my face expressionless. The urge to taunt her a bit longer is undeniable. I smirk while resting my elbows on the desk and steepling my hands. Her eyes flare in frustration, and one corner of my lips widens.

"Well, little sun, it's quite simple really." A near imperceptible gasp leaves her lips at the sound of her pet name. *Good.* I want her to unravel. I need her eager and pliant as I tug at the frayed edges of her self-control while I watch her remember who I am to her. I begrudgingly ignore how my cock responds to her small gasp and continue.

"Gary was found dead—"

"You killed him," she reminds me through clenched teeth.

Her bottom lip trembles but she quickly sucks it between her teeth in an attempt to hide it.

I stay silent, staring at her, matching the intensity I see in her stormy eyes. As soon as I discern the uneasiness behind the twitch of her hands I continue.

"As I was saying, since I *killed* Gary, as you so put it, and the bar was left without an owner it only seemed logical to purchase it. I won't bore you with the reasons as to why. Besides," I lean back into the office chair, widening my legs, my hands clasped casually against my stomach, "It's none of your fucking business."

Sunny takes a step back as if the words physically pushed her in the chest, her mouth opening and then falling shut. I can practically see her thoughts traveling at lighting speed behind her eyes before she finds the courage to bite back.

"None of my fucking business, yeah?" she repeats slowly, her head cocking to the side with a sly grin creeping up her lips. "If that's the case...then I can guarantee you that my state of undress is none of *your* fucking business. Besides," she says, tightly crossing her arms, her smile widening as if she won this little exchange of ours. "It's not like it matters when half the staff has already seen me naked."

At first I don't react, my jealousy burning so hot it almost feels cold. A near homicidal rage flares through me and it takes every ounce of control I have left not to let it show, settling back in the chair, my face wiped clean of any emotion.

"Careful..." I tsk, "It's almost like you forgot who you're talking to."

She flinches. And my mouth fucking waters. This really isn't helping my *she thinks you're a psychopathic murderer* dilemma but I can't help myself.

Even if it's fear I can see crawl across her skin, I am not above watching her breath hitch and her chest heave as she tries to compose herself. I can tell she's trying to resist the urge to tell me to go fuck myself. And I wish she would. It burns behind her eyes. And fuck, would it turn me on.

"I'll quit," she threatens, seeming to muster all the courage she has left.

I laugh. A condescending chuckle more like. I don't even try to resist the pull she has on me, standing up and stalking towards her. She goes on high alert but doesn't move as I inch myself closer to her trembling body. I lean over to her ear just so I can smell the delicate fragrance of her lip balm. Grapefruit—and a hint of sugar. What I would do to lick the seam of her lips just to have a taste.

"Don't kid yourself, darling. We both know you won't quit." I trail my fingers down her arm, chasing the goosebumps across her skin. "And if you do, well, we both know I'll always find you. You can't hide from me."

I straighten, staring her dead in the eyes, brushing my thumb against my bottom lip. "Besides..." I trail off. "I think there's a part of you who wants to be found. Isn't that right, my little sun?" I don't bother to stick around for an answer as I walk past her, leaving her dumbfounded in the middle of the office.

Chapter 15

Sunny

"None of my fucking business," I grumble under my breath.

None of my fucking business, my ass.

I've been stewing my entire shift while gossip about the new hot owner has traveled across the staff like wildfire. No one knows who Byzantine truly is except for Lenix and I. And her knowing is a secret of its own. There's no way I'm putting her in any danger if I have anything to do with it. Byzantine is my problem.

And what a problem to have.

I could tell he enjoyed toying with me. The initial fear I felt for him is slowly morphing into a barely contained rage after each encounter with him. They're brief but so fucking loaded. My body flares up anytime he's close.

Like a disease. A virus wrecking havoc inside of me.

His eyes drill holes straight to my soul. He unnerves me and he knows it. Relishes it even. The lethal way he carries himself only heightens my reaction to him.

But there's something else there. Something I can't quite put my finger on. His imposing influence scratches at the edges of my subconscious, pulling at something forgotten.

He feels...almost familiar.

And yes, I'm painfully aware of how ridiculous that sounds. But I can't shake the feeling.

"You done?"

My head snaps up and my eyes narrow as I watch Byzantine stroll into the main dining area like he fucking owns the place. Ugh, I guess he does own the place now.

He sprawls into a corner booth, his crooked grin dimpling his cheek as he watches me. A king on his throne.

"Why are you still here?" I pipe back. "I can close up, I've done it a million times."

Translation: Please leave me the fuck alone.

He chuckles, scratching his scruff with his hand. "Well, I wouldn't want to leave you alone, now would I? You never know what kind of evil is lurking in the shadows."

I wipe my hands on the rag hanging from my back pocket and cross my arms. "Pretty sure I'm looking straight at him."

A surprised laugh bursts out of him and he smiles. "Touché," he says, his voice full of mirth.

Technically, I'm done cleaning the bar, but my feet refuse to move, unwilling to get any closer to Byzantine. The entire dining room separates us and I'm very much okay with that. So I stay in place instead, and glare at him from afar while he takes out his phone and starts typing, either unaware or unbothered by the holes I'm trying to burrow into his skull.

"Have a drink with me," he demands, his eyes still glued to his screen.

"What?"

Oh, I heard him alright, but the word jumped out of my mouth anyway, surprised by his casual order.

He places his phone screen-down on the table and looks up, his features stoic. Not cold, but penetrating. A shiver trails down my spine as I gulp down my nerves.

"I said, have a drink with me," he reiterates slowly, each word emphasized with wicked intention, tapping two fingers on the table and making my body jolt. I suddenly want to break his fingers in half—or crawl across the floor to him.

Both are equally startling.

What the hell is happening to me? I quickly push the visuals out of my brain as if worried he can read my thoughts.

I finally make a move and grab a bottle of whiskey and two glasses before exiting the bar.

"Fine, but only because I don't really have a choice, do I?" I reply, my knees wobbling as I near the corner booth. Byzantine still looks like an arrogant prince, watching with a righteous air that I want to strangle out of him.

I slide into the booth, staying close to the edge and as far as possible from him. I place the bottle and tumblers in the middle of the table, lean back, and stare at him. I can tell he's amused and my blood begins to heat. He cocks a brow.

"Well?" he says, his chin pointing to the bottle of whiskey. "Aren't you going to pour us a drink?"

I cross my arms and dish out the same cocky grin. "I'm clocked out."

I bite the inside of my cheek, waiting for his reaction. He looks at me for half a second then laughs. It's warm, inviting even.

Still, I wince.

He continues to chuckle while reaching for the bottle and pours us each a generous amount of whiskey. He slides mine across the table. I wait till his fingers are clear off my drink before picking it up. Byzantine tilts his tumbler in the air giving me a small toast. I return it with a thin-lipped smile, bringing the alcohol to my mouth and taking a sip.

I'm going to need this drink if I'm being forced to have a casual, somewhat strong-armed, conversation with Byzantine at three o'clock in the morning. We sit in silence while he studies me from over his drink. My heart beats wildly in my chest, as I try to keep my composure and force a bored look on my face.

But he's like a bomb sniffing dog, only instead of explosives, he expertly sniffs out the fear I'm trying to conceal. I can tell by the way his lips curve up slightly, taunting and intimidating. And maybe some other emotions I'm currently refusing to admit even to myself.

His eyes shine with intent and my skin heats with anticipation while I squirm under his gaze. "You shouldn't fear me, Sunny," he finally says.

I scoff. "That's a laugh. You're kidding right?"

Shit. Maybe I shouldn't have said that. But how else am I expected to feel? The man oozes dominance and—oh right—killed Gary.

He grins. It's a feral rise of his lips that makes me lick my own. The silver rings ornamenting his tattooed fingers reflect the candle still lit between us on the table. The ice lightly clinks in his glass as he takes a casual sip of whiskey. His Adam's apple bobs up and down as he swallows and my eyes dip, following the movement and then linger on his scar.

I must have stared for too long because he reaches up and slides the pad of his fingers across his scar. Quickly, I glance down at my own drink, considering just downing the whole thing in one large gulp.

"Are you wondering where I got this scar?" he asks. I can feel Byzantine's eyes on me but refuse to match his gaze.

"Maybe once or twice," I mumble. *More like all the time.*

"Look at me," he orders sharply.

I train my attention on him and find his eyes flitting across my face as if trying to memorize it. My mouth suddenly goes dry.

"It involves Gary," he admits and my heart drops.

Wait, what? My mouth falls agape, the words melting on my tongue before I can speak them.

He looks slightly amused with my reaction and continues, "Five years ago, your previous boss tried to kill me, and almost succeeded, but Connor—" He stops, fixing me with his enrapturing stare. "You've met him actually." And then waves his hand around as if to say *'oh you know? The one who scared you half to death last time you saw him.'*

I'm still shell-shocked by the Gary admission and barely react. He grins and continues, "Connor found me," he states, his tone even but his eyes darkening as if remembering something troublesome. He takes a quick sip of his drink and continues, "Brought me to the hospital, but I had lost so much blood that they said I was dead for several minutes before they were able to restart my heart." He absentmindedly strokes his scar as if to soothe the memory out of his skin.

My mind is on fire and I don't know which thought I should land on so instead I blurt out the first thing that comes to me.

"How old were you?"

"Twenty-seven," he says thoughtfully, staring down at the table, but then continues, "When we finally went looking for him, Gary had erased himself from the city. All of our trails were dead ends." He pauses, and looks me straight in the eyes. "Until a few weeks ago, when we heard he was back in town, moonlighting as the owner of Sammies."

I don't know what to say or think, desperately trying to merge the two realities I'm currently straddling into one.

Gary tried to kill Byzantine? Did he deserve it? Who the fuck was he involved with? Did I even want to know?

Scrounging up any leftover courage I'm still holding on to, I push out the question burning on my lips. "Did you deserve it?"

Byzantine shrugs, all fucking casual and nonchalant as if we're not talking about him getting brutally attacked by none other than fucking Gary.

"Maybe," he deflects with an unnerving grin, making my stomach flip. I kick myself internally for finding him even remotely hot, especially now while we're deliberating if someone I knew had it coming.

"I'm just trying to make you understand why you shouldn't fear me, little sun. Gary deserved what happened to him. He wasn't a good guy."

My lips part ready to cut in but he raises his hand and I snap my mouth shut.

"No, I'm *also* not one of the good guys. I think that's been established already." He leans back against the booth, his green eyes sparkling as if he's getting off from admitting he's no saint. "My point is, I might have killed before," he continues, his voice dipping lower, causing my throat to go suddenly dry. I know this about him already but hearing him say it still makes my heart lurch and my stomach sink.

Abruptly, he leans over like he's about to tell me a secret, his arms resting on the table, a searing look on his face that makes me squirm in my seat.

"But I would *never* hurt anyone who didn't have it coming." He stays silent for one second too long while I attempt to merge with the booth behind me. I wait for him to continue while he locks me into place with his smoldering gaze. "Especially you."

My heart quickens and my mind goes suddenly blank.

I blink at him, unable to move or respond. Finally, Byzantine breaks the tension, and slides out of the booth as if he didn't just say what he just said.

"Come, I'll drive you home," he says.

"Oh no, that's okay. I live—"

"It wasn't up for debate," he drawls before he stalks out of the dining room and disappears into the back hallway. I'm left dazed and definitely confused, and I'm finding it hard to piece together what just happened.

But when I hear the back door open and shut, I finally blink back to life, scampering out of the booth then out into the back parking lot, quickly locking the bar behind me.

I'm glued against the passenger door, as if Byzantine has a contagious disease I'm trying not to catch.

I might just be trying to avoid how ridiculously good he smells. It's distinct and bright, like the fresh ocean air, and somehow it tickles my senses with longing. It's also impossible to ignore now that we're locked in the same vehicle together. His car's a manual, black in color and looks expensive.

That's as far as my knowledge of cars goes.

Ever so often his hand reaches down to shift gears and my body electrifies. Like a static current drumming morse code on my skin. I hate it. I love it. I can't stand it. I need to get out of this car before I implode from whatever tension is currently building between us.

I shift my body in the seat, my thighs sticking to the leather underneath me. I'm sweating like I have something to hide. Maybe it's just the leather. Truly, I can't tell.

Suddenly, a realization dawns on me. "Wait, how do you know where I live?"

Byzantine gives me a side look that has his eyes sparkling with mischief but doesn't answer.

Dread tingles my spine and I clear my throat nervously. "Have you been following me?" I ask tentatively.

"Didn't I just tell you not to fear me?"

"Yeah well, stalking is unbecoming," I volley back, trying to act less rattled than I currently feel.

Byzantine chuckles, the quiet sound feeling like a punch in the gut. I take a deep breath and try to ease my body language into something less terrified.

Furtively, I glance over and study him while he drives. I mean objectively, he's breathtaking. Unfortunately, he's also the kind of hot who kills people who deserve it—according to him.

His dark brown hair is shaved short, a scruff on his cheeks that seems intentionally there, the soft curves of his lips in strong contrast to the cut of his jaw. His skin, bronzed and golden, peeks through countless tattoos. The street lights intermittently illuminate his features and I notice a scar dipping low through his left eyebrow, traveling down to his eyelid. I swallow hard and look away. Scars shouldn't be this attractive. He shouldn't be this attractive.

I rest my elbow on the car door and stare out the window. We sit in tense silence until he turns on my street and stops in front of my building. I'm about to scurry out of the car and mutter a thank you when his hand lands on my arm. I freeze, turning back to find him staring at me intently.

"Stay," he orders, successfully paralyzing me to my seat.

He opens the car door, climbing out and heads towards the passenger side, looking like he's aiming to open the door for me.

Jesus Christ, is this guy for real?

I have the uncontrollable urge to open my car door before he gets to it just to spite him, and also maybe in spite of my body's reaction to him *opening* said car door.

When he finally does, I realize he's left me barely any room to climb out. I stretch out of the car, leaving me no choice but to stand much too close to Byzantine. The satisfied look on his face has me wanting to roll my eyes for the hundredth time, but I resist the urge.

I'm trying to act annoyed by his gesture, but the tremble in my shaky knees would beg to differ. I take a large step backwards as soon as I can, avoiding eye contact.

"Okay well, thanks for the ride. It really wasn't necessary, though, I walk home all the time," I grumble.

His posture shifts into something more rigid than a few seconds ago.

"You won't be walking home any longer. Not if I have anything to do about it," he declares.

I'm about to laugh it off but it dies in my throat when I notice the searing look he's giving me. Okay, wow he's serious. Anger spikes through me, now actually annoyed by his arrogance.

"I don't know what you're playing at Byzantine, but whatever it is, stop, 'cause I'm not interested," I say with a huff in my voice.

I close the car door in his stead, my heart in my throat as if I'm about to hurl right here on the sidewalk and stomp off towards my building. I can feel his eyes burning into my back but I refuse to look at him.

He can go fuck himself.

Chapter 16

Sunny

It's been over a week since Byzantine first drove me home. Surprisingly, Sammies has been running pretty smoothly ever since he took over. Even better than when Gary was running it, I must admit.

Connor and Bastian are becoming familiar faces too. They always sit in the same corner booth tucked into the shadows, drinking whiskey on the rocks while they speak in low tones away from prying eyes. Lenix has kept up the charade of playing the clueless waitress while Connor has taken a liking to her, requesting her service on any nights she's working. Knowing her, she doesn't care who they really are, she just likes the attention.

All three disappear into the office at least once a night for long stretches of time. But no one asks any questions. Especially Lenix and I.

Byzantine hasn't let up his quest of being annoying about driving me home. No matter how often I try to weasel my way out of it, he manages to catch me before I can slip away, and I reluctantly—or somewhat petulantly—march to his car and let him drive me home.

He hasn't gotten any uglier either which is the one detail that somehow annoys me the most. He hasn't missed any of my shifts since he took over, always sitting at the bar watching me work, if not busy with Connor and Bastian. My skin vibrates the entire time he's near, painfully aware of his deliberate gaze on me as I flit from one side of the bar to the other, serving customers.

But it's his other looks that rattle me most. The ones he thinks he's hiding from me, the ones I see when he thinks I'm not looking. I often catch small glimpses of those looks in the mirror behind the cash register when I have my back to him. Haunted looks that leave me breathless. On rare occasions, it's of a longing so intense, I have to avoid him entirely until I can shake myself out of how those fucking looks make me feel.

And then other times, his eyes on me trigger this indescribable pinch to my heart, usually quickly followed by a wave of nostalgia so fierce it feels like I'm drowning. Those are the moments I reach for the bottle of gin mid-shift just so the burn anchors me back into place—and the buzz is nice, too. I still can't comprehend why I often feel like this around him, and I flatly refuse to investigate it more closely.

I'm busy closing someone's tab when I notice Byzantine lead someone into his office. The man in tow is short and stocky, his head shaved to the scalp, showing off a tattoo of a symbol I vaguely recognise, his traps bulging high up his neck. He looks like a mean bulldog. His attention lands on me and I quickly look away, cold dread prickling at my nape. They disappear into the back and my gaze flits to Lenix near the service bar. She looks as frazzled as me. I walk over, resting my elbows on the surface separating us so our faces are as close as possible.

"Who the hell was that?" she hisses, while stuffing crumpled cash into her waitress pouch.

"I don't know...but did you see that guy's tattoo?" I ask, looking around to make sure no one is listening. "Isn't that from somewhere?"

Lenix's eyebrows scrunch together and then suddenly her eyes widen. She leans even closer to me before saying, "Holy shit, what if Connor, is actually Connor Maxwell?" she whispers, waiting for me to react but the name doesn't ring any bell. "Right I forget you've only been here a year," she adds, flipping her hair off her shoulder. "As in The *Sin Eaters*? They're like the most powerful crime organization in Noxport. The West Coast even."

My stomach sinks with this new information, but it all makes too much sense not to be true. With the way Byzantine and Connor carry themself—*especially* Connor—you'd think they own this whole damn city. And maybe they do. This realization only solidifies my suspicions. These guys are feared. As they should be. And one just so happens to have taken a liking to me.

The next day, I wake up from a nap drenched in sweat. I pinwheel, yanking my sheets off me with my legs. My chest heaves up and down as I try to regain my bearings.

"Fuck," I rasp out loud. The same dream again. Naps always seem to trigger it, and it always feels disturbingly real, too...just too fucking much.

I can never decipher it. And it's never those bizarre dreams either, where nothing makes any sense. No, this one is vivid, like being ripped out of a memory I can only revisit when I close my eyes and drift into sleep.

I lay a clammy palm over my heart and try to calm myself down. It's just a dream. Just a terror inducing fucking dream.

I look around my room and sigh. I fell asleep mid-clean again—a habit I started in my teens. My childhood bedroom always felt like the only place in the house where I had any real control. And when I could feel myself unraveling—when the black void would hover just a little too close above my head—I would stomp up to my room, slam the door shut, and *purge*.

I'd take everything out from my drawers, then the closet and pile it on the floor. Then, when I'd look around mid-clean, feeling like I had made everything worse, like I would never make it back to a clean and tidy space—I'd crawl into bed and curl myself amidst the mess.

Somehow, the chaos soothed me and I would drift into sleep, breathing just that tiny bit better. Then, I'd wake up rested, relaxed even, and tackle the mess until the chaos in my head no longer matched the chaos in my room. It's now become somewhat of a ritual.

But today, the pile of books and clothes strewn everywhere doesn't feel all that relaxing. It feels like an elephant sitting on my chest. I exhale loudly and fall back onto my pillows. My gaze lands on a random corner of my room while I curl in around myself, my mind eventually drifting to River. It's never long before I think of her. Especially when I feel like this. The one person I didn't have to pretend with. I took it for granted.

Here in Noxport, all I do is pretend. No one likes sad girls. And sometimes, it feels like that's all I am. So I fake it, and slip into the fun persona people expect of me. Because what's the other option? It's been established—I'm not ready to deal.

So, I continue to stare at my bedroom wall while I let my heart fall back into a normal rhythm. It's becoming harder and harder to ignore all these pestering emotions swirling inside of me. I much rather the general numbness I typically carry around in the chasm in my chest. I let out a heavy sigh, resigned to clean up the mess I've left around me.

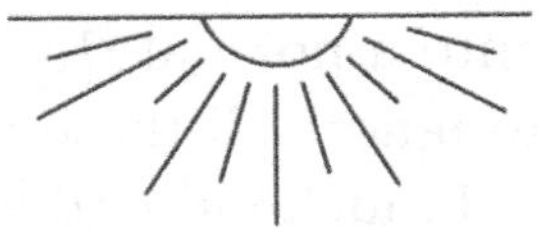

Chapter 17

Byzantine

My boots sink in the grainy sand as I walk towards the pile of clothes Sunny left on the beach. The sun is low on the horizon. It shimmers on the still water while Sunny bobs on the surface of the ocean, moving along with the gentle sway of the morning waves. I shouldn't be here—shouldn't have followed her like a lost pup looking for a treat.

Like a fucking lost case, alright.

I can tell Connor is on to me, with the way I can't keep my eyes off her when at the bar. Truth be told, I'm not trying to be subtle. But I'm spending too much time at Sammies and I have no one to blame but me. I'm distracted and he can tell. So, I've started bringing in the business to the bar to try to rectify my absence. Anything, to keep an eye on what's mine.

And Sunny has *been* mine for centuries.

But I can't tell her that without sounding unhinged, so I'm playing the long game. I'm not bothered. It feels like

I've spent my whole life searching for her. What's another couple of months?

Or, I hope it's a couple of months.

Sunny has walls higher than Mount Everest. Can I blame her? She might be a closed book but I'm privy to the lifetimes of reasons why she shouldn't trust me. And maybe she feels that. But it only makes me want her more.

I just have to convince her I'm not such a piece of shit. Which is proving harder than expected.

Fucking Gary.

Why did he have to lead me to her? Why couldn't I have bumped into her in the streets? I'm not ashamed of who I am but as far as first impressions go, mine has been far from stellar. And now I can't stop fucking stalking her.

I bought a bar, for fuck's sake.

You'd think after my near-death experience I'd be a changed man. I'd hear the angels sing and come back saved or some shit. That's just not how it works. I'm still me. I just have more insight now—a larger idea of what's to come when I do die. It's rid me of the fear of dying.

Could be considered a leg up in my line of work.

A lot of the in-between has faded. Those timeless pockets of existence before I'm birthed into yet another life are fuzzy and unclear. But the lives I've spent loving Sunny over and over again? Those burn bright like the force of a thousand suns. And yet...our demise was just as inevitable as our love.

Existing in different bodies, different personalities. Still, it was always *us*. The same souls forever bound. Forever cursed. Betrayal. Suicide. Murder. You name it we've done it to one another. Our paths always destined to cross. But maybe this time we can finally do better. Maybe this time we can succeed, finally learn our lesson and stop hurting each other.

That will be the fucking day.

How can I even begin to explain this to Sunny? Especially now when she doesn't even trust me. Her fear of me lingers and I'd be lying if I said it didn't turn me on. I'd be lying if I said I didn't try to instigate the feeling once or twice before just to watch her flush and her pupils dilate. Her body's reaction similar to what it could feel like to be buried deep inside of her.

Fuck.

I take a deep breath while I watch her walk out of the surf, her curves trickled with water. Her yellow bikini doing nothing to help suppress the growing erection pressing against the zipper of my jeans. I readjust myself and school my expression, my legs bent up towards my chest, my arms resting over them while I sit in the sand near the shit she left on the beach.

She walks up, pulling her hair on one side to squeeze the sea water out of her curls. Her face remains serious as she looks down at me, leaning over to grab her towel.

She quickly dries herself off and lays her towel flat beside me, plopping herself on top. Her body stretches out like a cat in the sun, her skin still dewy from the water.

Fucking kill me.

"What's your excuse this time?" she sighs.

Her eyes are closed, arms laid straight beside her as her toes burrow into the sand.

I clear my throat. "My excuse for what?"

She scoffs—she does that a lot—and looks over at me with one eye open.

"For you being here," she clarifies, lazily waving her arm in my general direction before continuing. "Your all black outfit doesn't strike me as beach attire."

I stifle a grin as I rub my hand across the stubble on my face.

"No excuse this time, little sun. I just knew you'd be here."

I knew she'd be here because she's here almost every single morning, rain or shine.

She stays silent for a while and then finally replies, "You're fucking creepy, Byzantine, you know that?"

I glance over, the sounds of the waves crashing close by, her eyes are closed to keep from the glaring rays, a small smile curling her lips.

"You shouldn't leave your shit unattended like that," is my only answer.

My ass is sore from sitting on the ground watching her swim for the past half hour, but I refuse to move an inch. Not with Sunny's body so close to mine. Not with her so relaxed. I need to soak up every second I can when she's like this. It never lasts. But it doesn't stop me from imagining what I'd do to her if she would only let me. If only she'd let me in.

The fantasy is easy to conjure up, even now—the tug of her bikini top as I push it aside. Her skin still cold to the touch as I'd glide my hand against her breast. Her pebbled nipple hard between my fingers, pinching it just to hear her moan.

I would stop time just to hear her moan.

"I don't have shit to steal, Byzantine, have you *seen* where I work?" she laughs and turns on her side to face me, the curves of her body a fucking crime in this position. Her voice snaps me out of my wandering thoughts, and I turn my gaze straight ahead.

But I'd much rather continue imagining all the dirty things I'd do to her. All the dirty things I will do to her.

"Have you even slept yet?" I ask her. "I dropped you off only a few hours ago."

"No, have you?" she responds, rolling onto her stomach, her feet up in the air, the yellow bikini barely covering the swell of her ass.

I swallow hard. My eyes linger on the smooth expanse of her skin while I answer her, my mouth dry. "No. But we're not talking about me," I say, flashing her a smile. "Come have coffee with me," I add, standing up to rub the sand off my black jeans, then hold out my hand for her to take.

She looks up at me, her eyes squinting from the sun, and I try hard to ignore how enticing it is to have her at my feet.

Sunny's answer lingers between the small intake of breath she takes. "I don't know..." she says, uncertainty coloring her tone.

Her hand rests near her eyebrow, shading her from the sun to get a better look at me. "Not sure what the etiquette is for having coffee with my stalker," she deadpans, but then laughs at her own joke, her laugh bright and sunny like her name.

I give her thigh a small shove with the tip of my boot, but say nothing and brandish my hand again, waiting for her to take it. Her eyes rove over my face, studying me, then finally she sighs and takes it.

"Fine, let's go."

Chapter 18

Sunny

We sit down at the same booth I sat at with Lenix when we learned Gary's body had been found. Now I'm having coffee with the man who killed him.

Funny how life is sometimes.

I stare down at my oat milk latte as Byzantine peers at me over his cup of black coffee. Of course he drinks his coffee black.

This feels too domestic. Us being here. I couldn't imagine Byzantine doing anything as normal as sitting at a coffee shop. He feels larger than life. Although, I have started to get used to him being around all the time.

"So what do you do exactly?" I ask innocently.

He watches me, a boyish grin on his lips. His eyes are bright in the early morning sun, and I hate how my stomach slams into my throat at the sight.

I hate it. I hate it. I hate it.

"You don't want to know what I do, little sun," he states, taking another sip of coffee.

"Like hell I don't. What is it? Drugs? Guns? All of the above?" *It's probably all of the above.*

"I'm part of The Sin Eaters, I'm sure you know that by now," he answers, his lopsided smile widening.

"I know that, I also know that Connor runs the entire operation but what I'm asking is what do *you* do?" I push.

We continue our little staring contest until he concedes and answers me, "I launder money and oversee most of the legal side of our business, like Sammies—amongst other things."

"Amongst other things..." I say sarcastically, "do you like it?"

"I'm the best at it."

"That's not what I asked"

"This isn't why I invited you here," he replies seriously.

"So why did you?"

Byzantine looks back at me now, his irises full of an emotion I can't place, and I can't help but squirm beneath his intense gaze.

"I want to get to know you," he replies.

"I was just trying to do the same..." I mutter with slight annoyance. I sweep across his features trying to find anything other than his favorite stoic mask but I get nothing.

I roll my eyes and reach for my latte just to have something to hold. We're getting nowhere.

Suddenly, the tension between us crackles when Byzantine leans over the table and snatches my left wrist in his hand.

"What's this?" he growls, a muscle ticking in his jaw.

His thumb digs into my skin while we both stare down at the scar on my wrist. It's an ugly thing, raised and angry. It begins at the edge of my palm and goes up my forearm, about three inches in length. I've managed to cover most of it with a tattoo of two snakes criss-crossing around my forearm, but at the right angle, it's still pretty apparent. I'm surprised he hasn't noticed it before today.

It's also obvious what it is if you have eyes and any kind of critical thinking. I know his question is rhetorical. But he has no right to ask about something so private. Shame burns my cheeks and indignation boils under my skin as I rip my arm away from his tight hold. Still, the loss of his touch is a dull throb I willfully ignore.

"It's none of your *fucking* business."

I throw his own words back at him and lean on my chair to get as much distance as I can from him. He studies me for what feels like forever, his eyes piercing through my resolve until finally, he leans back in his own chair and folds his arms across his chest looking defeated.

"Touché," he simply says.

We fall silent while we drink our respective coffees, the tension between us rippling like a lightning storm ready to strike. After stewing in silence for what feels like an eternity, I've had enough and grab my purse from the chair beside me, stand up, and clear my throat.

"I think I'll get going," I say dryly.

When he glances up at me, I nearly lose my balance. It's the most vulnerable I've ever seen him. Pain painted in broad strokes across his face. Then, he blinks and it's gone. Back is his steely gaze and debonair attitude.

"I'll drive you home," he murmurs, readying himself to stand. But I stop him with a hand on his shoulder, quickly pulling it away as if burned.

"It's okay. I want to walk. Clear my head," I rebuff. I'm certain he's going to object—he hasn't let me walk home alone in weeks—but instead, he just nods and settles back into his chair.

"You should get some sleep," he says quietly as he rests his chin in his hand, looking out the window again, averting his gaze. "I'll see you tonight at the bar."

I stay frozen to the spot for a moment too long. I can't help but to feel a bit jilted that he's letting me walk. "Right, um, okay. See you tonight...thanks for the coffee, I guess," I say, fumbling on my words and quickly walking out of the door.

I kick a small pebble further down the sidewalk as I near my neighborhood. What the fuck was that? Byzantine was acting strange all morning. I mean stranger than usual.

I know I shouldn't have bit his head off but since when did he take my snark to heart?

I can't shake the feeling I was in the wrong and I hate it. My thoughts travel back to earlier.

The way he grabbed my wrist like he had the right to demand the origin of my scar, as if angered someone had hurt me, even if the someone was myself. It made me seethe. I was right to shut him down. It's nobody's business but mine.

Besides, that scar happened forever ago. Old news. Big deal. I've moved on.

The week-long stay at the mental hospital might say otherwise though. I shake my head as if it could help stave off the intrusive thoughts. There's no need to think about that period of my life.

I'm here now and that's what matters.

I adjust the purse on my shoulder and head into my building. Byzantine was right about one thing, I need to sleep, and I need to sleep now. I dig the keys out of my purse and unlock my apartment door. I peel my clothes off my body as soon as I enter my studio, shrugging on an oversized shirt and crawl into bed.

Byzantine's face is the last thing I see before I give into the sleepless void.

I'm wiping down the bar with a rag, trying to get my blood down to a normal non-volcanic level as my thoughts go a mile a minute.

Byzantine hasn't left his office all night. He's never done that. He's always sat at the bar while I work—at least for a little while. Apparently him not doing so tonight is enough to piss me off. But are my angry thoughts directed at me or him? I don't know. And why is it bothering me so much?

I can't even describe the way he's making me feel. Is it guilt? Remorse? But I didn't do anything overtly wrong, and I'll be damned if a man is going to make me feel like this when I'm not even at fault.

I plop the wet rag on the counter, wipe the errants strands of hair off my face, then storm out of the bar and into his office, shoulders straight, head high. I don't bother knocking, I know he's alone in there.

I storm into the room, slamming the door shut behind me and stand there, murder in my eyes. Or what I hope translates to murder. Byzantine doesn't seem surprised by my sudden appearance, which only makes my blood run ten times hotter. I take deep breaths in and out, ready to pounce as I watch him recline back in his office chair, a tumbler full of whiskey in his hand.

"What the hell are you playing at Byzantine?" I snap. I cross my arms against my rising chest as he pins me with a heated stare, my throat suddenly tight, yet still I refuse to stand down. He told me not to fear him. So that's exactly what I'm doing.

"You've barely spoken to me since this morning and even then it was like pulling teeth. Let's all remember that it was you who invited me for coffee, not the other way around."

He takes a long sip before answering. "Not everything is about you, Sunny," he drawls. Then, he picks up his phone, effectively dismissing me.

I take a step back as if slapped. Oh, the *fucker*.

"Not about me?" My voice raises up an octave and I can hear the hysteria in my tone. I close my eyes and take a deep breath before continuing.

"I don't know what fucking games you're playing at but you have the wrong girl if you think I'm gonna take this laying down. Don't you dare start acting as if this is all in my head when you're the one practically stalking me. This hot and cold shit isn't cute, get over yourself," I hiss.

My whole body is trembling but I would rather die than let him win a game I didn't even agree to play.

Byzantine glances back up from his phone, his jade eyes penetrating as he coldly stares me down.

"Get over myself?" he says incredulously. He deliberately places his glass and phone on the desk without making a sound. Slow and calculated. Like a predator before the strike.

I swallow hard and lick my lips. I unfold my arms and begin to wring my fingers together. *Fuck what did I just start?*

He braces his hands flat on the desk, standing up. He looks every bit the gangster I believe him to be, straightening to his full height while glaring back at me. The intimidation is etched all over the hard curves of his body. It's too late to second guess my stance, so I raise my chin in defiance.

Finally, he moves, walking around his desk and towards me in quick strides. I can't help but to step back until eventually I'm leaning flat against the wall. Only inches separates us when he finally comes to a stop, pinning me to the spot with his glare.

I gulp loudly while his eyes darken. Heat blazes across his pupils, and a low rumble rises from his chest as he repeats himself. "Get over myself?" he growls.

It almost sounds like a threat. His eyes dip to my lips and then back up as he slowly raises his hand and collars my throat, his rings cold on my skin while his thumb presses against my thrumming pulse.

"Do you have any idea what you do to me, little sun?" he questions, his voice like flames licking across my face.

His other hand begins to trail up my arm, his fingers tracing a path of goosebumps along my skin. The hand against my throat squeezes lightly as he coaxes a small whimper out of me. I'm powerless under his touch.

"Do you know how hard it is to be around you and not touch you?" he says, low and almost threatening.

He leans closer, his lips barely a flicker against my jaw, then travels down my throat. Lust begins to curl low in my stomach.

His lips find their way back to my ear and he whispers, "The nights I've spent fisting my cock to the images of what I could do to you?" He presses his hips against mine, evidence of his desire hard against my thigh.

"What I *will* do to you?" he rasps. His hot breath wreaks havoc on my nervous system as I try to desperately regain my composure—and fail.

"The nights I've spent watching you work, thinking about all the ways I'll make you come with my tongue alone?" His hips press even harder, pinning me against the wall, my clit pulsing with what his filthy words are promising.

His thumb travels against my neck and pushes my chin up, effectively opening my throat to him. My body is frozen against the wall while his stubbled cheek rubs against the sensitive skin near my ear and I let out a moan, my lips parting with the sound.

Byzantine sighs and finally pulls away, his hooded eyes landing on mine. I can feel my cheeks flush as my body tingles at the sight of him. He grins and licks his lips—his hand still firmly placed against my throat.

"I don't play games, my little sun. You best remember that," he states, his mouth curving devilishly.

My heart plummets into my stomach when he finally releases me and steps further back.

"I'm just waiting for the day you'll be mine again."

And without a second glance my way, he reaches for the door and storms out of the office, leaving me panting against the wood-slatted wall. My mind is a lust-filled mess but his last words are still ringing in my ear.

You'll be mine again.

What the hell did that mean?

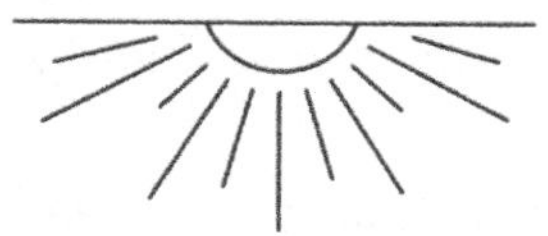

Chapter 19

Byzantine

Watching you fall from the cliff was not the last—or even the first—time I had watched you die. Like a sick joke between me and the karmic ties incessantly pulling us together. Our souls eternally enchained. Bound to you and your sweet carnal release. Destined to find you, again and again, until death would once more steal you away from me.

Until we met again under different faces, different names. Our souls reaching out, yearning for just a touch. Desperate for the familiar warmth of our noxious love.

I had arrived home late on that day. You were my wife then. I had spent the evening out. Drinking with coworkers to quell the bore of our marital bliss. I loved you, yes, I loved you truly. But I was lost. And so were you.

Months ago, we had sat in the wooden chairs of the doctor's office, listening to the doctor inform us that you were barren. Times were different then, different roles, different expectations. And mother was the most coveted role a woman could have. I had taken your hand in mine and watched the light blink out of your eyes as the doctor struck a match and lit a cigarette. He then coaxed us out of his office and bid us fair health.

We didn't know better. I didn't know any better. And I failed to know how to help you. How to reach through the darkness and find you. I watched you die before I ever found your lifeless body on the floor.

I watched joy never find you again. The clinks of ice in a glass full of gin becoming a melody to your sorrow. The sleepless nights spent staring, catatonic, at the waning moon. Waning like you.

My love. My light.

You were disappearing into the dark starry night, with only but a sliver of light left.

The house was dark. The yawing shadows of our home greeting me at the door. But not you. I assumed you had gone to bed. I took off my hat and coat and headed to the wet bar for a nightcap. I didn't turn on the lights as I sat in my favorite chair in the living room, finding comfort in the silent darkness surrounding me.

I took my time to find you, my love.

Please forgive me.

I didn't know.

With the last sip of whiskey still on the tip of my tongue, I made my way up the carpeted stairs to the second floor. I walked past the bathroom with the door ajar. I wanted to kiss your warm cheek first. To watch you stir in the wrinkled sheets, the sweet smell of sleep on your skin. The guilt of spending so much time away from you blackening my thoughts. I needed you. I needed us. I just...needed.

But a shadow on the bathroom floor averted my gaze away from the bedroom before me. A chill crawled down my spine like an omen destined to come true. Slowly, I turned to face the bathroom and reached for the light. Time stood still as I watched the overhead bulb illuminate your too-still body. Bathed in the truth of what you had done.

An empty bottle of pills tipped over beside you.

A half drunk bottle of gin.

Your hair soiled from your own sick.

I stood there for much too long. Paralyzed by the sight of you. Your lifeless eyes. Your graying skin. Your nightgown askew, bunched up to your thighs. Your hand reaching out as if asking for help.

Asking for my help.

And I had done nothing but let you die.

Upon your last exhale I had been buried deep inside a bottle. As your chest rose up and then down one final time, I had not thought of you. I had not even felt you.

I loved you.

And again.

I had failed you.

Music blares in my ears as I give the punching bag a few more jabs, sweat trickling down my naked chest. I'm in Connor's gym and I've been working the bag for over an hour but nothing helps to quiet the thoughts racing through my head.

Visions of Sunny, in another life, laying dead on the bathroom floor have plagued me ever since I found evidence of the same desires on Sunny's body. The scar on her wrist echoing lifetimes of wanting the same release. When I woke up this morning, the pain from that one life was so acute I could hardly breathe.

Especially the faded memories of the months following her funeral. I drank myself to death just to be with her. As if my soul couldn't bear another lonely life without her.

Instead, I followed her into the void. I didn't know how else to live with myself.

I try to rationalize my feelings, struggling to detach from the quicksand of the guilt trying to engulf me.

Sunny tried to kill herself and I wasn't there.

But I didn't even know she existed back then, how could I have done anything to stop it? I can justify it all I want, it still doesn't abate the guilt of me not being there.

Of failing her again.

I tried to avoid her last night until my thoughts weren't such a mess.

Then the office happened.

It took every bit of my self-control not to devour her. Not to feel her skin heat under my touch. My mind was on fire. Then I slipped. The words were out of my mouth before I could regain any sense of composure. *You'll be mine again.*

What a fucking idiot.

As soon as I realized what I said, fear seared through me and I had to leave. Had to run away from the one person I refused to run away from. I'm just hoping Sunny was too frazzled to register what I said. I didn't even drive her home. I left her alone in the pub and bolted, something I swore I would also never do. Such a fucking idiot.

I punched the bag one last time and take a step back, my chest rising up and down with the exertion. Catching my breath, I unwrap my cramping hands and reach for the bottle of water on the table. I pull my earphones out of my ears and head upstairs.

I pad through the kitchen and out the sliding doors, heading to the pool. Connor is lounging on a chair in only red shorts and dark shades, yelling at someone on the phone while a joint hangs off his lips. His skin is bronzed and gleaming because of the sun, his tattoos glistening from the sweat on his chest and arms.

I pay him no mind as I head for the deep end of the pool and dive in. I plunge through the water, and stay under for as long as I can hold my breath, swimming the length of the pool, the cold water cooling my heated skin and thoughts. But it's a waste of time. My thoughts will never forget Sunny's name.

Impossible.

Even if I could manage to stop obsessing over her, she would still haunt me under the guise of another. A ghost of many lifetimes. And in every single one, I've loved her in my own fucked up way.

We never seem to get it right. Why are we always bound to find each other if we're also destined to hurt one another?

I emerge from the water, gasping. I swim more laps, determined to tire myself out, still hearing Connor's angered voice pierce through the splash of the water.

Eventually, I drag myself out of the pool, the water trickling off my skin. I don't bother with a towel, plopping myself beside my best friend, who's finally done yelling at whoever was unfortunate enough to be on the other side of that call. A glass of whiskey sweats on the table beside him, so I lean over to grab it, but he swats at me, glaring while he hangs up the phone.

"What was that about?" I ask.

"There's trouble at the docks," he groans, swiping his hand over his face in frustration and handing me the joint but I wave it off. "There's a shipment missing and everyone is too simple-minded to know what the fuck to do about it." He reaches for the liquor. "Why am I always the one having to clean up everyone's mess?"

I know it's rhetorical, but I can't help myself.

"'Cause you're the face of this organization, brother. Your good looks don't only exist for the purpose of getting your dick wet," I goad, popping my shades on my face and leaning back into the chair.

If looks could kill, it would probably have succeeded if it was anyone else but me telling him that.

"I should wring your neck and bury you six feet deep," he bites back, his eyes glinting with mischief. "If only you could just stay dead."

I grin. "I'm a fucking cockroach. You'll never get rid of me."

Connor lets out a low chuckle and looks up to the sky, appearing deep in thought. After a long pause he adds, "Speaking of getting my dick wet, let's go to the club tonight."

I scoff. Should have known his thoughts weren't that deep.

"I know you've grown rather attached to *Sammies*—" He side-eyes me over his shades while saying the name of the pub, as if alluding to something or *someone* else. But I don't react.

"But it's definitely not where I'll find what I'm looking for tonight." He licks his lips and waggles his eyebrows as if already imagining it.

I laugh. "Sure, I'll come. But if you whip your dick out in the VIP section again, I'm punching you straight in the balls and leaving you there."

Connor snickers. "I can't promise anything."

Chapter 20

Sunny

Lenix and I spill out of the taxi, half-drunk from pregaming at her place while getting ready for the club. We're both off tonight, and there's only one sensible way to celebrate. And that's to get drunk at a bar other than the one that pays our bills.

Lenix waves goodbye to the cab driver as I riffle through my purse for my lip balm. The streets are packed with people as we walk up to Vinyl.

We rarely come out to this neighborhood, but after what happened between me and Byzantine in his office, I needed a change of scenery. Most importantly, I need overpriced gin and sodas, loud blaring music, and maybe someone to make-out with.

Lenix listened with rapt attention, her mouth agape with equal shock and fascination as I told her what Byzantine had done—or promised to do. I happened to omit one thing—the sentence that still rings so clear in my head.

You'll be mine again.

But tonight, I'm filing it all under lock and key in the deep recesses of my mind, determined to forget about it while I distract myself by flirting with the entire club—if I so happen to feel like it.

I picked out a black nylon bodysuit to wear, paired with the shortest jeans shorts I could find in my closet. I know I look hot, and I'm going to use it to my advantage for the distraction of a lifetime. Lenix didn't hold back either. People can't help but to gawk while she saunters up to the bouncer, her neon pink heels and black bodycon dress turning heads.

She knows the bouncer, which is why we're here in the first place. She leans over and whispers something in his ear, causing him to smirk and step aside, letting us skip the line. She gives him a quick peck on the cheek and I follow her into the club, thanking the bouncer with a nod on my way in.

The club is packed even on a Wednesday, and I let out a long happy sigh when the deep bass spilling out of the speakers hits my bones, causing me to finally relax.

Lenix grins and takes my hand, weaving us through the club and leading me to the bar. Once there, we squeeze into the tight crowd to lean our elbows on the bar, and order a round of drinks and shots,

This is my first time here so while my best friend is busy texting god knows who, I take a look around. The theme of the club is dark and moody. Deep booths with large black cushions are strewn around the back wall, and the dance floor takes up most of the main floor, the only pop of color in this place is the neon light show above.

I glance up and notice the second floor is cordoned off. Must be the VIP section. Because of the way the lights are set up, I can only see the outline of the people upstairs. Not that I really care, it's certainly not what's calling my name tonight. It's the dance floor as always.

"Let's have another shot and go dance, the music's too good to stand around," I yell over the music to Lenix as she stuffs her phone into the side of her bra. She always refuses to bring a purse when we go out.

Her eyes light up. "Okay!"

She waves the bartender back over and orders two more tequila shots. We pay and down them fast. Then, it's my turn to pull her through the crowd, and right into the middle of the writhing, sweaty bodies.

The alcohol tingles through my veins as I close my eyes and soak in the drumming beat of the song blasting through the speakers. I drape my arms over Lenix's shoulders and her hands wrap around my hips, tugging me closer to her body.

We sway back and forth with the beat, our hips grinding against each other while we both get lost in the music. We haven't hooked up in ages, but her body against mine is familiar—safe—and I slowly let my guard down.

That's when a strong hand around my arm pulls me out of my reverie, forcing me to swivel around. The breath is knocked out of me when I realize who's holding on so tight, his light green eyes nearly black as he stares straight at me.

"Byzantine..." His name is lost in the swell of the crowd while I lose all sense of reason. He looks over to Lenix, whose shock matches my own. Rage vibrates off of him as he points a finger over my shoulder to her.

"You stay right there," he barks and unceremoniously pulls me out of the crowd. I stumble behind him, struggling to keep up.

Lenix is hot on our heels. "Like hell I will!" she yells at him.

But Byzantine ignores her small barks of protest as he leads us to the stairs up to the VIP area. "Let her go Byzantine! I swear to god, I'll have you kicked out. I know the bouncer—"

We're halfway up the stairs when Byzantine stops and turns around to face her. Meanwhile, I'm still too shell-shocked to even mutter a single word.

"You mean Hugo?" Byzantine grins. "Considering I'm the one who hired him, I'm sure I'll be *just* fine."

Lenix sputters out a retort, but realizes quickly she's on a sinking ship. As soon as we hit the second floor, Byzantine turns to her, pointing to the booth where Connor is busy making out with a brunette.

"You sit right there and mind your fucking business," he orders.

She glares at him, but says nothing and slinks over to the booth, sitting as far away as possible from Connor, arms crossed and pouting like a petulant teenager.

Byzantine's grip on my arm doesn't lessen as he drags me over to a private room near the back.

"Let me go, you're hurting me," I whine.

He's not actually hurting me, but seriously, fuck him.

He swings the door open and shoves me inside, then flips the light switch on, bathing the room in a low red glow. Crushed velvet couches fill the room and oversized throw cushions litter the floor. It's giving off major porn vibes, but I'm too fired up to comment on it.

"So what," I laugh dryly, glaring at him. "You own every bar in the city? Is that it?"

Byzantine stands still near the door, his rage barely contained while his chest rises up and down. His usual all black attire is crisper tonight, like he made an effort. His jeans hugging a little tighter, a black henley instead of his usual hoodie. It's hard not to concentrate on anything else, but I hold strong.

"Oh my god," I exclaim, throwing my arms in the air. "What the hell is wrong with you? You're acting as if I killed your first born or something."

"*What* was that?" It's barely a whisper. But it sends a chill down my spine.

"What was what?" I ask, stumbling on my words, and swallowing hard, unable to hide my growing anxiety.

"You and Lenix."

I stare at him, stunned, then finally snap out of it.

"You must be joking," I say, my tone barely amused. I study him closely, trying to read his expression, but as usual, he's a brick wall. Great.

A wicked grin forms on my lips while I step closer to him.

"Are you jealous?" I ask, coming out as more of a taunt than I intended.

His stare is unrelenting, his eyes like daggers on my skin.

"Tell me who she is to you," he demands.

I should tell him it's none of his business, but I chicken out under his heavy glare.

"We used to hook up. We haven't slept together in over a year," I finally answer, crossing my arms. "Happy?"

His eyes darken. "No," he says sharply.

But then a cocky smirk slides across his face, nearly knocking me off my feet. He looks me up and down, the dimple in his cheek making my heart stutter.

"But I'll live," he quips, stepping closer to me and with a flick of his wrist in the air he orders, "Sit."

I'm sitting before I can even protest, stunned by how quickly I heeded his command. Byzantine keeps his distance and I feel my cheeks flush beneath his penetrating stare. My chest is tight while my heart slams against it.

Abruptly, he stalks towards me, and I sink deeper into the couch cushions with every step he takes. My knees are squeezing tightly together by the time he looms over me. I swallow hard as I peer at him through my lashes.

His pupils are blown wide, his eyes now a much darker shade of green. He runs his tongue across his bottom lip as he stares down at me. It looks like he's preparing to eat me alive. The anger I felt earlier slowly morphs into something much more dangerous. An urge that leaves me breathless and needy. I lick my parched lips, attempting to appear unbothered and failing.

"Open your legs for me, little sun."

I nearly choke on his words. My heart pounds even louder as I let out a shocked gasp.

He's crossing a line that I'm not even sure I want crossed, yet that doesn't stop my legs from falling open. He steps in between my thighs and leans down, bracing one of his hands behind me on the couch. The heady smell of him ensnares my senses, like the fresh ocean breeze and cozy rainy days. It's like taking a hit of the most expensive drug, a high I will most likely chase for the rest of my life.

With his other hand, he runs his tattooed fingers down my cheek, then slowly cradles my chin, his thumb pulling at my bottom lip.

"I don't think you understand me, Sunny," he rasps.

He examines me, his intent now crystal clear in his eyes. He slowly pushes his thumb into my mouth forcing my jaw open.

"You and I?" He slides his thumb further into my mouth and I can't help but to curl my tongue around it. This small taste of him evoking the promise of so much more.

"It's only the beginning," he vows, tugging his thumb from my mouth and swiping the wetness on my parted lips like a priest blessing a parishioner. "I will make you mine whether you like it or not." His low voice vibrates against my skin, his breath fanning across my jaw while my fingers clutch to the cushion under me. "Your head might be resisting me but I know I can make your body yield to me."

He then leans ever closer, his hot breath fanning across the side of my neck until I feel his teeth graze my earlobe, his warm tongue flicking it gently as I stifle a moan, biting my lip.

"Tell me," he continues, his hand just a whisper against the side of my hip. "If I would reach down right now and trace my fingers against your cunt, would I find you wet?"

The tension is near suffocating, my skin tingling with electricity as he stills close to me, waiting for me to answer but I've lost all ability to string a coherent sentence together. I slowly nod my head instead.

I can feel him grin against my ear, "Good girl."

My body lights up to the sound of his praise. He straightens, his heated gaze undressing me while I'm on the verge of passing out.

I don't have time to question what's happening between us before the door slams open and a disheveled Connor appears in the doorway, Lenix trailing right behind. He glances at me first, then Byzantine, who's still setting me aflame with nothing but a stare.

Connor snickers but walks in anyway. "Sorry to interrupt whatever the hell is happening in here but Bastian needs us at the house."

He waves his hand around like a bored king. "You know, no rest for the wicked and all," he adds.

Finally, Byzantine's eyes dart away from me and turn to Connor. "Fine," he snaps.

Lenix shoves Connor over and runs over to me.

"Babes, are you alright!?" Sitting beside me while I try to regain a sense of sanity.

"She's fine, Lenix, don't be dramatic," Connor answers for me. She glares at him but he just laughs it off. "Anyway, see you at the pub. This has been...fun," he says, walking out the door.

I look back at Byzantine, who hasn't moved a muscle. Finally, he rolls his shoulders and lets out a disgruntled sigh.

"This isn't over, little sun," he warns, before following Connor out the door.

Lenix's head swivels back at me. "What's not over?"

Chapter 21

Sunny

The hangover pounds in my skull before I can even open my eyes. It's as emotional as it is physical. Doesn't help that I'm also the horniest I've ever been in...maybe forever.

I groan, pressing my palms to my eyes and turning on my side to face Lenix, who's still passed out in yesterday's dress, face first in the pillow. Byzantine might have been jealous of her and I, but she's my best friend and there's really nothing he can do about it.

After both him and Connor left, we found a full bottle of vodka still sitting chilled in their VIP booth, and we obviously had to take advantage. Lenix ended up making out with the same girl who had previously been locking lips with Connor. Pretty sure the brunette said she was straight but Lenix can easily make anyone question their sexuality, if only for the night.

The rest is a blur.

Byzantine's words are still ringing in my head even now. A part of me craves the submission he demanded of me.

Craves him pushing me to my knees, slowly twisting his hands in my hair, and ordering me to do whatever deviant act he can think of. Lust cuts through me at just the thought.

Then, there's the *much* louder part of me that balks at being told what to do. The way he spoke of me with such propriety—he's lucky I didn't fuck someone in the bathroom just to spite him. But I knew I'd be disappointed.

And if I'm being honest, I didn't want to.

Not when Byzantine can turn me on with just a curl of his fingers under my chin. As if he somehow knows how to reach into the deepest parts of me and light me on fire. I'll be cinders after he's done with me.

The rational part of my brain continues to nudge at me, reminding me who Byzantine truly is—and how I met him. He killed Gary. Like, actual murder.

But somewhere between then and now my fear of him has dissipated. I know he's not a good guy, but is he evil? My beliefs of right and wrong keep getting murkier the more time I spend with him.

Anyway, the verdict is still out. I wake Lenix up with a shove to her shoulder. Her head snaps up, bewildered. Pushing up onto her elbows she drops her head into her hands with a loud groan.

"Ugh, Sunny, what the fuck," she whines while rolling on her back, her dress hiked up to her hips with one leg hanging off the edge of the bed. Her mascara is smudged under her eyes as she looks at me with the same gaunt look I'm probably looking at her with.

"I need a mimosa," she declares.

I rub my eye, likely worsening my own smudged mascara. "Same."

We shower quickly in a futile effort to find our will to live—it barely works. Lenix borrows some sweats and I shove into another pair before we shuffle out the door.

We slink through the shadows like vampires, making our way to the waterfront, hoping maybe the sea breeze will help our crippling hangovers. We find a cute bistro with a patio facing the water, sit down, and finally order what will hopefully help alleviate our throbbing headaches.

While Lenix takes a sip of her mimosa, she looks at me with a smirk. She raises her perfectly tweezed brow, waiting for me to speak. To annoy her further, I play dumb,

"What?" I stare down at my own drink, playing with the strawberry stuck on the rim of my glass. I then reach for the basket of fries between us, grabbing a handful and stuffing them into my mouth.

Lenix sighs dramatically. "Don't even, Sunny! Go on. You can't avoid the subject forever. Spill."

"I mean, there's nothing to tell. Nothing really happened," I evade.

"Please," she scoffs, theatrically rolling her eyes at me. "You can't tell me nothing happened when you had a glazed *please fuck me* look on your face when Connor and I walked in," she smirks. "I should know, I've put that look on your face before." I kick her shin under the table. "Hey, that hurt you bitch!" she whines, rubbing her leg while still grinning her Cheshire Cat smile.

"We didn't even kiss..." I trail off. Would we have kissed if Connor hadn't come in when he did? It certainly felt like it. "Honestly, I'm kind of relieved nothing actually happened. Like, what the fuck was I thinking? The guy's low-key psycho."

"And probably fucks like one too," Lenix adds, raising an eyebrow suggestively.

"That's the point, isn't it? He's already acting all possessive and we haven't even kissed. What would happen if we end up hooking up?"

I'm playing with fire. Lenix may be cracking jokes but she knows it, too. Byzantine isn't the type who seems to have *casual* anywhere in his vocabulary. But then, something tells me I wouldn't want casual with him, either. I would want to lose myself in him and never be found again. I'd want to sear my soul to his and go beyond what I've ever experienced with anyone before.

And that terrifies me.

I mean, I don't even know the guy. The things I do know about Byzantine don't really spell out citizen of the year. But then he looks at me and my soul flares like a supernova in my chest. Nothing about him makes sense, except that I should fear him. But I don't. Instead, my skin heats with the thought of his body against mine. Hard and wanting, the taste of his sweat on my tongue, his fingers finding a home deep inside of me.

"Sunny, are you even listening?" Lenix waves her hand in front of my face and I snap out of my daydream. "Oh my god...were you thinking dirty little things you perv!" She laughs as I bury my face in my hands, my cheeks burning. Lenix stands up from the table and holds out her hand. "Come on, let's go for a swim. It'll make you feel better. You don't need to make any decisions right now. Especially when you're in the throes of the boozy blues."

I sigh and take her hand. She's right, there's nothing I can do about it now.

A few hours later, after a swim in the ocean and one more mimosa, I feel a bit better. Lenix left to get ready for a date, leaving me solo.

I'm browsing the aisles in a bookstore when my phone buzzes in my bag. I fish it out, and see a text from an unknown number.

It doesn't take a genius to know who it's from.

Unknown: How's your hangover?

I roll my eyes, thinking up a quick answer.

Me: I'm sorry, who is this?
Unknown: You know exactly who this is.
Me: As your employee, this is considered harassment, I could sue.

The ellipses appear, disappear, then reappear again. I can't help but grin.

Unknown: Fair. Should I be punished?

I swallow hard, my phone buzzing again before I can come up with an answer.

Unknown: What if I get on my knees for you? Would you like that?

Oh fuck.

I'm gawking at my phone in the middle of the aisle, the image he just painted making it hard to swallow. I scramble to come up with a quick comeback but I'm so turned on that I can barely see. I settle on a classic—act unimpressed.

Me: Sounds intriguing I guess...

A low chuckle comes from behind me and I freeze.

No fucking way.

I turn around slowly, phone still in hand. My heart squeezes tight, butterflies exploding in my stomach, when I find Byzantine standing right behind me. His eyes twinkle, a grin just wide enough for his dimple to appear. Ever so casually, as if it's totally normal for him to have stalked me all the way in here, he shuts off his phone and shoves it into his pocket.

"Hello, my little sun."

Chapter 22

Sunny

"Hello, my little sun?" I whisper-yell across the aisle.

My eyes are ready to pop out of my head but instead I turn around and head for the check-out without acknowledging him for one more second. He trails behind me, unfazed and takes the book I'm holding out of my hands.

"Here, let me get that for you."

I snatch it back and glare at him. "No thank you, I don't accept gifts from strangers," I bite back with a saccharine smile.

He smiles, and then shrugs, stuffing his hands into his black jeans. "Suit yourself."

I swallow back the retort burning on my tongue and pay for the book, thanking the cashier and practically running out the door.

I was not ready for Byzantine today.

By the time I'm outside, something dawns on me and I swivel back around almost bumping into his chest.

"Jesus, stalk much?" I say, annoyed.

I take a large step back and squint at him as if trying to catch him in a lie.

"How do you even know I'm hungover?"

I mean, I was a bit tipsy when he saw me last but not like, *drunk* drunk. I'm also side-stepping the fact he knew where I was just now.

He doesn't even bother acting guilty and gives me another one of his unassuming shrugs.

"Cameras," he replies.

"You were *watching* me?" I say, trying for it not to come out as a shriek, but it's close. Seething, I fight the urge to shove him hard in the chest. "What? Worried I'd get too close to Lenix again?" My question drips with indignation.

He's full of arrogance when he opens his mouth next, "Looked like she had her hands full, actually."

I want to scream. I stomp my foot on the sidewalk instead, my hands in tight fists.

"You're literally insane, you know that?"

I turn around and try to get away but he's faster. Next thing I know he's pushing me against the brick wall, his hands cradling my face, his hips rocking into mine. Shocked, I stare back at him, his roguish smirk leaving me breathless.

But then he turns serious, any hint of amusement gone. He leans closer, his lips brushing against mine and he says, "Forgive me Sunny."

His apology tastes almost sweet on my tongue.

But why does it also feel so loaded? Like he's apologizing for something much bigger than just this. I shiver as he breeches the final distance between us and finally presses his lips against mine.

His mouth is searching and hungry as my lips open to him and I sink further into his touch. His tongue sweeps in, wet and hot and eager. He swallows my moan, his hands dropping to my hips and then slowly trail up my stomach while his hips grind harder into mine.

"Please forgive me," he repeats, breathing against my lips. The sound of his voice finds a home inside my bones. Suddenly, the urge to cry overcomes me. A wave of emotions dragging me under as I struggle to breathe. He holds me tightly to him, biting my lower lip, tender but so full of need. I'm lost. Drowning, while his tongue finds my own, a desperate need pulling me even deeper into the depths.

Then, like a dagger to the heart, terror tears through the lust and my body locks up. A fear so visceral it ravages through me, making me gasp out for air and break away from our heated kiss.

The words stick in my throat while my eyes desperately search his. Byzantine says nothing but holds me even closer, wrapping his strong arms around me before I have the time to push him away. He kisses my temple and caresses my hair as if soothing a frightened animal. My body begins to shake as he continues to hold me.

What the fuck is happening to me?

My breathing is shallow, the panic starting to rise. I try to fight Byzantine off but he refuses to let me go. I can either fight him and let the panic take over or allow him to hold me like this—and neither feels safe. Eventually, my arms fall limp to my side, my face finding the crook of Byzantine's neck. I squeeze my eyes shut and relent, seeking the undeniable comfort his body offers.

Somehow, the soothing smell of him grounds me back to reality. Even if I hate to admit his calming effect on me.

Byzantine mutters low, pacifying words as he cradles me. I hear him whisper "My windflower," into my hair but I'm too far gone to question what he just said. Suddenly, a wave of embarrassment takes hold of me and I struggle out of his embrace, mortified by my reaction to our kiss. I try to take a step back but he snatches my hand, seeming to ensure I don't escape.

I rub the top of my shoe against my calf, like a child caught red-handed and let out a small shameful laugh. "Well that was weird..."

Byzantine doesn't answer, and stays silent, his eyes looking almost vacant, lost deep in thought.

Finally, he lets go of my hand and I bring my fingers up to my lips. I can still taste him on my tongue and I wince thinking how badly I ruined the moment. I have no clue what to do so I just turn around and head the opposite direction. That seems to snap Byzantine out of his trance and he catches up with me.

"Sunny stop, don't run away again."

Again?

There's enough of a plea in his voice that I stop in my tracks and glance back at him. His eyes hold a similar desperation to the words he just uttered.

What the hell is happening?

It was just a kiss.

A kiss that almost sent me to my knees and left Byzantine with a cursed look on his face.

He holds his hand up in offering. "Come for a drive?"

There's an innocence to his question, as if a drive will solve the quicksand we happen to be sinking in.

I look down at his hand, my thoughts a terrifying swirl in my head and then back up at him. He smiles and I sigh. I place my hand into his. "Okay."

Byzantine's car speeds down the winding road. The windows are open, billowing in the fresh oceanside wind while I rest my head in the nook of my bent elbow.

We haven't said much since the kiss that sent me spiraling. He's been quiet, his stormy eyes the only indication that he might be as rattled as me. Luckily for me my brain is still fried from my hangover, plus I have an uncanny ability of compartmentalizing anything that may threaten my more than fragile status quo.

I'm sure the therapist I ghosted a few years ago has a more technical term for it. So for now I focus on the air brushing against my cheeks. The wind is tinged with cold humidity, carried from the water to our left. I breathe in deep, enjoying the fact that I'm outside city limits for a change. Maybe I should be worried that I have no idea where Byzantine is taking us but I'm too tired to ask nor do I really care at this point.

If he wanted to kill me, he would have done it already. Although, he might be trying to kill me in different ways—much deeper than physical.

I can't shake the feeling he's hiding something from me. Like he's hiding something about him and I. About this crackling tension between us.

I let out a breath and readjust my head on my arm. Maybe I'm just imagining things. Wouldn't be the first time I read into things. I look over and idly watch Byzantine drive, his toned arm flexing ever so slightly anytime he reaches over to change gears.

He senses me watching and peeks over, a playful side grin suddenly appearing but it's gone as fast as it came. My heart pinches while I continue studying him. The scar on his neck is always so stark against his skin. His casual black tee hugging his shoulders and biceps.

The man only wears black. I don't hate it. At all.

Then, my mind drifts back to the night he told me Gary was responsible for him almost dying. I swallow down the knot in my throat at the thought that Byzantine nearly died years before I met him. Is it weird that it bothers me? I didn't even know him then and I'm only now starting to get to know him. I guess we both have that in common.

The almost dying part.

The scar on my wrist suddenly itchy at the thought.

The crunch of tires on gravel snaps me out of my gloomy thoughts as Byzantine parks the car. A small alcove faces us, the beach deserted and tucked out of sight from the road. I look over to him, sporting an air of victory as if he knew I'd love this place.

I grin. "Good thing I'm already wearing a bathing suit."

He lets out a throaty chuckle while giving me a once over. "Wouldn't mind if you weren't."

I ignore the way my body flushes at the implication and playfully shove his shoulder. "Perv," I volley back.

He laughs as he opens his door and climbs out. Weeks of Byzantine giving me a ride home has trained me into knowing there's no use fighting his overbearing need to open my car door for me, so I sit and watch him walk around to the passenger side.

He opens the door, offering his hand and I take it. He winks at me when I step out, letting go of my hand as he turns towards the back of the car. He pops the trunk and pulls out a blanket for us to sit on and a small picnic basket.

A fucking *picnic basket*.

I blink back at him and then raise my brow in slight surprise. "Came prepared, I see."

He shrugs, looking sheepish as his eyes catch the light. "Maybe just hoping," he says.

I pretend not to hear the intent behind his tone and look over to the waves crashing on the rocks further out to sea.

Then, I follow him down the small trail and flip off my slides as soon as we hit the sand. I wiggle my toes and smile. The sand and water, the cure for most of my problems.

Although one of my problems is currently staring at me with a pleased smile on his face as I glance over at him. The blanket and basket still tucked under his arms as if he stopped in his tracks just to watch me dig my toes in the sand. I blush and hurry along, letting him pick a spot for us to sit.

As soon as we're settled, I take my clothes off and drop them beside a gaping Byzantine. I'm wearing the same yellow bikini he last saw me in.

"What?" I stare back at him, popping my hands on my hips like I have absolutely no idea why he's gone slack-jawed.

He seems to realize he's staring at me like a horny teenager and shakes it off.

"Nothing," he mutters, looking away towards the ocean, green eyes squinting against the sun.

"You just look good in yellow," he adds, before looking back up at me.

A deep pang of want overcomes me. I swallow hard trying to shake off the flush I can feel tingling across my skin. I watch Byzantine notice it, along with the small rise of my chest, his eyes darkening as he follows the blush up to my cheeks.

"Anyway," I say almost shyly, clearing my throat. "Aren't you coming in?"

He looks down at his black jeans and Doc Martens and then grins. "I'd rather watch."

I respond with a small shrug. "Suit yourself." Turning around, I jog into the warm afternoon waves.

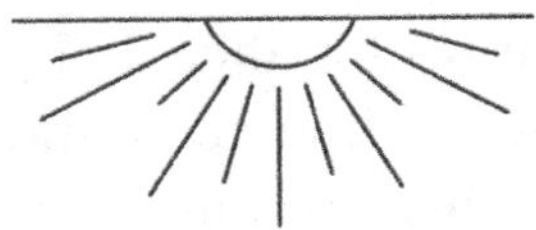

Chapter 23

Byzantine

"So..." Sunny trails off, I can hear the tremble of uncertainty in the tone of her voice. "Should we talk about what happened earlier?"

She's laying on her stomach beside me, her legs raised up, slightly swaying them back and forth as if trying to unconsciously self-soothe. Her bathing suit is slowly drying on her smooth sun-kissed skin, the book she just bought flipped over and resting in front of her. She's chewing on the skin of her thumb and I reach over to swat at her hand.

"Stop that, you'll chew your arm off at this rate."

She laughs, full of nerves. "Nervous habit."

She flips her wet hair from one shoulder to the other while still looking at me with a searching gaze. "Well? Should we?"

I'd rather gouge my own eye out then talk about the kiss.

So I decide to distract her instead. Reaching over, I trail a finger down her spine. Her shoulder blades tighten and then relax as she lets out a slow sigh. Her skin is still cold from the water as I watch the goosebumps erupt across her back.

She looks over to me. Her words now a stutter on her lips. She tries to resist the feeling of my fingers light on her skin but finally relents and rests her head atop her folded arms.

Her head tilts, her eyes hooded while she watches me. I can tell her question is still burning on her tongue but I'm determined to make her forget—even if it's just for now. My hand reaches the small of her back, her hips lifting ever so slightly as if chasing my seeking touch.

My balls tighten at the sight of her so pliant, so hypnotizing. My fingers slide against the seam of her bikini bottom, my thumb slipping under the fabric and then back out. Her legs, which were still up, now fall back down to the blanket, crossing one foot over the other.

I can tell she's trying to act unbothered. It only fuels me further. I lick my lips and swallow hard and continue to trace a path along her body. My palm, barely a whisper against the swell of her ass. I manage to stifle the groan rising deep inside my throat, the silence between us is electric—palpable—and only punctured by the sound of the waves crashing behind us.

There's still so much left unspoken between us. And maybe some things will always remain unsaid. An entire lifetime with Sunny wouldn't be enough to tell her everything I want—no, need—to say.

My windflower. My little sun.

Kneeling closer to her, I shift my position, freeing up the hand I was resting my weight on and making sure to dust the sand off my palms. She's like an offering on an altar laid out in front of me while I graze my hands down her thighs and then down her calves.

With her eyes now closed, her furrowed brows are the only hint she's not drifting into sleep and as if on cue, she places her foot that was crossed over the other back down on the blanket, uncrossing her legs. Opening up for me.

My cock aches as her body responds to my touch exactly how I knew it would. Reaffirming what I whispered to her last night—her body's mine. It's always been mine.

I trail my fingers all the way down to the arch of her feet. She twitches and giggles but says nothing. Then, keeping my hands flat on her calves, I move over so that I'm now kneeling in front of her feet. Her long legs parting ever so slightly as I caress her legs back down and then gently pick up her left foot with both hands. I place a kiss inside the arch, then do the same with the right.

I kiss her next on one calf and then the other. Her skin tastes like sea salt and I fight the urge not to lick her skin all the way up her parted thighs.

Sunny is keeping still but her breathing betrays her, as does mine. I silently readjust my position and place my knees on either side of her legs, leaning down to gently place an open mouth kiss to the top of one of her thighs, my tongue dipping out for a quick taste. She lets out a small gasp and squirms almost imperceptibly underneath me. I smile against her skin, pressing another kiss on the other thigh.

Sweat trickles down my back and I finally give in to the heat of the sun, tugging my shirt over my shoulders and tossing it beside us on the blanket. When she hears the rustle of clothes above her, Sunny's eyes snap open.

Her body grows unnaturally still as her eyes rove over my naked chest all the way down to the small trail of hair disappearing into my jeans and then back up. It's hard not to preen under her loaded stare but I do my best to hold her gaze while my cock strains against my zipper.

Without breaking our gaze, still kneeling over her, I reach down and palm my cock over my jeans. Her eyes shift as if fighting the urge to look down again but still, she continues to look me straight in the eyes—straight into my fucking soul.

Eventually, I lean back over to resume my languid worship of Sunny's body while she closes her eyes back shut. Nestling back into the crook of her arm, she sighs deeply. As the lust builds low in my spine, I gradually lose my gentle touch. I knead her ass with both hands, giving it a nice squeeze, my thumbs caressing her cheeks in the process.

She moans into her arm and my chest squeezes along with the sound. I palm her ass, my hands dipping closer and closer towards her center. My thumb trails further down as Sunny pretends not to notice but opens her legs even wider. Gently, I graze over the fabric between her legs and try not to lose my fucking mind at the sight of her beneath me.

Her body is so willing, so open, to my now near desperate touch. I lean closer to her, one hand now cupping her pussy entirely. I can't help but to grind into her as she wiggles against my hard length. My naked chest presses against the heated skin of her back and I let out a low groan when I hear her breath hitch. I lean back on my heels, my thumbs hooking around the ties of her bathing suit.

"Lift your hips for me," I say, my voice low and gravelly.

Her hips pop up as soon as the words are out of my mouth. Grinning, I give her earlobe a quick nip and press a kiss to her neck. "Eager little thing," I taunt against her skin.

I straighten back up and find her smirking like she's been caught doing something wicked but still keeps her eyes closed, unencumbered.

Ever so *fucking* slowly, I pull her bathing suit over her ass and then down her legs. I chuck it over my shoulder, truly not giving a fuck where it lands, then slide my hands up her thighs, gently parting her legs even wider. At the sight of her glistening pussy under the hot sun, I nearly go blind, licking my lips and looking up at the sky thanking the gods above.

I slide two fingers through her wet slit and she lets out a small whimper. The sound like opium spiking my veins.

"*Fuck* Sunny," I groan out. "You're so fucking wet."

Her body shudders under me, reacting to my words and she answers with a pleased hum. With my fingers, I trace a lazy circle around her entrance and then down to her clit as I watch her react to my touch. Then, grabbing her hips and pulling her up so that she's now on her knees, I crouch down behind her.

"Let me see that pretty little cunt," I groan, squeezing her ass in my hands and parting her cheeks open. "I need to taste you," I say, my tongue licking a slow broad trail from her clit to her entrance. She bucks against me, finally making a sound louder than a small moan. Her head falls between her shoulders while I continue to lick and suck and bite. I can taste her getting wetter against my tongue. I need more. I'll always need more. I dip my tongue inside her and she lets out a small cry.

I could listen to those sounds fall out of her lips forever and it would still never be enough.

I pull back and she whimpers at the loss which makes me grin. Reaching over, I slowly untie the strings of her top, like unwrapping a gift, and watch it fall from her breasts, nearly coming at the sight.

"On your back," I order.

Sunny turns around on a dime, resting on her elbows, naked, flushed and panting. She watches me wide-eyed as her chest rises in anticipation. Her breasts are full and so fucking perfect, her nipples a deep pink, strained and hard. I take a moment to sear the sight into my brain and then bend over her once again.

I close my mouth around her nipple and suck gently, catching it with my teeth, and giving it a small bite followed by a soothing lick.

"Byzantine..." she finally speaks.

My name is the only word out of her mouth as I growl into her skin, my hand finding its way back to her drenched pussy. I slide a finger inside and she clenches around me in response.

"Such a needy little pussy," I grunt, pushing a second digit inside and curling them against her inner wall. Her hips buck with the intrusion as I begin to pump in and out. She squeezes her eyes shut, biting her lip and then whispering my name again and again.

I trail kisses down her stomach while she continues to writhe against my palm, my thumb making slow hard circles against her clit.

"Are you going to come for me, little sun?" I growl, staring at her as I speak, the sound of her arousal against my fingers so fucking erotic, it only makes me want to pump faster just to feel her unravel against me.

She looks almost stunned as her eyes roll back, her head falling beneath her shoulders, moaning loudly.

"Yes, Byzantine, please...*please*."

I know she's close by the way her pussy pulses around me. I lean down, craving another taste and replace my thumb with my tongue. It only takes a few rapid strokes for her to dig her nails into my shoulder while she comes against my tongue.

My name, a quiet prayer on her parted lips. My body heats up at the sound. As if I'm chasing the echo of a thousand moments spent like this with her before today. The satisfaction is instantaneous, like a piece of me finally locking into place.

I keep my fingers buried deep inside of her while she comes down from her climax, her hand still gripping me tight as if scared I'll disappear under her touch. I pepper kisses along her thigh, a silent promise that I'm not moving, I'm not leaving as I finally pull my fingers out slowly.

I'm here. I'm here. I'm here.

I settle next to her and she cuddles into me, sighing into my chest, her eyes slowly drooping closed. Wrapping an arm around her waist, I pull her even closer and listen to her breath slow down until she gradually falls asleep against me. The smell of her grapefruit lip balm lingers in the air between us as I watch a small cluster of clouds slowly drift across the sky. I lose myself in thought. Lost in feeling. Just...lost.

Chapter 24

SUNNY

The drive home is as quiet as the drive up to the beach, mutually lost in our own bubble of deafening thoughts. Byzantine woke me up with a small kiss on the temple, wrapping himself around and over me. His weight was like a warm blanket around my limbs. He looked at me then, with such longing that I locked up under him.

He must have felt it but said nothing. Only giving me a small kiss on the nose and rolling back over. The tenderness of his actions gave me an emotional whiplash. I'm so used to experiencing a much sterner side of him that this version of Byzantine left me weak in the knees.

Well, my weak knees probably had more to do with the mind melting orgasm he gave me in the middle of a secluded beach. But that's neither here nor there. Either way I felt skittish as I watched him shake the sand off the blanket with quick snaps of his muscular arms. My clothing now securely back in place.

What was I thinking? I wasn't.

It felt natural to let him seek the curves of my hips in near worship. I felt wanted. More than wanted. More than seen even. I fail to even find the words to describe how it felt to have his hands burn against my own scalding skin.

But this doesn't need to mean anything. It's just a bit of fun. I scoff internally, chastising myself. What a blatant lie.

I exhale deeply and look over to Byzantine, his eyes fixed on the road ahead. His full lips are rounded in a concentrated pout while he changes gears, his hand grazing my thigh before pulling away to rest it on his own. Long fingers curve around the leather of the steering wheel, sometimes drumming against it, and sometimes simply gripping it. The broad curve of his chest against his shirt makes my throat tighten and suddenly it's all too much.

I tear my gaze away from him as I feel my core clench, liquid heat traveling down my spine. God, he's beautiful. Why did he have to be so good looking? He's impossible to resist. I roll my eyes, annoyed by my body's reaction to this man and cross my arms in protest.

I'm so fucking screwed.

But I'm also not an idiot, I know he was trying to distract me from talking about the kiss. It was a very good distraction. I'll give him that. It dawns on me then, that he avoided kissing me our entire time at the beach—well on the mouth at least. I swivel my head around to say something but then realize Byzantine is parking the car in front of my building and I lose all courage to say anything.

He keeps the car idling as he pops out to come open my door as usual. I step out, suddenly feeling awkward. But he doesn't seem to care and takes my hand in his and kisses it. He's so gentle today it's almost jarring. And then, while his eyes are still locked on mine, he slowly turns my palm over, uncovering the raised scar on my wrist and my brain goes quiet.

He stops as if to wait and see if I'll pull my hand away but I can't move. Slowly, he leans down and brings his mouth to the scar, pressing his lips up the length of it. I watch, entranced and slightly shocked, as his tongue swipes out, a small hot lick and then it's gone.

My body trembles with the sensation of his reverent kiss along such an intimate place. A part of me I'd rather not look at too closely.

But his actions are saying much more than his lips ever could. *I see you,* they say. It feels like he's asking for forgiveness for something he had no control over. Had no way of knowing. I'm on the edge of panic when he finally lets go of my wrist and smiles up at me. I swallow loudly. He raises his hand to my face, my chin settling into his palm while his thumb traces the now familiar path of my bottom lip. I chase the feeling before it's gone and look back at him. He holds my gaze for a little while longer and finally steps away.

"Sweet dreams, my little sun," he says into the night before climbing back into the car, the sound of the door slamming shut making me flinch.

Eventually, I shake myself out of this day long fever dream and turn towards my building door knowing he won't leave until I'm actually inside the building. I give him a small wave and turn the key into the lock, open the front door, the sound of his car driving up my street the last thing I hear before climbing up the stairs and into my apartment.

The next morning I wake up with the familiar black void hovering above my bed threatening to swallow me whole. Byzantine's repeated interest in my scar must have triggered it. I've been able to dodge it for a few months but it's never far away or gone too long. The last time this happened I stayed in bed for over a week. Lenix, bless her, managed to cover my ass at work.

I turn onto my side in a meek version of the fetal position, dragging the sheets over my shoulders even if it's sweltering hot inside my room.

Not again. I squeeze my eyes shut hoping it's just a lingering effect of a night spent tossing and turning but the anxiety like wet sand in my stomach informs me otherwise.

The unease is here to stay.

All I want to do now is drift back to sleep and pretend for just a little while longer.

That word again. Pretend.

Pretend I'm normal and don't wish I could die when I wake up like this. Pretend I'm anyone else but me, anywhere but here. Make up a life where I had a happy childhood. A life where River didn't leave me here alone. Pretend this choking feeling will ever disappear and that I know anything else but *this*. The familiar sinking feeling of emptiness deep in my bones, constantly rewriting my DNA with feelings of unworthiness and nothingness. It's exhausting.

I curl even tighter into myself and let out a sob, somehow knowing I have no other choice but to cry if I ever want to escape this fucking feeling. If I ever stand the chance of surviving this all over again. Surviving the sudden need for a life so much fuller than this. A life spent happy, whatever happy means to that unbroken version of myself. It's such a waste of time to feel, so much easier to just...not.

But I can still feel Byzantine's kisses searing the length of my scar and I can't look away. Can't look away from the reason this scar even exists in the first place. The reason I left as soon as I had the strength and money to escape the memories. But the cruel joke is I can never escape. To escape would mean taking a scalpel to my soul and cutting out all of the ugly pieces of myself. Cut out all the parts of me I've tried to leave behind. It's never worked. Why was I so shocked when it still didn't work this time?

I wipe my tears off my face with an angry swipe of my hand, and text Lenix to come over before our shift tonight. The void might be back but I refuse for it to take over my life like all the other times. I have bills to pay, it can wait. I drag my tired body into the shower and let the water wash away some of the melancholy. It only lasts long enough for me to dry my skin and put some clothes on. I sit in a catatonic state on the edge of my bed until the intercom buzzes for me to let Lenix in.

My head rests on Lenix's lap, her back against the wall, legs sprawled on the bed as she absentmindedly plays with my hair while some tv-reality show plays on my laptop.

Lenix has seen me in worse states than this, the scariest are the ones I slip into while blackout drunk. It's not a pretty sight according to her. I wouldn't know, I never remember those moments. There's a reason she calls me her gloomy baby. The nickname makes me cringe every single time she says it, but how can I deny it when she's had to console me more than once while crying on a dirty sidewalk at three in the morning while stuffing cold pizza in my mouth.

In the morning, when she graciously hands me back the missing pieces, I can't help but to feel the shame crawl under my skin like cockroaches. I don't understand how she puts up with me. I'm exhausting to be around and she basically spends most of her time making sure I don't fall off a cliff somewhere. Figuratively...most of the time.

"We have about an hour before we need to start getting ready," she says, her voice rumbling against my ear. "Do you want to talk about it? I mean, *is* there something to talk about? You know I'm cool either way," she reassures, continuing to play with my hair.

I can't help but to smile and sit up to look at her.

"I love you, you know that right?" I tell her.

Her eyes soften, "I love you too babes, and of course I know that." She squeezes my hand and pauses still looking at me. "So...that's a no on the talking then?" she teases, a sly grin on her face as if she already knows the answer.

I laugh and give her an eye roll that says *yeah we're avoiding the subject for now.*

"I have a joint in my purse if that'll help," she offers.

"No thanks, I always get paranoid when I smoke before a shift, thanks though."

She shrugs and jumps off of the bed. "Suit yourself," she replies, fishing out the joint from her purse. She opens the window, sitting on the ledge, legs up to her chest and lights up, the soothing smell of weed slowly wafting into the room.

I sheepishly realize then that I haven't told her about what happened between Byzantine and I yesterday.

But the thought of even formulating the words to explain what the fuck happened between us leaves me mentally drained so I watch her smoke her joint instead in easy silence. I'll tell her later. Or tomorrow. Or never.

A tiny shameful part of me wants to keep it a secret. Or just pretend it never happened.

It's hard to feel anything with the void currently taking up so much space anyway. I sit up in bed and let out a long dramatic sigh. I can't believe I have to work tonight when I feel like this.

I slide out of bed and start rifling through my closet for the sluttiest outfit I can work in, determined to fill the void with a distracting outfit and Lenix's company.

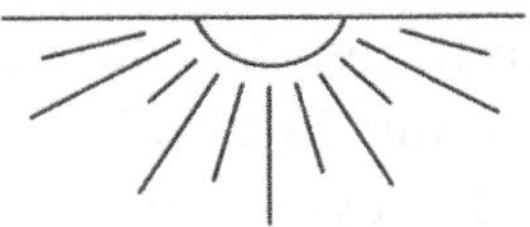

Chapter 25

Byzantine

I'm scowling at the sun, lost in thought while sitting near Connor's pool, the tumbler full of whiskey I'm holding sweating from the heat.

Sunny has been distant since our time at the beach over a week ago. I knew she would be. Retreat into her little shell, locked up surrounded by her familiar walls. She's avoiding me as much as possible, the only real time we have together is when I drive her home after her shifts. I can't stomach the thought of her walking home alone so late at night.

But even then she seems distracted or just not quite there. She has this vacant look to her that I've seen before.

Before...when she was already mine and I didn't keep her safe. When I failed her and the price was her life. The vision of her on the bathroom floor from another lifetime follows me around like a noose around my neck.

It makes me avoid her in turn. I avoid the bar as much as possible, busying myself with the other businesses we own around town.

It's a familiar pattern to fall back on. I've done it so many times, you'd think I could make myself stop. But avoidance is something we both have in common. We have lifetimes of practice.

But I also have a nagging feeling it's not just what happened between us that's making her distant. It's something else entirely. I can't bring myself to ask.

My thoughts keep drifting to the scar on her wrist. My mind aches to know what happened, what made her take a blade to her wrist and press so deep it left a mark like that. Sunny's body locks up whenever I come too close to the truth.

For now we both just aggravate this yawning distance between us and pretend nothing ever happened between us.

I let out an irritated groan, gripping the glass I'm holding far too hard when Connor strolls in.

"Do you ever go home brother?" he drawls.

I glare at him, not bothering to answer and finish off my whiskey in one large gulp.

"Where's Bastian?" I ask instead.

"In the office hunched over like, three laptops, busy being a genius I think," he says, plopping on the lounge chair beside me.

"Do you still go to those fights in the West End?" I ask, out of the blue. I need to let out my frustration before I lose my fucking mind. Maybe punch something in the process.

"Once in a while," he answers with a grin, his eyes glinting at the promise of physical violence. "Why? You itching for a fight?" He leans over conspiratorially. "Wouldn't have anything to do with a long-legged bartender I caught you with the other week?"

I say nothing. An answer in itself.

"I fucking knew you buying that shithole was not for *profitable business endeavours,*" he mocks, air quoting the last part just to drive in his point and I fight the urge to sock him right in the nose.

"Don't read into it asshole, you're the one who told me to keep an eye on her."

"You're keeping an eye on her alright," he snickers.

I punch him hard in the bicep before he has time to react.

"Asshole. Fucking *chill,* I was only joking," he says, glaring at me, but the amused glimmer in his eyes remains. "Just make sure we can trust her, alright? That and her little friend of hers. I can tell she's in on the secret. But if I catch just a fucking whiff that one of them have been talking," his face now as deadly as the next words out of his mouth. "You know what needs to happen."

Dread washes over me but I don't react and match his stare instead.

"Don't worry your pretty little head about it brother," I say sardonically. "I've got this under control."

Connor keeps his icy stare for a second longer, and then, like flipping a switch, he shifts from lethal to playful.

"So bare knuckle fighting, yeah? Will you be watching or participating?"

"Participating," I grunt back.

He arches his brow and reaches for his phone. "Let me find out the details for tonight and we can head out." I settle back into the lounge chair, relief washing over me. Itching for the sick thrill of my fist colliding with someone else's face.

The underground fight is taking place in the basement of Danny's butcher shop up on 3rd avenue. I didn't bother asking why.

A hard punch slams into my chin and my entire body flings backward with the force, stumbling a few steps trying to regain my balance. The crowd roars around me as I bring my hand to my lips, the familiar taste of copper filling my mouth. I glare up at my opponent, he looks like a raging bull shuffling back and forth around me in a half-circle.

The pain blooms in my jaw, and I can feel the blood seep through my teeth as I smile at him. The crowd grows even louder at the sight. I savor the pain, the endorphins traveling down my body and grounding me to the moment. This is exactly what I needed.

My naked chest drips with sweat as I roll my shoulders and stretch my neck left to right. I spit blood on the floor and wipe my hands on my jeans. We've been at it for a while now, I can tell the other guy is getting winded and I'm just biding my time, looking for an opening for the final blow. I stalk towards him as he tries to intimidate me with his fancy footwork and I struggle not to roll my eyes at him.

He thinks he's in the MMA or some shit.

It only takes a small indecision on his part for me to finally find the opening I've been waiting for. I lurch forward slamming my fist in quick consecutive jabs to his side and then finish with a solid right hook to the face before he face-plants to the floor—unconscious.

I glare down at him, smirking boastfully while blood trickles from a cut into my left eye, wiping it away mechanically. I'm watching the loser get dragged out of sight, when I feel hands grab my shoulders from behind, and I flinch until I hear Connor's laughing yelp in my ear, swiveling me around.

"You were ruthless, brother," he exclaims, handing me back my shirt. "We should do this more often," he says, waving a wad of cash in my face.

"Yeah, no thanks. I'm good," I respond, heading for the exit, the fresh air hitting my lungs in relief.

"You sure? You might have missed your calling," he continues.

"Or maybe you're just a greedy son of a bitch," I say as we both head towards Connor's SUV.

"Yeah, also that," he answers, chuckling as he climbs in the car. "Did you want to go for a drink or are you all beat up and shit?"

I grunt out a yes, settling into the seat. "I just need to shower first."

"Sure thing, and let me guess..." he says, turning the keys in the ignition, music already blaring through the speakers, a taunting smirk on his lips. "Sammies?"

I don't give him the satisfaction, dropping my head onto the headrest and closing my eyes instead, savoring the pain drumming through my body. "Just shut up and drive."

Chapter 26

Sunny

I'm deep in the weeds when I notice Connor and Bastian walk in, followed closely behind by Byzantine. I nearly drop the two drinks I'm making when I notice his face.

His chin is bruised, his left eyebrow split open, the eyelid underneath slightly swollen. What the hell happened to him? The most confounding thing about it is the almost serene smile he's sporting as he prowls into the bar looking more like a champion and not like he just got jumped in an alley.

It's a Saturday night so the place is packed but their usual booth is now permanently reserved for them. A detail that annoys the entire staff since it's prime real estate for actual paying customers. But the three always leave *very* generous tips anytime they're here so no one's really complaining.

Byzantine's eyes drift to mine before he settles into the booth. I quickly glance back down to the drinks I'm making, frazzled that he's caught me staring. But before looking away, I can't help but notice the attention the guys are gathering in the bar. It's inevitable whenever they walk into a room. People might not know how deadly they are but the unmistakable air to them can't be ignored. It literally rolls off of them.

Women and men can't help but watch and stare. Not to mention all three are confoundingly gorgeous. Like how is that even possible?

Bastian and Connor are related so I guess it runs in the family but Byzantine? Well, he's just in a league of his own. Or maybe I'm just biased. Everyone loses their shine when he's around.

A tendril of jealousy curls around my throat at the thought of someone else trying to catch his attention tonight. It's not unusual but Byzantine typically doesn't bother with any of it.

Now I'm not so sure.

We've been avoiding each other. I have absolutely no idea where we stand, and I honestly don't have that much of a desire to figure it out. It's not from a lack of caring, I just haven't felt like myself since I woke up so far deep inside this dark hole that I'm having a hard time finding my way back out. Lenix has been sleeping over more often than not. Probably picking up on the fact that I would rather die than be left alone right now. So you know—fun times all around.

I try to keep my attention on the customers in front of me but my attention keeps drifting back to their booth. Of course, Byzantine looks sexy even with a busted face and I chastise myself at being so fucking basic that a man who's been caught in a brawl makes me hot and bothered.

I'm not the only one with that train of thought according to the tables of women glancing over hungrily every so often. I resist the urge to chuck ice at their faces and dip my head back down, trying to concentrate on my task at hand.

After a few minutes, Lenix calls me over to the service bar. As usual she's serving their table as per Connor's long-standing request, a detail I haven't failed to notice.

"Have you seen Bizzy's face? What's that about?" she whisper-yells, her tray covering half her face as if trying to hide behind it.

"Yeah, it's hard not to fucking notice," I bite back, my frustration obviously aimed at the man in question and not towards her. "Not like I'll find out..." I trail off as I watch Lenix punch her order in. She glances over to me, the glare of the computer illuminating her worried features.

"So nothing's changed?" she asks.

"Nope." I shrug my shoulders in defeat. I finally cracked a few days ago and admitted to Lenix what happened between Byzantine and I.

She was mad at me for a whole three seconds before relenting her grudge for all the *juicy details*—as she would say.

"Well maybe this is your opening," Lenix says as she leans over the bar giving me a mischievous side glance. "You know...kiss and make it better, kind of thing?" she adds, wiggling her eyebrows playfully.

I throw my rag at her and she giggles, catching it mid-air before it hits her face.

"I'm just saying."

I don't bother giving her a response and quickly make the drinks she just punched in. With a thanks and a wink she pops them on her tray and saunters back to their table. I notice Byzantine watching me before I turn back around determined to ignore him for the rest of the night.

My heart is in my throat as I rap my knuckles on the office door.

"Come in." I hear Byzantine's voice echo from behind the door before I creak it open and inch my way into the room.

He's sitting on the couch to the right of his desk, some type of frozen *something* that he probably stole from the walk-in freezer slapped over his eye. I lean on the wall behind me, having lost the ability to stand without looking awkward in front of him.

"I was starting to think you didn't feel pain," I mutter.

He side-eyes me with a grin. "What does that mean?"

"Well, look at you." I wave my hand up and down at him as if it's obvious. "You just waltz in looking like this, and then order a drink as if nothing's the matter."

He chuckles but says nothing.

"You look awful by the way," I bite out just to spite him, my arms crossed squarely on my chest, a well-curated bored look on my face.

"Is that so?" he says calmly, placing the frozen bag beside him and looking at me inquisitively. "Why are you here, Sunny?"

My eyes lock with his as I stutter out a response, "Well...I mean...I'm done closing the bar so..." I stare at my shoes, unable to finish my sentence, suddenly feeling like a complete idiot as if it's too bold for me to assume he'll be driving me home after weeks of doing exactly that.

"Is that all?" he asks cooly, his question weighted down by all of the other unanswered questions attached to those three simple words.

I slink towards the two-seater facing him and sit down, drumming my fingers on my knees while the left one bobs up and down, anxiety coursing through me. I swallow hard and finally say, "I know I've been acting strange since, well since—"

"Since I made you come against my tongue?"

I nearly choke on the lust that barrels through my chest as I watch him proudly lean back on the couch. His arms laid out behind him, his legs wide and relaxed, an arrogant smirk curling his lips. I bite my own lip while I try to scrub the image of me kneeling in front of him out of my head.

"Well, when you put it that way," I answer, having no clue what or how to reply.

He stays silent, studying me for far too long before finally speaking, "Are you naked under that skirt?"

Half-shocked and half-burning up I sputter out, "What? Of course I'm not. It wouldn't be professional you fucking weirdo." I cross one leg over the other now worried he can see under my skirt from his vantage point.

Well, worried maybe isn't quite the right word to describe how I'm feeling right now.

Byzantine, looking every bit the smug prince, watches me as I squirm from the opposite couch, his eyes darkening as he licks his bottom lip slowly.

"Take them off," he demands.

"Take what off," I reply quickly, playing dumb while resisting the urge to obey his command, my core tightening with the thought.

He lets out a dark chuckle and it travels straight down my spine and all the way down to my toes.

"Take. Them. Off," he repeats, leaning forward, elbows resting on his knees, hands hanging loosely in front of him. "Stand up, reach under your skirt and slide your panties down your legs before I do it myself," he orders while he leans back on the couch resuming his original position.

My heart is practically exploding behind my ribcage, the lust so thick in the air I can practically taste it. If this was anyone else I'd be laughing in their face. But his words hang heavy between us and I can tell he knows I'm resisting, but he can also tell that I'll eventually concede.

I roll my eyes and let out a long huff.

"I fucking hate you, you know that?" I tell him while standing up and doing exactly what he ordered. With my black thong now in my hand, I brandish it in the air.

"There, happy now?"

"Very," he drawls. "Now hand them to me."

My throat goes dry as he just sits there. Waiting. The annoyed act I was holding onto for dear life evaporates with every step I take towards him. I've suddenly fallen very serious by the time I step into the space between his spread legs.

Unhurriedly, he reaches over and takes them out of my hand, promptly shoving them into his pocket. I waiver in place while I watch the same hand now glide up my parted legs, stopping in the middle of my thigh as I hold in a small frustrated whimper. He leans over, giving it a small squeeze and then a lingering kiss while slowly looking up at me with his hooded eyes.

"Thank you," he whispers, pulling away and leaning back.

"Now," he says darkly. "You're going to walk back over there, hike up your skirt, sit down and open your legs for me."

I hold his stare for another tense moment, my thighs growing slicker while his command still rings in my ears. Finally, I turn around and take one shaky step after the next back to the opposite couch. My mind goes absolutely blank when I finally sit back down, facing him. Skirt hiked up to my hips.

Just like he ordered.

I take a second to steady my breath before looking back at Byzantine. His eyes—they burn into my fucking soul.

They're the only tell he's even remotely affected by the sight. I swear I see a flash of pain travel across his face but he quickly blinks it away. I don't think I would be so obliging if he didn't look equally untethered.

Finally, I slowly open my legs and I can practically see his pupils dilate with every inch I offer him. My body burns hot, now desperate for his touch, my legs open wide—waiting.

Then, he smiles. Predatory. Lethal.

"Good girl."

With the sound of his praise, my eyes close, his words reaching a part of me that has been dormant until now. His voice, the only sound able to coax it to life.

"Now, my little sun," his voice practically a whisper, deep and low. "You're going to place your heels on the couch, spread wide and show me how wet you are."

My body quivers with want, yearning to follow his filthy words down the abyss we're tumbling into. I do as he says and rest my feet on either side of me, my legs falling even wider open. I reach down and glide my fingers through my arousal, and then raise them up to show him, as they glisten with the evidence of my desire.

"*Fuck*," Byzantine rasps out, heat branded on every single letter of the word.

I can tell by the twitch of his hand and the bulge in his jeans that he's as turned on as I am, but he doesn't move an inch. His eyes steadfast and wanting. "Now," he growls, his voice more urgent than before. "Take those same fingers and spread yourself open for me."

A breathy moan slips out as I follow his orders blindly, parting my pussy open for him with trembling fingers. The lust builds and builds inside of me and I resist the need to let my head fall backwards onto the couch and close my eyes shut with the pleasure I'm currently experiencing.

"That's it, little sun," he says through clenched teeth. "Let me see what's mine." I barely recognize Byzantine's voice, his eyes near feral as they lock with mine and I shudder under his stare.

The tension is coiling deep inside of me, my legs shaking with both need and desperation, the urge to touch myself and release some of the ache near excruciating. Instead, I steady my gaze and look at him from beneath my lashes, my chest rising up and down, waiting for him to tell me what to do next.

"Fuck yourself with those pretty little fingers while I watch," he finally says darkly.

I exhale with the sheer relief of now being allowed to touch myself more fully. My hips hitch as I bite my bottom lip and start pumping my fingers in and out.

"That's my good girl...just like that."

"Oh my god, Byzantine..."

My eyes fall shut, lost in the pleasure of his voice and my touch. But when I hear the rustle of his belt buckle and the glide of his zipper, I snap them back open, my mouth salivating at the sight.

His hand is firmly on his hard length, giving himself long languid strokes as he watches me come apart. My movements falter for just a second when I notice the two daggers tattooed along either side of his cock. I'm too far away to study them closely, but it doesn't prevent me from being captivated.

A spike of pleasure makes me clench around my fingers as I stroke my throbbing clit with my other hand. I'm hypnotized by Byzantine's steady gaze and the increasingly urgent strokes of his hand.

"You're so beautiful like this, little sun," he groans out.

I whimper, having trouble even concentrating while he continues. "Look at you. Your cheeks flushed, your pussy so wet for me, so fucking perfect."

I'm barrelling towards the edge as he continues to pump his cock into his fist at the sight of me.

"Are you going to come for me?" His hips jerking up as he strokes his shaft, my eyes rolling back in pleasure.

"Yes...yes," I moan. "Byzantine, I...I'm..."

As soon as the words are out of my mouth, my orgasm rips through me and I implode. I push my fingers even deeper trying to chase the feeling while I cry out.

I hear Byzantine's low groan and my eyes fall back to him just in time to watch his cock twitch and spill out onto his hand. His eyes squeeze shut and then quickly open again, his breaths heavy and ragged as he slows down giving his cock quick jerks, chasing his own release.

Finally, our gazes lock. Enraptured.

A loaded silence fills the room as a residual tremor of pleasure wracks my body. I continue to watch him from across the office, both speechless and breathless.

Finally, a slow pleased smile appears on Byzantine's face and without breaking eye contact he reaches for a tissue, wipes his hands clean, shoves himself back into his jeans and stands up.

"Come, I'll drive you home."

Chapter 27

Sunny

If I would let my wet tongue slip out of my mouth and taste the air right now, I'm sure I would get zapped by all the electricity crackling in the air between Byzantine and I.

Shockingly, we're both as closed off as ever as I sit in the passenger seat of his car, the music filling the void we can never seem to fill with our own voices. Byzantine seems to only be vocal when his voice is hurtling me over the edge.

I mean, I'm not complaining, I guess.

Still doesn't change the fact that we've been avoiding the subject of our kiss and the one time I tried to bring it up he made me come instead.

Now I can't help but wonder if the kiss was just that—a kiss. Was it really that big of a deal? Did I imagine everything else besides the kiss? The way he stroked my hair and murmured soothing words into my hair. The way it felt like free falling. And not the good kind of free fall. More like the kind where you know you're about to die as soon as you hit the ground.

So...kissing Byzantine felt like dying? That's pretty macabre.

I shuffle in my seat, looking out the window with a sigh. It's late—or early—depending on how you see it. We're on the precipice of dawn, not quite but you can still feel it in the air with the birds chirping the upcoming sunrise. I should be rather relaxed after what happened in the office, but my brain is rattling off every worry I've ever conjured up at a neck breaking speed.

What if? What if? What if?

But then, Byzantine turns left on Billow street and my head pops up.

"My apartment is the other way," I say.

"I know," he replies as he shifts gears.

Annoyed, I glower at him.

"Let me guess, you aren't going to tell me where we're heading?" I ask.

Byzantine smiles while keeping his eyes on the road.

"What's the fun in that?" he answers, amusement lacing his tone.

I'm too tired to argue so I just settle back against the window in a huff. After longer than expected, having driven outside the city, he finally parks—a large field of wildflowers sprawling in front of us. He kills the engine and leans back into the seat, his hands laced together across his chest, looking straight ahead seemingly unbothered.

"What are we doing here?" I finally ask.

"Watching the sunrise."

"Oh."

I don't know what else to say so I say nothing. Quite a regular occurrence between us. We sit in silence for a while as I try to pick out the first hints of pink in the horizon but only the navy blue stares back at me.

My gaze drifts near a patch of flowers on the outskirts of the field, wondering what kind they are, but then a thought suddenly pops into my head.

"Windflower," I blurt out.

"What?" Byzantine turns his head over to look at me.

"You called me windflower the other day. Why?"

I catch the guilt in his eyes before he turns away, back to the non-existent sunrise. After a long beat he finally answers.

"It's my favorite flower."

I can't hold back my shock and bark out a laugh. "You have a favorite flower? I don't even think *I* have a favorite."

Byzantine keeps his gaze straight ahead. "Why? Because I'm a man I'm not allowed to have a favorite flower?" he says plainly.

I drop the smile. "Well no, it's not because you're a man—that's besides the point. It's just...have you met yourself? You just don't really strike me as someone who has a favorite flower, that's all." I fall back in my seat a little unnerved. "Sorry if I offended you or whatever," I grumble.

He peers over with his boyish grin that makes me want to kiss him—or punch him, I'm never too sure.

"I'm full of surprises aren't I, little sun."

Realizing quickly that he's alluding to what happened earlier in his office, I roll my eyes.

"You're an ass."

His laughter rolls over me, warmth enveloping me as I watch his eyes glint with mirth. My heart pinches into a tight squeeze and it makes me look away.

We stay like this in now comfortable silence, for a change, until finally the first rays of the sun yawns into existence. Purple bleeds into pink into orange and I'm lost in the simple beauty of the moment.

Then, Byzantine's voice floats over to me, it's barely a whisper but it slices into me nonetheless. "Will you ever tell me why you have that scar on your wrist?"

The sunrise blurs as I blink back the tears his words are evoking, unable or unwilling to even acknowledge his question. I breathe in a heavy sigh and watch the sun illuminate the field instead. The rays bounce off the early morning dew collecting on petals and grass as they gently sway against the breeze.

Eventually, I feel Byzantine move beside me. His hand slowly wraps around my wrist, his thumb gently pressing against my scar, stroking my skin in small circles round and round and round.

My body implores for him to never stop touching me, while it also yearns to run as far away as possible.

"I wish you would stop asking," I finally whisper back, letting one single tear fall down my cheek and over my lips, my tongue darting out and catching it so as to hide it from Byzantine.

He leans over and with his free hand, tucks a strand of hair behind my ear. His touch, so light I can barely feel it. His hand lingers there, tracing the wet path of my one fallen tear until his hand falls back on his lap. I glance over to him then, the sun reflecting back the yellow in his eyes. He studies me, his features so serious. So sullen.

"I don't think I can do that," he whispers.

Suddenly, I realize I've never seen his face so open—so raw. I let out a small sigh, trying to memorize what I'm witnessing inside his soulful eyes. They seem boundless, endless, a sea of overlapping emotions that would take me lifetimes to decipher. I choke back the sob traveling up my throat, my eyes burning from the effort.

I can tell he knows that I'm seeing a part of him that I've never been privy to before. And a part of me feels oddly honored. The same pang of nostalgia I've felt before, whenever I'm in Byzantine's presence, slices me deep. He sighs and blinks and suddenly the veil is back and all I see is myself reflected back.

My hand nearly flies up to his face, desperate for him not to disappear behind the mask I'm now becoming so familiar with. I should know, I wear a similar one anytime he's near. And with that he finally lets go of my wrist, settles into his seat, turns the key in the ignition and drives us back into the city.

I haven't slept yet. It didn't take long after Byzantine dropped me off to traipse back out and head to the beach. I count the strokes one after the next until my lungs burn, then turn on my back, the waves only a weak push and pull—just enough to rock me back and forth as I catch my breath, bobbing on the surface of the ocean.

I'm trying to tire myself out, hoping the exhaustion will hit and maybe I'll get a chance to sleep for once. I haven't really bothered to try lately. Sleep evades me and I let it. My thoughts are a constant nuisance lately that just never relents and it's not as if my dreams are any better.

Most of them leave me with an ache so deep I can barely breathe.

The only soothing thought I can muster up lately is Byzantine's lips on mine. But then again, how soothing is it really?

It's becoming an obsession. Anytime he's close, I hyper-fixate on the fact that he hasn't truly kissed me since that first time outside the bookstore. It feels childish to even bring it up. I lack the courage anyway. Let alone try to kiss him myself. We deliberately tip-toe around each other. Even the way we lust over each other is distant.

Watching me like he owns me from across the room as I finger myself under his careful instructions. It was so fucking hot, and yet so unbearably cold.

Maybe this is all part of his master plan. To make me crave his touch until I beg. And I'm very *very* close to begging. I can't go a few hours without the thought of his hands on me rushing back in full force. The hot need for release is beginning to permeate my every thought.

Let me see what's mine.

I didn't bother correcting him. Was he wrong? It seems he claimed me the moment he wrapped his fingers around my throat in that dark alley. Maybe even before then. Even when I feared him.

I still do. Only now, the reasons I fear him have changed, morphing into something different—other-worldly—slowly pulling me into his orbit.

It's only been a little over a month since Byzantine walked into Sammies with his deadly presence and promised Gary a slow death. How could I think of him in any other manner than what he is?

A killer. A criminal.

But does it matter?

That version of Byzantine pales in comparison to the one who spoon feeds me his quiet presence in small bites. Like a delicacy. And I crave more and more. Then there's the unexplainable familiarity. Like a favorite blanket, soft and full of the comforting scents of home. Nothing about it makes sense.

Especially, when it seems like he seeks a level of intimacy I don't even know if I possess, let alone can reciprocate. A closeness shared through heated looks and probing questions that threatens to topple the walls I so willfully hide behind.

I hate the way he asks about my scar like he's owed a confession. What was I going to tell him anyway?

That Death showed up one day when I was a teenager and never left? How Death became an intimate friend, rolling itself in a ball at the feet of my bed like a cat while I slept. How I'd write Death poetry while pretending to listen in class or how it would hold my hand in the shower while I cried, the fresh blood on my thigh flowing down the drain.

How Death would whisper in my ear *not yet*. Over and over again until one day it stopped. One day it just unfurled its bony hands and told me it was time.

Twenty-three was old enough to die. And finally, I had a legitimate excuse. A tragedy that could explain why living always felt so hard. Finally, I could leave this plane with purpose. Death handed me the blade and promised me relief. Release from the anger and the constant ache of living. And I was tired. So fucking tired.

But Death had been full of treasonous lies.

I was unconscious before the blade ever reached my other wrist. My roommate found me in the bathtub. Like a fucking cliche. Waking up in the hospital with my parents hovering over my bed, the same parents who pretended to care if I lived or died, had been one of the worst days of my life.

I had failed. And Death had lied.

Four years later, I was still here.

So no, there was no point in telling Byzantine about my scar.

Finally, I close my eyes, focusing on the warm sun washing over me for a little while longer. Eventually, I swim back to shore, plopping myself on my towel, and try to catch my breath. The exertion must have helped because I slowly drift into sleep a few minutes later.

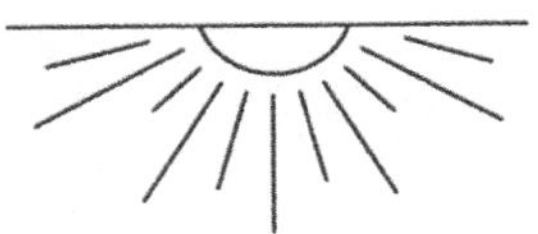

Chapter 28

Byzantine

There was no body for me to mourn. No way for my tears to fall on your skin, promising to love you until my own dying breath.

Why Gabriel?

Why did you have to be so foolish? So close to the edge when the wind had snapped your coat in warning. But it was my fault you were gone. It was my fault—all of it.

This pain was both my solace and my torment. I could still picture you falling from the edge, your hand reaching out to me. A plea for my help. I had failed you Gabriel. I had watched you fall. And did nothing.

What hurt the most was the inability to mourn you publicly. To our peers, we were merely business partners. Not lovers. What we shared was whispered in the dark of nights as I thrusted into you. The feeling of you so hot and tight and perfect.

No one could know. And now? No one would ever know. You were perfect Gabriel. And so young. So full of life. Why did you have to leave me like this? Who was I now without you?

I was a pit of secrets. And you had been my most prized one. You had loved me so freely and I never knew how to reciprocate, the tight confines of society like a shackle to my throat.

I stood in my room, lost in thought, trailing my fingers against a book sitting on the table. I opened it and found the pressed flower hiding between the pages. Your voice floated back to me. Memories of the day you had gifted it to me.

You seemed so humbled by your love for me while I sat beside you, holding your gift in my hands, unable to feed you the words you so desperately needed from me.

"It's a blue windflower," you had said in a low whisper as if not to disturb the silence coiling between us. "It means 'I am faithfully attached to you.'"

You had looked up at me with adoration and I had cowardly looked away, your love like honey to my sore throat, so sweet and yet, so overwhelming.

"Legend has it, the flower was created by the goddess Aphrodite when she sprinkled nectar on the blood of her dead lover Adonis," you continued. "It became to symbolize her eternal grief, representing Adonis' life—beautiful, graceful and short-lived."

I had smiled back at you, brushing my fingers into your blond curls.

"Only you would find such a tragic story romantic," I had said softly.

You chuckled, looking down at your hands.

"Thank you Gabriel." I had leaned into you, touching your lips with mine. "I will cherish this book, like I cherish you."

You had beamed so brightly and I kissed you once more, chasing the feeling of the moment into the next.

Now, I looked at the pressed windflower and wanted to scream my pain into the very pages of the book you had so lovingly given to me. How ominous your words now rang in my ears.

Beautiful.

Short-lived.

Eternal grief.

I lay in bed, unable to sleep. I'm not even trying to distract myself, just staring at the wall, so full of thoughts, it feels like they're seeping out of my pores like noxious fumes ready to kill me. Sunny asking about the significance of a windflower has left me agitated and battling memories from so long ago that I can't seem to suppress. All they do is hurt like a sore that never heals, reminding me of all the ways Sunny and I have failed each other over the centuries.

Even saying that sounds ridiculous, but finding it fantastical has never quelled the pain before and certainly doesn't now.

I swipe my hand over my scruff, sighing loudly into the silent room. I throw the duvet off my body and climb out of bed, feeling more restless by the second like an electric charge radiating through my veins. I pace around the room, my muscles tight and corded, with nowhere to go so early in the morning. My mind is eating me alive and all I do is feed it more and more and more.

Sunny's still resisting me, but I won't relent. I'm not letting her escape now that I have her in my grasp. I can tell that she's still grappling with what I've done to Gary. She won't let herself open up and trust me completely. And it grinds on me more than I would think.

And yes, maybe objectively, I'm not a good man. She deserves so much better than what I have to offer. But I'm not ashamed of who I am. I don't fear the darkness inside of me, I never have—and one day soon she won't either.

One day soon she will give in to me, to us. No matter what it fucking takes, I will have her, mind, body and soul.

Chapter 29

Sunny

I hear the buzz of my phone on my nightstand as I walk out from the bathroom, my wet hair sticking to my shoulders, cinching my towel tighter around me. I've been off for a few days and for a split-second I wonder if it's Byzantine calling.

But when the same number I've been avoiding for over a year flashes on the screen, my throat closes up and my heart squeezes hard inside my chest.

It's my mother.

I could ignore it. It's been established that I'm quite good at that—ignoring things. I could just let it go to voicemail.

Yes, ignore it. Easy.

But my hand reaches for the phone anyway, ultimately making the decision for me. I don't know what compels me to pick up now but I do. I tap the screen and answer the call.

"Hello?" I say tentatively.

"Hello Sunny," my mother snaps.

The grip on my phone tightens, my eyes falling shut as I try to keep my breath even.

"Oh hey mom—"

"Don't *hey mom* me," she sneers, interrupting me as always, her voice icy against my ear. "Do you really think you could ignore me like this and I would just...just let it go? How could you!?" she shrieks.

Her shrill voice makes my skin crawl and I curse my impulsive decision to even answer this call.

I try to keep my voice leveled but the snark in my tone is sharp like a blade, "How could I what, *mother*?" I put emphasis on the word knowing she hates it when I call her mother and not mom.

"Don't you play your silly games with me missy. You are still my child and you *will* respect me," she seethes, making me clutch the phone even harder. "You left without even telling me or your dad you were leaving. How could you? And *then*...then you ignore us like we're complete strangers to you?" she says with indignation, her voice rising higher with every word.

I can picture her now, in my childhood house, her fingers tangled in the telephone cord of the old landline they still have attached to the wall in the kitchen. A full face of makeup even in the house, her eyelashes heavy with the blackest mascara she can find, the blush on her cheeks a shade of pink that has always clashed with her skin tone. Stuck in a decade long passed. A decade when she still felt beautiful. An era when men still gave her the attention she so desperately craves from her husband—my father.

I hit the speaker button and place it on the dresser, the towel puddling to my feet while I riffle through the heap of clothes on the chair—washed but never folded. It takes every single ounce of strength I have not to take the bait she's carefully laid out in front of me.

Before I left for Noxport, we hadn't spoken in months. I know, although she'll never admit it, that the actual reason she's upset is because she can't uphold the picture perfect illusion of our tight-knit family if I'm gone. Especially after River. My absence is creating a tear in her carefully constructed mirage. Her worries are self-serving, they have nothing to do with me.

"How did you get this number anyway?" I quip. This woman doesn't believe in boundaries. Whatever excuse she'll give me probably won't be the truth so I'm not surprised when she skirts the question and skips right over it as if that detail is insignificant.

"I have the right to speak to my own daughter. Is it such a chore to speak to me that you had to leave like a crook in the night? I had to learn about it from Catherine since you blocked me from seeing your life online. Do you know how embarrassing that was?" she sniffs.

Catherine is my cousin. We're not close.

"Is there a reason for your call or did you just simply need to act the victim?" I bite back.

I hear the sharp intake of breath through the speaker before her piercing voice fills the room.

"Sunny Constance Delarue, I did not raise you to speak to me with such insolence!" she screams.

You didn't raise me at all.

I shimmy into a pair of leggings as she continues to chastise me and I let her run out of steam, pulling a dark green crew neck over my head and falling into bed, my phone on my chest. Finally, she falls silent.

"Are you coming back for the memorial?" she asks.

I put an arm over my eyes, my anxiety rising like a quick tide.

"What memorial?"

"It's been five years since—"

"And?" I groan through clenched teeth. "No one does a memorial after five years. What's the fucking point? Who's this even for?"

It's for her. It's always for her.

"Language, Sunny," she tuts. "Well, you might not see the point but I thought a small memorial would be a nice way to mark the event."

The event.

I can barely breathe, listening to her prattle on about the guest list while fury slices through me like a hot knife. Eventually I regain my voice and cut her off.

"I'm not coming back for the memorial. Or at all for that matter, so you can make up whatever excuse you want for my absence, I really don't give a fuck. We're done here," I snap. I don't wait for her rebuttal before hanging up, blocking her number out of spite. I fight the urge to throw my phone across the room and instead scream into my pillow, my hands in tight fists.

Why did I even pick up? I knew exactly how this was going to play out. And in one simple phone call she managed to stuff me so full of anxiety and guilt that I can barely swallow, her influence still so suffocating even this far away.

I hate her. I hate her. I hate her.

The memories I've been forcefully suppressing threaten to come back up like bile burning up my throat. I don't want to think. I don't want to look. I don't want to feel.

"Fuck!" I scream it into the pillow, biting my inner cheek so hard I can taste blood. I need to get out of here before the comforting pull of a blade on my skin makes me spiral even deeper into the void. I pick up my phone with shaky hands.

Me: Feel like day drinking?

Lenix: Always! Beach?
Me: Duh. Meet you there.

She sends me a string of emojis to accentuate her excitement and a half hearted laugh escapes my lips while I head to the dresser to fish out a bikini.

The small portable speaker sits between us, blasting the perfect curated beach day playlist courtesy of Lenix. The sun is red against my closed eyelids while I try to shade my face from the early afternoon rays. We're a bottle of Prosecco deep already, when Lenix rummages through her beach bag and pulls out a mickey of tequila.

"I knew it was in here somewhere," she exclaims, wiggling her eyebrows in my direction, the freckles on her nose that only seemed to come out after a full day in the sun, heightening her natural beauty as she twists the cap off.

"You're like Mary Poppins but for sad alcoholics," I remark between mouthfuls of chips from the bag beside me.

She scoffs, taking a swig of the bottle and handing it to me. "The only sad alcoholic here is you, thank you very much," she says, pushing her long black hair off her shoulder with her usual faux attitude.

"I'm just here for the good vibes..." she trails off, looking over my shoulder and into the distance. "And maybe a few cute boys too." She flashes a toothy smile and settles back on her elbows, closing her eyes against the rays, her face seeking the warmth of the sun.

I turn around to find Byzantine, Connor and Bastian heading towards us.

"You *invited* them?"

Lenix simply shrugs her shoulders. "Connor gave me his number last week. Thought it would be fun."

I narrow my eyes. "Lenix, are you fucking Connor?" I whisper, as if the guys could hear us from all the way over there.

Her gaze pops open, looking over my shoulder and waving. "God Sunny you don't have to be so crass," she reprimands but still winks at me deviously. "No I'm not *fucking* Connor. We're just friends. Besides, he's basically a male version of myself. He's just fun to be around," she replies noncommittally.

"He's *fun* to be around?" I repeat dumbfoundedly.

Doesn't she remember how I met him? But then, I swallow any more of my retort, feeling like a hypocrite.

"Just be careful, Lenix, yeah?"

She slides her sunglasses on her face. "Always babes," she promises, and rolls on her side as the three of them reach our spot.

"Hiya boys!" Lenix says as she twinkles her fingers at them. Byzantine brittles at the word *boys* but says nothing, while Connor flashes his famous smile and drops the cooler he's holding near our heads. Bastian hangs in the back, holding a huge umbrella in his arms, Byzantine carrying the beach chairs.

I need a moment to recalibrate. They all seem so—normal. The thought of them having a normal beach day like us mere mortals is currently fighting against the larger than life image I have of them.

And...is Byzantine wearing swim trunks?

This feels all too casual but I bite down on the feeling and smile up at him. I'm casually trying to hide my annoyance about them crashing my "let's avoid all my problems at all cost" drinking party. The man currently staring at me being one of my most crucial problems in question.

"Came prepared I see?" I note, just to have something to say.

Lenix and I only brought the essentials—towel, bathing suit and booze. But these guys strolled up as if they were going camping or something.

Connor lets out a small chuckle while he watches Bastian struggle with the large beach umbrella then glances at me.

"Why would I lay on a lumpy towel like a peasant," Connor drawls while fishing out two beers from the cooler and handing one to Byzantine. Lenix mocks outrage but he only laughs. "Besides," he continues, falling into one of the beach chairs, his toned legs splayed out in front of him, chest gleaming with sweat while taking a long swig of beer. "I refuse to wash sand out of my ass."

With that, Byzantine swats Connor behind the head. "Idiot," he grouses.

Connor simply chuckles at his own joke, watching Bastian still grumble over the umbrella.

I watch Byzantine situates his chair so he's facing me, and the image of him makes my mouth go dry. His face is still bruised, but even in this casual environment, he looks as regal as ever. I take my time taking in the sight while he gives me a small knowing smirk.

His shorts hit the middle of his thighs and it only accentuates his strong legs straining against the fabric. My gaze slowly trails over his crotch, his fingers twitching ever so slightly seemingly reacting to my slow perusal.

Pleased, I continue my inspection upwards. The light dusting of hair on his chest is almost invisible in contrast to his tattoos, shiny from the suntan lotion he just slathered on. Every inch of him is defined like he's spent countless hours in the gym perfecting his physique and when I finally reach his face, I feel light-headed and I'm not sure if it's from half a bottle of Prosecco or him. He peers down at me, his smile wicked while he raises his beer up to his lips.

A small shriek pulls me out of my trance, realizing Connor placed a cold can against Lenix's back making her yelp.

"Asshole!"

Connor cackles while still brandishing the beverage towards her. "What?" he asks innocently. "I thought you were thirsty?"

She glares at him but still reaches for the beer anyway. Bastian, after finally winning the fight against the umbrella, has settled beside Connor. Never one to be talkative, he just grins watching our friends bicker back and forth.

Smiling, I lie down on my towel. But even when surrounded by the best distraction in Noxport, my thoughts stray to the conversation I had with my mother earlier. Her voice is stuck on a loop in my head.

It makes me want to seek the anesthetic comfort of apathy—and maybe some more alcohol.

I'm doing everything possible to avoid the hurt, but still it burns and burns and burns. Like a knife to the throat, I pretend not to notice the threat. The ghost of my past haunts me even here, where the sun shines bright and the boys are notoriously hot.

I reach for the tequila bottle and take a hefty swig while I avoid eye contact with Byzantine. Drinking is always a dangerous gamble when I'm trying to avoid my feelings. And I'm currently walking a fine line between the comforting numbness of the drink and the deluge of emotions threatening to explode like a cracked dam.

Thankfully, he doesn't mention my aloofness, dragging his fingers along my warm skin instead, leaving a trail of goosebumps on my thigh in his wake. The warmth of his hand is overwhelming, the dam cracking wider as I try to fight it.

Luckily, Connor is a hell of a diversion.

"So this is how the other half lives," he states, taking another sip, and looking around.

"What other half?" Lenix asks, slightly peeved.

"Plebeians," he deadpans.

The word isn't even fully out of his mouth before Bastian is swatting him over the head, but he just shakes in laughter.

"What? You know I'm right," he snickers, his toothy grin bright as he tries to avoid Bastian's next swing. "Don't you two pretend you can remember the last time you spent the afternoon at the *public* beach."

"Jesus Connor," Lenix states. "How rich are you?"

His eyes twinkles as he looks at her. "Darling, don't you know it's impolite to ask? Where are your manners?"

"Connor, do us all a favor and shut up would you?" Byzantine says piping in.

Suddenly, he sits up and playfully tries to wrestle Byzantine out of his chair, but the man is a brick wall and just sits there glaring at him. I smirk and can't help but to laugh, the weight on my chest a little easier to ignore while I spend the rest of the afternoon in easy company.

It's spent swimming, sunbathing and watching Connor chase Lenix around with half-dried seaweed. Meanwhile I try to keep up the precarious charade of being just fine. It leaves me feeling like I'll always have to pretend to be happy, even for just an afternoon. So I retreat into my shell, continuing to get even more intoxicated, unable to avoid the pain while Byzantine notices but says nothing.

Chapter 30

Sunny

It's dark out when we leave Lenix, Connor and Bastian in the beach parking lot, debating over which club to head to tonight. I slink off with Byzantine, following him to his car. I noticed he barely drank today, must be because he drove here.

"You dropping me off?" I ask, proud I didn't slur my words while asking my question.

"No you're coming home with me," he clips.

"Jeez, so bossy," I grumble.

"You're drunk, I'm not leaving you by yourself," he says while opening the passenger door for me to get in.

"I am not," I counter back.

"Sure you aren't," he mocks while walking around to the driver's side, climbing in.

"I can take care of myself, you know, I don't need your help," I mumble, feeling like my words came out all squished together.

"I know you can." He reaches over and gives my thigh a small squeeze. "Just let me take care of you for once," he adds, his thumb stroking small circles on my skin.

My throat grows tight, tears burning the back of my eyes. Fuck, I'm too drunk for this. The warmth of his hand is overwhelming, the dam splintering even wider as I take large gulping breaths, trying to continue to willfully ignore all my problems. All the morbid reasons that make me reach for the bottle in the first place.

I can feel myself spiral and there's nothing I can do to stop it.

When Byzantine finally parks his car in the underground parking lot connected to his condo, I say nothing. I'm paralyzed, barely registering what's happening around me.

"Sunny? Sunny..." I glance over to his worried face but can barely perceive him. I'm locked away somewhere. "Are you okay? You're starting to scare me."

I'm slowly shutting down, but can't do anything to prevent it. There's nothing I *can* do. Byzantine cradles my face in his hands, his eyes troubled, searching my own for any sign of life. Whatever he sees makes his features go blank. He disappears behind his mask just like I have.

Saying nothing more, he lets me go and climbs out of the car. I barely notice him when he opens my side and drags me out by the arm with gentle force.

I blink and we're in the elevators.

I blink again and we're standing in his living room.

Time is slipping through my fingers. It stopped being linear as soon as I slid down the dark hole I'm currently free falling into.

It's not my first free fall. But it's Byzantine's first time witnessing it. And the barely lucid part of me is absolutely mortified. It's locked behind a glass door, observing everything but unable to do anything about it. I'm hurtling into the past and I'd rather go blind than to look at the memories resurfacing. But the past doesn't listen, knocking at the door of my consciousness, demanding to be heard.

I barely feel his arms wrap around me as he ushers me to the couch. I'm near catatonic. I notice my cheeks are wet. When did I start to cry? I bring my fingers up to my face, in disbelief, my lips salty with the taste of the tears I've been shedding.

I can't tell how much time has passed but Byzantine reappears with a cup of steaming tea and a glass of water. He makes me gulp down the water and then hands over the hot mug.

"Sunny," he says, his voice luring me into the present moment—at least a part of me is here. "Talk to me. Did something happen?"

I close my eyes. The warmth of the cup searing into my palms while I try to call back the broken parts of myself into the present. Here, now, with Byzantine. Lies are useless, my current state is betraying my well kept secrets.

Resolved, I take a deep breath and begin, "Five years ago, my sister River—" I pause, searching for the right words.

"You have a sister?" Byzantine asks, filling the empty space between us.

I swallow hard, taking a slow sip of tea before answering. "I *had* a sister, yeah. She was my twin actually," I admit.

I watch Byzantine's face morph into a horrified understanding of what I just confessed. I hate that look, I spent years avoiding it from everyone around me.

I chew on the inside of my cheek and continue, "One night, we went to a party at our friend's house. There wasn't much else to do but drink and do drugs, so that's what we did most weekends."

Byzantine begins to slide towards me on the couch and I freeze up, my vulnerability already unbearable without him trying to comfort me.

"Don't. Please," I beg, my voice cracking while I look down at the mug in my hands, holding on to it like some kind of life raft. He stills but says nothing and settles back into the cushions.

I take another breath and continue, "I was busy hooking up with *Dave Phillips* when I heard a scream coming from the backyard. One of those screams where you just know something's wrong. The rest of the night is blurry. All I remember is seeing River laying near the pool. Someone had dragged her out before I got there. She wasn't breathing. Her lips were blue. As soon as I saw her, I knew."

I watch my tears fall into the now lukewarm beverage. My lips tremble, looking up at Byzantine. "I was her twin, her fucking twin and when she needed me the most, when she was fucking *drowning*," I say through clenched teeth. "In the moment where her heart stopped beating, I didn't feel a thing. Not a fucking thing. I was nowhere in sight. Too busy giving head to some loser with a lip ring."

"Sunny..." Byzantine croaks.

I stare at him, pleading with every emotion spilling out of me. *Please don't say it wasn't my fault. Please.* So he says nothing.

"My parents and I were never close but it just worsened after River died. A part of me died that night, like a piece of my soul was just ripped out then and there. Extinguished the moment I saw her dead in the wet grass... It'll be five years next month." I mutter while looking out the window at the starry night sky and wishing I could be anywhere but here. "My mother called this morning. I hadn't talked to her in over a year. She said I should come home for this stupid fucking memorial she's organizing. But I'm not going. I refuse to go back to where I lost River."

Finally, Byzantine moves. He leans over and takes the cup out of my hands, placing it on the coffee table nearby. A small piece of me knows exactly what he's about to do. Slowly, he takes my wrist in his hand and strokes the raised scar with his thumb and I shudder under his touch.

I take a deep breath before speaking again. I hate being this emotionally naked, but still I power through. "It took me a few years to find the strength to do it. I needed her. Every day I needed her. But she was gone. And I was still here. Every fucking day I was *still* here. Until one day I knew it was time..." I whisper, looking Byzantine in the eyes as he continues to stroke my wrist with his thumb. "It didn't work. Obviously. When I woke up in the hospital bed, still alive and not with River, the pain was comparable to her own death. I knew then that I had to leave. If I couldn't die then I would at least leave. And eventually, I did. Ended up in Noxport. And I don't plan to go back—not ever."

The words dry up in my throat. Now, I'm just numb. Speaking the words out loud helped me stop the spiral but the haze of the alcohol is still heavy on my senses. My blinks are slow, heavy and I need to sleep. Forever maybe—hopefully.

Still holding on to me, Byzantine stands up from the couch, pulling me off it, and into his arms. My head falls into the crook of his neck, breathing in his calming scent. He smells like the ocean. Like sun-soaked skin and the afternoon breeze. I nestle in closer, inhaling deep while he caresses my hair. His touch is a soothing balm on my searing thoughts.

Gently, he leads me to his bedroom, instructing me to sit on his bed with only his hands and a soft touch. I'm barely here. And he can tell. Slowly, he peels my shirt off, kneeling in front of me and kissing both my palms. His hands graze the length of my arms and over my shoulders, reaching over to untie my bikini top. Then, he slides it off and over my head to join my shirt on the floor. He tugs on my shorts and I lift my hips, sliding both shorts and bikini bottom down my legs.

This isn't sexual. It's comforting. It's care.

The urge to cry is heavy in my chest but I swallow it back down. He heads to his closet and comes out with an oversized t-shirt.

"Lift your arms," he whispers.

I lift them mechanically and he tugs the shirt over my head. It smells like him, soft to the touch like it's been washed over and over. He then pulls the duvet down, telling me to crawl under and I do what he says. I curl on my side as I listen to Byzantine move about the room. Finally, he slides next to me, only wearing a pair of fitted boxers and pulls me into him. I have a fleeting thought of thanking him for tonight. But my eyes grow heavy and I fall asleep in his arms instead.

Chapter 31

Sunny

I'm bored.

My mouth is wrapped around Dave Phillips's dick and I'm bored. My eyes flit to the alarm clock flashing red behind him checking the time. Is this dude ever going to come? He probably has whiskey dick and I'm too drunk to care. Ugh. My jaw is sore and cramping, and did I mention I'm bored?

The coke I snorted earlier is starting to wear off and I'm wondering if I can find anyone willing to share another bump. It's then I hear a shriek coming from outside, it's loud enough to pierce through my drunken haze and I freeze.

"Don't stop," Dave grunts above me. "I'm almost there, don't stop." His hand finds the back of my head, letting him set the pace and after a few thrusts he comes down my throat with a long groan.

I'm quick to my feet, happy it's over and eager to wash him down with another drink. I leave Dave with his pants still down and walk up the stairs and out of the musty basement bedroom.

I can already hear River's comment about my tryst with Dave Phillips.

"Real classy Sunny," she'll say. I smile at the thought until dread slams into me. The echo of the scream I heard earlier floating back to me. I must be way more wasted than I thought to have already forgotten about it.

As if conjured, I hear it again, followed by another scream and then another. Pure unadulterated fear locks my limbs in place mid-way into the kitchen. It takes me a groggy second to locate where the commotion is coming from. The backyard.

Something's wrong.

I don't know what but I just know. I force my legs to move and jog outside only to find my friends crowding the pool. Curious I look around, it's a cold late summer night, no one has been using the pool. So why is everyone here?

But somehow, I know the truth before I can even explain yet. As if the emotions of my impending reality hits me faster than the sight of what's to come. As if my mind time-traveled into the future but my body is still walking up to the sullen crowd, wondering what would warrant such a scream.

I look for River, now desperate to find her. I try to ignore the voice inside that's already aware. Or maybe it's some psychic twin shit. Nonetheless, I know. But I wish I didn't.

My eyes are ricocheting between familiar faces trying to find the only face that matters. The crowd parts expectantly, as if they were waiting for me. All I see are pain-stricken faces and I almost choke on my fear. Suddenly I'm pulled aside and into someone's arms, forcing me to face away from the truth.

The arms belong to a friend and I hear her urgent whisper in my ear as if she screamed it. "Don't look Sunny. Don't look." I can hear the tears thick in her throat. My movements are slow, still inebriated even if I now wish I wasn't.

"Where's River?" I croak.

I shove her away but she grabs my shoulder.

"Sunny," she murmurs.

"River?" My voice is shrill and the crowd silent while I turn back towards the reason why everyone is milling around the pool.

Then I finally see her.

River.

The only time in my miserable fucking life where I wished not to find her.

Wished she was far, far away from here. And maybe she already is.

I must have screamed her name. Maybe I never stopped. I don't remember. All I remember is slumping beside her body. River's clothes soaking wet, blue-lipped and waxy skin. Voices telling me she was found face down in the pool. I numbly hear the ambulance wailing in the distance.

But everything is muted as if I'm drowning myself. As if I'm being swallowed up and suffocated. I fist her shirt into my cold hands and lift her into my arms. She's so heavy, so fucking heavy. I can't help but to shake her. It's like shaking a doll. My reaction is distressed like I could shake her soul back inside her body.

"River," I plead. "Don't do this to me," I sob into her soaking wet chest. "Don't leave me here. You promised. You fucking promised me," I choke out. I'm emptied out. I can't catch my breath as I fight against arms stronger than mine. They pull me away from her and I try to resist but I'm fucking drowning. I'm drowning. I'm drowning. "River!"

I blink against the bathroom light, padding across the floor towards the sink. I need to drink water before I turn to dust. I don't know what's worse, my hangover or the shame I'm feeling about last night, while still fighting off the memories of that dreadful night years ago.

This isn't how I wanted to tell Byzantine about River—or anyone for that matter. I teeter between guilt, full blown embarrassment and gratitude, remembering our conversation.

Not even Lenix knows about my sister. Realizing that I told Byzantine before my best friend, I try not to add more weight atop the existing guilt. I had my reasons not to tell her. Noxport was my clean slate. A place I could become another version of myself. Someone else other than the girl whose twin died.

I splash water against my face, find a towel and rummage through his vanity looking for some pain relievers for my pounding headache. Finding some mouthwash, I gargle some for good measure.

Before walking back into the bedroom, I take a quick detour to snoop around, since I was in no state to take in my surroundings last night and I'm too curious not to. His loft seems to sprawl the entire floor of the building, perched high up from the city below, the view overlooking the ocean.

The entire condo is decorated in muted tones of brown, black and gray. Very Byzantine, and very *not* surprising. God forbid he owned anything with a pop of color.

It feels cozier than I expected. Honestly, I don't know what I imagined. Something colder maybe. Instead, this looks lived in, traces of him everywhere I look. From a large bookcase in the corner of the living room to the framed art on the walls. A perverse thrill takes over me from just being here. I try not to peer too closely as to why I'm feeling this way.

Byzantine is still sleeping when I sneak back into the room and into bed. I lay on my side watching his chest rise and fall, and despite the hangover, heat envelops my body as I recall how he took care of me last night.

I place my hand on his torso, trailing through his chest hair, following the path downwards to his boxers. I hear Byzantine's breath hitch and I glance up. His eyes are still closed but a subtle crook of his lip lets me know he's awake, when my palm grazes over his crotch. His cock stiffens under my touch, my fingers gently curling around his length through the fabric while I begin to stroke him.

Lust dips low in my stomach and I swallow hard, licking my lips in anticipation. I disappear under the covers only to reappear in between his legs eager to continue what I started. Byzantine lets out a low grunt when I give his balls a slow squeeze, my mouth hot against the cotton. I reach over to pull his boxers down but his hand locks on my wrist.

His eyes are open, piercing and serious.

"You don't have to," he grits out, sounding breathlessly tentative and my heart squeezes. His abs are tight, seeming to hold himself back while his breath continues to quicken.

I tug on his boxers again. "I *want* to," I assure.

I don't want him to take pity on me after last night. I don't want last night to define me or us. I want to feel something other than all-consuming sadness for a change. He takes a second to study my features, seeking my open willingness to continue. Eventually, his eyes soften and he lets go of my wrist.

A small victorious smile crosses my lips, finally pulling his boxers down and then off. The covers slip down, uncovering Byzantine's toned body, his leg bent to the side, open and ready for me, his arm tucked behind his head, stretching him into the most mouth-watering position.

His cock lays hard and heavy on his taut stomach while I pull myself closer.

"Did those hurt?" I can't help but ask, referring to the tattoos along his shaft as I wrap my hand around him and gingerly drag my tongue along the length of him.

He groans, his eyes closing but still answers with a smirk, "What do you think?"

I smile, circling his broad head with my tongue but don't bother answering. I give him a few long strokes with my hand until I can't wait any longer and wrap my mouth around the tip, my tongue trailing smoothly over the slit.

"Fuck..." His hips buck, pushing further into my mouth and I eagerly swallow around him. "That's it, little sun, just like that."

I hum my satisfaction, my mouth chasing the taste of him on my tongue while I reach down and stroke his balls, massaging them in my palm. His hand falls to my head, tightening in my hair while his cock throbs deeper into my mouth. I can tell he wants to set the pace and I let him, relaxing my jaw as he starts thrusting into me.

"You're such a good little slut, aren't you? So fucking perfect," he purrs.

My thighs clench at the sound of his voice, his words igniting a fire inside me, his words so filthy all I want is to hear more and more and more.

Swallowing him even deeper, I suck harder, my cheeks hollowing out, tears springing to my eyes when the tip of his cock hits the back of my throat. I moan around him, my hand wrapping around the base, stroking him up and down, his hard length pulsing against my wet palm. When his hips fall out of rhythm, I can tell he's close.

"Fuck Sunny, you feel so good," he growls, while I give him a long broad lick of my tongue before claiming him back inside my mouth. "Are you going to swallow me all down? Lick me clean like a good little whore while I come down your tight throat?"

Jesus, the mouth on this guy. I'm so fucking turned on I feel I could come just by the words spilling out of his open lips. I give a small nod of approval, my mouth still wrapped around him, locking eyes while he stares down at me with such fierceness that I can't help but moan in appreciation.

He smirks, keeping his hand tight around the back of my head, his fingers threaded through my hair. He only lasts a few more jerks before his eyes flutter shut, his mouth opening on a near silent groan as I feel his release hot and salty down my throat. As promised, I swallow every last drop while his face paints the most alluring picture of pleasure, his climax a masterpiece I want framed in my mind forever.

I don't think I would ever tire of watching him like this. Kneeling exactly here between his legs, the taste of him still lingering on my tongue.

He smiles at me, a look of deep satisfaction etched across his face as he pulls me up and over him, claiming my lips with a searing kiss. It takes me a moment to realize that this is what I've been waiting for.

He's finally kissing me. My body flares with so much heat, I can hardly breathe. His tongue, wet and hot and wanting against my own as I moan into his mouth. Thankfully, this time I don't unravel and just revel in the sensation of his lips on mine. He then rolls on top of me and deepens our kiss, his hands roving across my body, and for a while I lose myself in him. Time slows down and nothing exists but the warmth of his body against my own.

It's the middle of the afternoon and the hot sun makes me wince, pearls of sweat rolling off my stomach and onto my beach towel. *Too hot.* I stand up and stretch—maybe a bit more sensual than usual knowing Byzantine is staring at me with unfettered heat, almost as scorching as the midday rays on my skin.

I turn around to start towards the water but hear him behind me say, "Let me come with you."

I turn on my heels, surprise arching my brows. "You want to come swim with me?"

He grins. "Why are you acting so shocked?" he replies, amusement in his tone.

"Because I've *never* seen you get wet, like, ever?" I say.

His gaze travels to my hips and then up, his head tilting. "Is that so?"

I roll my eyes and flip him off. "Gross."

Byzantine chuckles, the vibrating tempo of his laugh zipping through me like lightning, rocketing against my heart like a pinball. The sensation makes me take a step back like I was physically pushed. Quickly, I shake it off and simply give him a coy smile.

"See you in the water then," I say, sultry as can be.

The water rises up my body as I walk deeper and deeper into the ocean. Eventually, I dive under the waves curious to see if Byzantine will follow me out this far.

I resurface, satisfied and refreshed, turning over to my back to float, hearing his quick splashes growing near as he swims towards me. I peek over to him while he floats nearby, his whole body disappearing under the waves, his mouth half-submerged in the water.

Fuck. It's alarming how beautiful he is. The water glistening on his dark bronzed skin, the sun reflecting off the droplets sluicing down his face. Whatever I was idly thinking about is quickly replaced by one single thought. To trace my tongue against every inch of him. Somehow, Byzantine can tell where my thoughts are straying and a hungry grin slowly appears across his face. I swallow hard.

"Come, let's get closer to shore," he suggests, his voice traveling across the waves and into my ears like a siren's song.

"Why?"

"Because I want to hold you without the threat of going under," he answers.

"Oh."

I turn back on my stomach and swim over the rising waves and back to shore, Byzantine trailing close by. My toes hit the wet spongy sand, the water now just past my chest as I turn to face him. He looks even more like a carnal deity in this light, but I evade his space while I stare at him, my body gently swaying with the tide.

He inhales deeply before speaking. "I'm surprised you like the water this much," he admits.

"Why? Because I have a dead sister who drowned?" I state, my answer so carelessly flippant that I have half a mind to apologize but don't.

I keep my face blank while he studies me. His silence is calculated but I can't help but to fill it anyhow, squirming under his serious stare.

"Actually...River and I always dreamed of living somewhere warm, close to the ocean. We used to spend afternoons pouring over wildlife encyclopedias and promising ourselves we'd see whales in real life one day." I shrug my shoulders in defeat. "If anything I feel closer to her when I'm in the water, like maybe the water is this weird conduit between us—maybe she's closer this way..." I say, my words stuttering to a stop, almost feeling embarrassed about this silly belief I've constructed of our two souls trying to connect through the medium that ripped her away from me. "I find comfort in the water. Not fear."

"Are you scared of dying?" he asks.

His question doesn't surprise me and I answer immediately, "No," I admit, while we stay motionless, staring at each other across the water. "I fear the way I'll die, like, what happens to my body. But no, I don't fear death. It's a comforting thought even. And maybe that's all kinds of fucked up, but living is hard and death feels...easy," I say, taking a deep breath and avoiding his gaze while I gather my thoughts.

"You?"

The green in Byzantine's eyes reflects the sun bouncing off the waves while he walks closer to me. A knot suddenly forms in my throat making it hard to swallow.

"No. I don't fear death," he states, his hand trailing up my arm, his fingers digging into my bicep as if fearing I'll float away. "I've already died, remember?" His face is so serious like his eyes are seeking a path straight to my soul, his touch searing me into place. "I've seen what happens when we die. There's nothing left to fear."

"Wait," I say incredulously, studying him now, searching his face for the answer to a question I haven't even formulated yet. "You never told me that."

"You never asked."

My laugh is hollow as I continue, "Are you telling me you saw, like what? Heaven?" The question comes out more like a scoff as if I find this line of questioning ridiculous. But my drumming heart doesn't seem to find it silly at all. A private part of me yearns to know the place where River exists now. Does she look like herself? Does she remember me?

Byzantine somehow feels me slipping into the quicksand of my thoughts, and pulls me into his arms, his hands flat against my spine holding me close to his chest. His nose trails up my neck, and I shiver under his touch. But it helps. I dig my toes further into the bottom of the ocean, reminding me where I am.

I'm here. I'm here. I'm here.

Byzantine's voice is low when he finally answers, "I've seen much more than just the afterlife."

I know Byzantine's words mean much more than what he's letting on, but then his teeth catch my bottom lip and I can't help but to melt into him, his mouth the ultimate distraction as my arms wrap around his neck.

His kiss deepens, his hand grasping the back of my neck to angle me better into an exploration of his mouth on mine. Yet again, this feels like much more than just a kiss and it's dancing dangerously close to the first time his lips caught my own. It's as if the fabric of reality can't help but to unravel between us, melting from the heat of our embrace. Finally, I pull away and try to catch my breath, my chest rising up and down, cheeks flushed.

"You're doing it again Byzantine," I say sternly.

His kiss-swollen lips pull upwards. "Doing what?" he asks innocently.

"Distracting me," I say, crossing my arms for extra effect.

"Is it working?"

"Yes. But that's besides the point and you know it," I say, jamming my index finger into his hard chest to cement my point. "What the hell did you mean by you've seen more than just the afterlife?"

Guilt flashes in his eyes but as always it's gone before I can delve deeper.

"It's complicated, I shouldn't have said anything," he says, locking me out behind his hard, unreadable exterior. He pulls me into his arms again and whispers, "just let it go—please."

There's enough of a plea in his voice that it rattles me into complying. I follow him out of the water, convinced the amount of unspoken words we harbor between us is enough to drown us both.

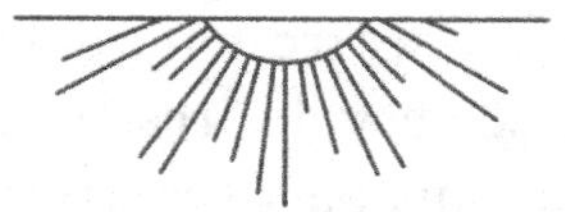

Chapter 32

Byzantine

I'm sitting in a meeting with Connor and I should be listening but I'm not. We're upstairs in his office, but luckily it's not just me in here, and the attention is on one of our lackeys droning on about this week's intel.

My mind couldn't be further away from this place.

I fucked up.

I shouldn't have said what I said. It slipped out, like my secrets are constantly near the surface waiting to be let out. Similar to when I so carelessly called her windflower. My words act quicker than the more rational part of my brain, as if my lips would rather listen to a much more ancient piece of me. The one who's known Sunny for what feels like forever.

I can't help but to whisper secrets into the soft shell of her ear. My desire to have every piece of her—own her like she already owns me is burning me from the inside out. It leads me to tell her things she's not ready to hear.

Will she ever be ready?

What was the fucking point of dying if only to watch her slip through my fingers again? To stand stoic and listen to Sunny tell me she would rather be dead than here.

She might have worded it differently but I knew. I know that a part of her is far away from here. The scar on her wrist is a testament to those very desires. And once again I'm an onlooker to her pain. But at least this time, *this* fucking time I am not the cause...yet.

The possessive part of me wants to lock her up somewhere and never let her out. Or at least strong-arm her into wanting to live. But I've been here before. She needs to save herself. She needs to figure out how to breathe without hurting. My fear of this pattern repeating in this lifetime strangles me, a tight grip around the scar on my neck. I feel powerless.

I am powerless.

Sunny is an enigma I've failed to decipher through time itself. Every time I feel close to unlocking her she disappears under my touch. What's different about now? Here in this life. What can I do to make her stay?

I don't think I can survive one more life without her. Another life without her soul seared to mine. I need to tell her. I just don't know how.

An idea starts to form in my head but I'm not sure it would even help. Or even *do* anything. I'm reaching for anything and everything hoping something will stick.

"Byzantine." I hear Connor say and I glance over only to realize we're the only ones left in the room. *Shit.*

His stare is somber, and I shift in my seat, clearing my throat but saying nothing, feeling like a child being reprimanded.

"Am I going to have to take care of your little distraction?" he says, his tone cold against my skin, my stomach roiling at the sound. I know he has every reason to say that but it doesn't prevent me from wanting to kill him just for saying it.

I avert my eyes feeling like a caged animal. "No. It won't happen again," I mutter, finally staring back at him so he knows I'm serious.

He taps his finger on his mahogany desk seeming to be mulling something over. "What the hell is wrong with you? You've been acting shifty for weeks now," he finally says.

I know then, I have to tell him. I'm losing my fucking mind keeping it a secret. At this point, I don't even care if he actually thinks I did lose my mind. If only I can stop shouldering all this weight alone.

"I need to tell you something," I say, cold sweat trickling down my back. Connor cocks a brow, but says nothing, letting me continue. "You're going to think I'm crazy."

"I already think you're crazy," he replies.

I grunt in disapproval and cross my arms, closing off.

Connor grins, his demeanor suddenly shifting from boss to best friend and settles into his large leather chair. "Just fucking tell me already."

I stare at the clouds through the window behind him, biting my inner cheek, unsure where to start. Maybe if I don't look at him it will be easier.

"I never really told you what happened when I died," I finally say, giving him a quick glance to make sure he's listening. He's fallen serious and simply nods as if to tell me to go on. I look back over to the window before I continue. "I saw...things. A lot of it is a blur now but some things still stick out. Some things I'll never forget."

"What things?" he asks, his voice slightly incredulous.

I take a deep breath, my eyes closing with the swell of my lungs. My eyes land back on him, my nerves crawling down my spine.

"I saw...well, I saw the lives I've lived before this one."

I can hear Connor's hard swallow before he speaks, "Are you fucking shitting me Byzantine?"

"I wish I was," I laugh dryly.

I shift in the chair again, feeling like I would rather just stand up and run.

"But that's not all..." I continue, swiping a hand over my face. Fuck, this is harder than I expected. "All the lives I saw, I was with someone else, in love with someone else," I clear my throat, searching for the right words. "And it's...it's hard to explain but...even if the faces changed, I still somehow knew the soul was the same. I knew them. And, well, they knew me. They loved me," I say, cringing at every single word that just came out of my mouth.

I can tell Connor is trying to absorb everything I just told him. The tightness of his shoulders, the quick tap tap tap of his fingers on his desk. I don't blame him. Five years later and I'm still not sure what the hell is happening.

All I know is that Sunny belongs to me.

"Do you believe me?" My voice cracks and I wince at the vulnerability I unwillingly let slip.

"I mean, you've never lied to me before. I'm just trying to wrap my head around what the fuck you just told me," he replies.

"There's more."

"Great," he jests and his sarcasm is like nails to a chalkboard.

"Fuck off, Connor," I mutter, scowling and tightening my arms across my chest like a shield.

"Oh c'mon, I was only joking." His face drops all traces of amusement. "I'm serious, tell me."

I take a few moments to collect my thoughts again and lick my lips as I think. "When I woke up that day in the hospital bed, I had a hard time deciphering what was real, or I mean, what was real from *this* lifetime and what were memories from before. But something was crystal clear. I knew I would eventually find that—soul again," I say, almost shyly, my breath coming out ragged but I push through. "Then five years passed and I thought maybe I had been wrong. That I had just imagined it all—until the night we found Gary. The night I first saw Sunny."

The silence is thick in the air as I let him sit with what I just told him. How I've known Sunny from before.

I loved her before. A thousand times before.

"How did you know?"

"I don't know...I just knew. I can't explain it, I just fucking knew."

"Does she know?" he asks.

I look over to him, hoping to god my eyes don't betray the pain behind them and simply shake my head. Connor's face is a mixture of surprise and total confusion. But then he breaks into a smile and says, "I fucking knew you had it bad brother. I just didn't know *how* bad."

His laugh is pure. And his easy tone acts like a balm to my nerves. I let out a sigh and give him a half smile, feeling somewhat relieved.

"So?" Connor says, leaning his elbows on the desk conspiratorially. "What are you going to do about it?"

Chapter 33

Sunny

My feet are killing me.

I shrug my purse onto my shoulder and mechanically shove my hair into a messy bun while I walk out the back door of Sammies. It's only midnight but it was a slow night, and I was the lucky one who got cut early. Byzantine disappeared mid-shift promising to come back, but since I finished earlier than expected, he's not here to drive me home and I don't plan on telling him.

He's been acting a little strange ever since he opened up about his near-death experience. Well, stranger than usual. He opened up and then shut right back down again. Like a frightened clam. But I don't think it's just that. I think what I told him the night I confessed about River spooked him.

Probably the whole part of me being suicidal. Yeah, that'll do it. It's the reason why I've always kept it secret—aside from River. She knew all my secrets. People look at you differently when they know. Like the only feeling they can conjure up is the sad saccharine taste of pity.

Although what I see in Byzantine's eyes when he stares back is not pity. It's something else entirely, something I can't quite place. All I know is that it doesn't feel hollow like pity, nor does it feel like he's treating me like I'm this fragile broken thing either. I could ask him. But he'd most likely try to distract me again instead of answering the question.

Maybe deep down I'm the one seeking the distraction.

I inhale deeply, breathing in the fresh nighttime air, cutting through the parking lot and turning the corner on King Street. I've only taken a few steps down the sidewalk when I feel something hard jam itself between my shoulder blades and freeze.

"If you run, I'll shoot," the man behind me growls, shoving what I'm now assuming is a gun deeper into my back. My hands go up on instinct, adrenaline coursing through me. "That's it," he says while pulling the gun away from me only to shove my shoulder with the barrel. "Now turn around nice and slowly and no one is going to get hurt, you understand me?"

"Y—yes," I stutter, facing him with my hands still raised above my head. Despite the fear clawing at my throat, I try to take a quick inventory of the attacker. Male, short, long stringy brown hair, blue eyes, stained gray hoodie, and a rose tattooed on his neck.

"Hand me your purse," he barks and I wince.

I'm about to hand it over when the sound of screeching tires pierces the night, dragging the man's attention away from me. His eyes go wide and without another word, turns on a dime and sprints down the street, disappearing into the alley up ahead. I turn towards the car, relief flooding my body as I see who it is.

"Byzantine..." I manage to say, realizing every muscle in my body is wound so tight I can barely breathe.

He stalks towards me, expletives flying out of his mouth, fear written clear across his face.

"Are you okay?" he asks, grabbing me by the arms, giving me a once over, before finally bringing me into his arms. I try to answer him but I can't seem to find my words. "Talk to me, Sunny. Are you okay? Are you hurt?"

"Y—yes, I'm okay," I finally say, curling my hands into fists, trying to keep them from shaking. "I'm just...I'm just a little rattled I think..." I trail off, curling into him. "I can't believe that just happened," I stutter out as an after-thought. "Should I call the police? You know, give them a description?"

Byzantine's body tenses around me.

"I'll take care of it."

Surprised, I unwind myself from his embrace, glancing up at him. "How?" I ask.

His features are stoic as he tugs my arms, leading me to his car.

"Just trust me," he replies, opening the car door for me and helping me in.

I don't know what to say, so my mouth stays shut as I settle in my seat. We both fall into silence while he drives. I don't need to ask, I know he's bringing me back to his place.

After a while, I finally say, "I do, you know."

He glances quickly at me, then back at the road.

"Do what?" he replies.

"Trust you," I add, a small smile sweeping across my face. His eyebrows shoot up in surprise as if he didn't expect me to say that. He doesn't reply, grinning instead while his fingers drum the steering wheel, his mood shifting into something a little less dour.

Eventually, he drives into the underground parking lot and he leads us into the elevator, the doors dinging open thirty-three floors later. Byzantine takes my hand and tugs me inside, my body lagging behind still slightly discombobulated from what happened.

Standing near the kitchen, he stares at me, his eyes roving over my face. “Are you sure you’re okay?” he questions again.

I take a second to answer, making a quick assessment of my feelings.

“I’m okay now,” I finally reply, squeezing his arm in reassurance.

His expression is of sheer relief when his hand finds my cheek, grazing it softly.

“Go wait for me on the couch, little sun. I need to make a call, I won’t be long,” he says softly.

I acquiesce and plop myself on the L-shaped couch, watching him disappear into the bedroom. The black leather feels cool against my skin as I gaze around the living room. A plush dark gray carpet takes up most of the floor space with a low oval coffee table perched on top. All so very Byzantine.

After a few minutes, he strolls back out and heads to the wet bar.

“Gin?” he asks, and I nod, pouring whiskey for himself. He hands me the tumbler and I reach up to take it but he keeps it in his hand, his eyes worried as he stares at me.

“Are you *sure* you’re okay?” he finally says.

I muster up my most reassuring look as I take the glass from his grip.

“I’m fine, Byzantine. Truly.”

He sighs and then sits down opposite of me on the couch, still staring at me as he takes a slow sip of his whiskey. I do the same while I try not to squirm under his reaching gaze.

“Stop looking at me like that,” I say exasperated.

“Like what?”

"Like *that*," I reply, waving a hand at his face. "It feels like you're staring straight into my soul, it's quite unnerving if you must know," I quip.

"Is it?" He takes another sip, his eyes now undressing me with just a look.

"Yes *Byzantine*, it is," I respond, leaning over and placing my glass on a coaster before raising my knees up to my chest as if it will protect me against his stare.

"Maybe I am," he says seriously. I fight the urge to scoff but before I can even mutter out a, *what do you even mean by that?* He adds, "Come here."

I stop short and look back at him, my entire body pitching forward like it has a mind of its own but I keep my ass firmly on the couch cushion and cross my arms instead.

"I'm good here, thanks," I mutter, glaring at him from across the sectional. But what I find behind his blown wide pupils makes my skin buzz with anticipation.

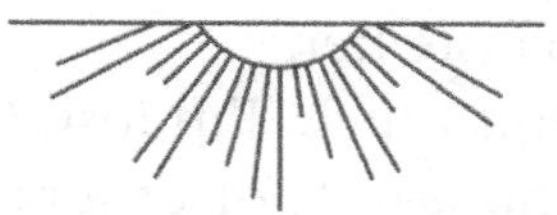

Chapter 34

Byzantine

I watch Sunny cross her arms in protest. She thinks I can't see the rise of her chest or the squeeze of her thighs. I lick my lips, suddenly salivating at the sight.

"Sunny," I growl, my voice an octave lower than before. "Come here before I make you."

Her eyes squint in defiance and a slow grin appears below her flushed cheeks.

"*Make me,*" she replies.

My cock jerks awake with the potent promise of those two words. But instead, I stare at her some more, my face a blank mask as I watch her squirm, unable to read my intent. Then, very slowly, I place the tumbler I'm holding on the floor next to me.

And pounce.

Her eyes go wide as she reacts on instinct and scrambles off the couch, trying to get away from me. With a small shriek, she manages to circle around the back of the sofa but I'm faster and catch her halfway to the bedroom. I slam her into the wall next to us, her hands flying up to my chest.

Before another of her many snarky remarks leaves her mouth, I drag my hand into the hair at the base of her head, pulling and tilting her face up to me. My other hand digs into her hips as I push into her, a small gasp leaving her lips. Fuck, I need to taste her.

The second our lips touch, I'm lost. Just like before, the kiss morphs into thousands of others. But this time I'm prepared for the feeling. I tug on her hair deepening the kiss, her chest heaving into mine. I resist the free fall as I lick the seam of her mouth, her hands sliding down my stomach, eagerly letting me in.

She sighs into me and every atom in my body pleads for repentance if only to hear Sunny's small sighs as long as I'm alive. I bite her bottom lip, her tongue wet and hot against mine as my thigh finds the crook of her legs.

Pulling away slightly, I trail kisses down her jaw, along her throat and up again. I nip at her earlobes and she lets out a small whimper, making me press my hips harder into her warm supple body. I slide my hand up her shirt, already knowing she isn't wearing a bra, groaning when my hand smooths over her naked breast. I give it a long squeeze, toying with her hard nipple between my thumb and finger.

"Don't you like it when I give you orders?" I ask, in between open mouthed kisses to her neck.

Her head falls to the wall behind us, her eyes closed, before she answers, her voice breathy and full of lust, "Yes."

"Yes what?" I urge.

"Yes, I like it when you give me orders," she answers with a small whimper.

I release the grip I have on her hair, reaching down to cup my hand over her pussy, and give it a small patronizing pat.

"Does it make you wet?" I whisper while I bite the soft skin below her ear, watching her back arch off the wall in response.

She nods, licking her lips and releasing a slow exhale. I breathe her in deeply and then step away. A pang slits through me as I watch her catch her breath. She's so fucking beautiful. And she's here. With me.

Her eyes pop open, wide and yearning and my cock throbs at the sight, I stroke it through my jeans as I watch Sunny's gaze fall to my hand.

"Take your clothes off," I demand.

She blinks at me owlishly, but eventually springs to life, quickly yanking her shirt over her head, followed by her shorts, which she kicks off with one foot. She then does the same with her thong and I try not come just at the sight of her standing naked in front of me.

So fucking responsive.

All I want is to sink my teeth into her skin until I taste blood. Taste *all* of her.

I stalk back towards her, her body slamming against the wall once more. I trail my lips down her clavicle, and then up over her shoulder, stepping into her legs and giving her feet a small kick to open them wider. She sinks into me, wrapping her arms around my neck as I continue kissing up her throat.

"Would you do anything I tell you, little sun?" I rasp out, my fingers grazing her pussy as I feel her legs tremble against my thighs.

"Anything," she says quickly—breathlessly.

She shivers and kisses me, her lips desperate and seeking. Slowly, I slide a finger into her wet cunt while her tongue finds my own. Digging my throbbing cock against her stomach, she moans into my mouth, trying to catch her breath while I pump in and out of her. Whispering into the shell of her ear, a trace of deviancy in my voice I taunt.

"Would you crawl for me?"

I hear her breath hitch as her pussy clenches around my hand and I lean back to study her reaction. Her mouth opens and then closes, her pupils blown wide. I pull my finger out and lift it to my mouth.

"Is that a yes?" I say, tasting her on my tongue as I watch her swallow hard.

Slowly she nods, and my heart hammers wildly at the sight of her falling to her knees without breaking eye contact.

Half of me is shocked she agreed and the other half is so fucking pleased that all I want to do is drop to my own knees and mutter praise against her warm skin.

"Sunny..." I croak out.

I fight the urge to take my dick out right this second. The thought of her hot open mouth around my cock almost better than having her crawl for me.

Almost.

"Stay," I tell her.

I leave her kneeling on the floor and walk to the bedroom doorway. She watches me wide-eyed as I unbutton my jeans and slide the zipper down. She licks her lips and my cock swells at the sight.

She's mesmerizing. And she's all fucking mine.

I pull my dick out and slide my thumb over the slit. I give it a slow tug, watching Sunny sit on her heels while she wiggles her ass, seeking some friction. I let out a low growl, the pleasure almost too much.

"Now, *crawl*."

Her mouth lifts in a slow lustful smile at my command and carefully she places her hands in front of her. Without ever lowering her eyes to the floor, she crawls towards me, her heart-shaped ass swaying back and forth as she inches forward in small sultry drags of her hands and knees.

I squeeze my dick harder, tension coiling tight at the bottom of my spine. Her knees softly trail against the floor as her eyes fall to my throbbing cock and then back up. When she finally reaches me, she sits back on her heels and gives me a slow blink but doesn't say a word.

"You're a fucking vision, you know that?" I tell her, reaching down and twisting her hair into my hand once, twice.

"Open your mouth," I order, my hips hitching forward at the sound of her soft whimper, shooting straight to my balls. Her mouth falls open, her tongue flat and wide resting on her bottom lip.

I'm trying to keep a level head but Sunny is undoing me faster than I can think. I breathe through the memories of her doing exactly this, as if her body still remembers all the other times we've enacted these same roles. Her eyes are inviting and serene as she waits for my next order.

"You're such a good girl," I praise. "So fucking perfect."

Her only response is a coy smile and a long drag of her tongue over her bottom lip as if eager to taste me. I notice her hand reach between her legs, and give a small tug on her hair, followed by a quick *tsk*.

"Not yet."

She moans in protest but still complies, placing her hands flat on her thighs. Pushing her head towards me, I hold my cock at the base and finally—fucking finally—slowly slide into her mouth. As soon as the head touches her tongue, she wraps her mouth around it and moans. The vibration travels straight through me, up my spine and into my brain.

"Fuck," I groan out. "You feel fucking amazing."

This only makes her suck harder, swallowing around my thick shaft. I let out another low groan as I thrust even deeper into her mouth.

"That's it, little sun, suck my cock just like that," I say, feeling almost fucking euphoric. The words coming out of my mouth are barely registering, lost in the sensation of her hot mouth until I feel my dick hit the back of her throat. All I want then is to feel myself come down her throat and watch as she swallows every last drop. But it's too soon. Way too fucking soon.

Sunny's mouth is making me question if there's anything better than this. But finally, I coax her off me, and she relents with one final broad lick down my length, my hips jerking forward. Her eyes are glazed when she peers up at me, and I hold out my hand to her.

"Stand up."

Placing her hand in mine, she stands up on shaky legs and I can't help but to stare at her, my adoration most likely obvious in my eyes. But I don't care.

"You've been rather quiet since the couch," I remark, combing my hand in her hair and leaning in for a hungry kiss.

When our lips part, she grins at me.

"I like the sound of your voice much better than mine," she whispers, reaching down and wrapping her hand around my cock, still wet from her own spit, giving it a long hard stroke.

I grunt into her shoulder, nipping her skin. Without looking up, I push her into the bedroom and lead her to the king size bed. When her legs hit the edge, she falls onto her back, her knees up and feet wide. I can see how wet she is as I tug my shirt over my head. I hurry to take the rest of my clothes off, eager to have Sunny under my hands once again.

Her eyes rove over my tattooed body, as if she's soaking every single detail into memory. I give her a devilish grin, wrapping my hands around her thighs and yanking her towards me. She lets out a small shriek and giggles.

It quickly turns into a long mewl when I drop to my knees and give her clit a broad lick. I bury my nose in her cunt, high off her very essence and then push my tongue inside of her while I reach over and pinch her swollen bud with my fingers. She says my name, slow and breathy and it's an aphrodisiac I can't help but try to recreate again and again as she grinds into my face, chasing the pleasure I'm drawing out of her.

I stand back up, slowly drinking her in, the taste of her potent on my lips. The way she's eagerly splayed open for me, her skin flushed, her hair disheveled, it's enough to drive me crazy. And I guess I already am.

"*Fuck*," I grunt, sliding a hand over the length of her leg. "Look at you."

She pushes herself further up the bed, beckoning to me and I follow her onto the sheets, stroking my cock while I inch my way towards her.

"Birth control?" I ask.

She nods and answers, "I'm clean. You?"

I nod in reply, my brain turning fucking primal at the thought of her tight pussy wrapped around my cock. My fingers find her slit, pushing two fingers into her, curling them against that sensitive spot inside.

"Byzantine, please," she pleads, writhing underneath me. "I need to feel you inside me—*now*."

She doesn't need to tell me fucking twice. Getting on my knees, I nudge my cock at her entrance, coating the head with her arousal. Steadily, I push myself inside, letting her adjust to my size while her cunt clenches around me, so hot and perfect. With a final thrust, I bottom out and we moan in unison.

I slowly drag my cock out, Sunny's nails digging hard into my back and quickly slide back in with a hard grunt. The sensation of being so deep inside of her slams into me and

I nearly choke on the feeling. It feels better than I could have ever imagined. Better than before, better than every fucking lifetime before *this*. She's the perfect culmination of what I've desired and ever needed.

I fuck her unhurriedly until I can't control myself any longer. With a long, feral lick up her chest, I begin to thrust harder, her whimpers chasing the slam of my hips against her skin as I lose myself in the feeling of her cunt wrapped tightly around my cock.

I piston in and out, my thumb rubbing her clit in tight circles. Her eyes fall shut, her hands roving down to my ass, her nails leaving small divots in my skin. Her pussy gushes around me and I know she's already close. I give her breast a quick slap and squeeze her nipple hard, coaxing her into a response. We lock eyes, and she lets out a long moaning scream as I lift one of her legs over my shoulder, deepening the angle.

"This pussy is mine, you hear me?" I growl, accentuating the words with hard rolls of my hips, her eyes still fixed on me, her mouth open in silent pleasure.

I know my words are hurtling her over the edge and I rut even harder, continuing to rub her clit.

"You tell me whose perfect little cunt this is before you come all over my cock," I demand, pinching her bud and feeling her pussy flutter while she arches her back. "Say it," I groan loudly.

"Y—yours Byzantine. It's yours," she says breathlessly, her face the most beautiful rendering of pleasure I've ever seen as she whines loudly, her pussy clamping around my cock while she comes—my name still on her lips.

Before she can even catch her breath I flip her over and drag her up on her knees.

"Hold on to the headboard," I order, her breath still coming in small stutters while she does what I say. I lean down, my hands squeezing her cheeks open and drag my tongue from her clit up to her asshole.

"Fuck Sunny," I curse, licking her again. "You taste like life itself."

Finally, without any warning, I thrust back into her and she screams out in pleasure.

"You feel so fucking good around my cock, little sun. I could fuck you for days. Your pussy was made for me," I grunt out, setting a brutal pace while I lean over, pulling her towards me. My hand collars her throat, her back against me as I continue to ram into her cunt, her small gasps frying my brain, drowning me in ecstasy. She reaches down, her fingers finding her clit while her lips part seeking mine.

"Fuck, Byzantine," she breathes. "Please don't stop."

"Your greedy little cunt wants more doesn't it?" I taunt, digging my fingers into her hips. "You're going to come for me nice and loud?" I say through clenched teeth as she sobs out a yes.

It only takes a few more pumps for my vision to start blurring at the edge as I feel her unraveling against me. I let my head fall on her shoulder, my balls tightening as I come inside her hard and fast. Like a detonation, I am ripped apart, the feeling only heightening with her soft sighs of satisfaction.

I still, trying to catch my breath, our skin sticking to each other as I slowly pull out. I watch my cum slowly leak out of her swollen pussy as she falls onto her elbows and I can't help myself. I reach down and push my release back inside of her with a slow drag of my finger.

My name falls out of her lips in a small gasp. The sight of her still so responsive and open is so fucking erotic, I fight the need to claim her all over again.

I settle onto my back beside her instead and she wraps a leg over me in a satisfied hum. I lay there, still trying to regulate my breathing, seeking to regain some clarity.

The pull to lose myself in her is so strong I can barely hold on. Lost in the feeling of finding her. Lost in the terror of losing her again. Lost in the feeling of feeling.

Again and again and again.

Chapter 35

Sunny

I lay limp, nestled close to Byzantine's body, his arm wrapped tight around my waist, my leg folded over his. My mind takes its time meandering back to earth from the sex we just had. Neither of us have spoken since he plopped onto his back next to me. I shouldn't expect anything different from the two of us at this point.

I can already feel the familiar terror of over-thinking crawling its way back inside of me. For now, I refuse to focus on anything but Byzantine lying naked beside me.

And what a glorious sight that is.

His entire body is adorned with traditional tattoos, bold lines and hard edges, reminiscent of the sailors who inspired the style. They cover him from his feet up to his shoulders. Lazily, I trace my finger on his stomach over one of his tattoos—a skull with a dagger through its head—and his abs contract with the touch. A small thrill zips through me at the sight, trailing my fingers even lower, needing to explore and discover every inch of his skin by touch alone.

Byzantine lets out a low groan and I shoot him a devious smirk. I want more. More of him. More of this moment that feels so fragile yet so potent. With one swoop of a leg over his hips, I straddle him, his hands landing on my own hips, his thumbs digging into the soft skin where my thighs and hips meet. He gazes up at me, his features relaxed. It's a rare sight.

"Let me see you," I simply say.

I place my palms flat on his broad chest and settle into my position with a small wiggle of my ass.

"Easy," he mutters, his hands squeezing my hips harder.

A small giggle escapes my lips as I continue my exploration. All of his tattoos are black. Except for one—a blue flower over his heart. I pass my hand over it and Byzantine's body twitches under me as if I burned him. My eyes pop up to meet his and I study his expression. The question dies on my lips when he just nods and then looks away.

It's a windflower.

My heart squeezes when I see him try to hide that same damn haunted look he typically gets when I get too close. Too close to what? I don't even know. I just know that when it happens, he slips behind his favorite mask just like I watch him do now.

This suddenly feels much larger than *just* his favorite flower. Heavier than just a word spoken softly into the air after we first kissed. I swallow hard, dread sticking to my chest like tar. It's my turn to look away, and eventually I slump down into the warmth of his chest, my cheek resting close to the tattoo near his heart. There's a desperate need to just hold him like this forever, especially now, when the air is thick with the unspoken truths still existing between us.

But just as fast, reality crests over me, the enormity of what we just did and what it all means feeling like it could suffocate me half to death. The need to self-sabotage takes hold of my limbs and I slink off him, crawling out of bed and pretending I didn't just have an existential crisis within the span of a few seconds.

"Where are you going?" he asks, his tone severe. I glance at him, his arm bent behind his head leaning against the pillow, his eyes betraying his casual pose.

"Home?" I meant it as a statement but it comes out as a question instead, feeling suddenly ridiculous as I stand awkwardly beside the bed—naked. Byzantine doesn't even bother to speak, his body does it for him. His muscles tighten, his jaw clenches and unclenches, and his eyes describe in vivid detail how wrong I am to have thought he would let me leave after all this.

My mouth opens and then shuts, until I finally let out a huge sigh and crawl back in bed and under the soft covers, finding his body heat like a moth to the flame.

The sense of falling jolts me awake. Startled, I sit up in bed, taking a few seconds to situate myself, the room still dark because of the black-out curtains in Byzantine's room. The man in question stirs beside me as I gulp down air, my lungs burning as if I had been holding my breath while asleep.

That damn dream again.

"You okay?" Byzantine mumbles his voice thick with sleep. His hand reaches over, pulling on my arm and I follow his tug without any resistance. He settles behind me, his arm wrapping around my waist, dragging me even closer. My body is still coiled tight as he runs his nose up my neck, his lips tracing a path over my frantic pulse.

"Talk to me," he whispers into my ear.

My eyes flutter shut at the sound of his voice.

"It's silly. It was just a dream."

"I don't care. Tell me," he says, his voice low and dreamy still as his hand ghosts over my hip and down my thigh, goosebumps flaring across my skin as I try to relax into his touch.

His soft caress centers me enough to collect my thoughts and I finally speak. "It's just this recurring dream I keep having. It wasn't always this frequent but ever since I moved to Noxport, I've been having it almost every other week..." I trail off as Byzantine's hand moves back up and across my stomach, slowly tracing the curves of my breasts and then up my neck.

"It's always the same, I'm at the edge of this tall cliff, the wind pushing against me."

Byzantine's hand stutters to a slow stop, his body growing rigid behind me.

I notice the shift but continue. "There's always a person standing in front of me, their face too blurry to make out. And it always ends the same way...it feels like I'm falling off the cliff and then wake up"

Byzantine feels like he's stopped breathing altogether and I move to turn around to look at him but his arm squeezes me like a vice around my waist, forcing me to stay facing away.

My curiosity is peaked but still, I choose not to pry. Unsure if I even want to know why he's reacting so strongly to a dream of mine. He seems to realize the shift in the air and clears his throat.

"That's strange," he simply says, his body relaxing behind me as his hand slowly wraps around my neck. My heartbeat ramps up while his thumb strokes the column of my throat

I can tell he's trying to distract me again. And fortunately for him it's working, my mind losing its train of thought as I feel Byzantine growing hard against my back, his free hand nestling between my legs. My body turns liquid as I sigh into him and forget all about the dream.

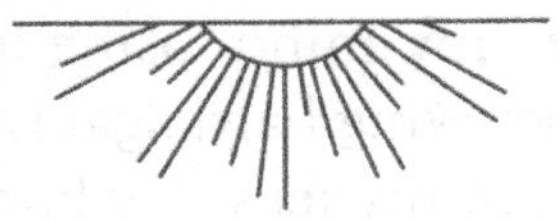

Chapter 36

Byzantine

I'm back in Connor's basement. I haven't been down here since Gary.

Fucking Gary.

I still hate him. But maybe just a little less now. How that fucking rodent was the reason I found Sunny I still have trouble wrapping my head around. How the hell was he the catalyst for the worst and best thing to ever happen to me.

Regardless, he deserved to die and I won't ever regret it.

I also won't feel sorry for ending the life of the fucker sitting in front of me either. The one who thought he could threaten Sunny and live.

No, this one I'll even relish.

It only took Bastian a few days to find the mugger. He hacked into the city's surveillance cameras and found footage of him fleeing the scene. That, paired with Sunny's description was enough for our favorite hacker to track him down.

Now the loser's here, duct taped to a chair, squealing like a trapped pig, while I approach him with my favorite switchblade.

"P—please," he sputters, his greasy hair covering half his bloodied face. "The gun wasn't even loaded man, please, I just needed some cash, I wasn't going to hurt her, I *swear*," he blubbers some more, rambling on like his bullshit story will give me a sudden change of heart.

I stop in front of the chair, glaring at him and smile. A smile taken from Connor's arsenal, cold, flat—unhinged.

"Makes no difference. You were dead the second you touched her," I state flatly.

My answer unnerves him and he thrashes against the chair, yelping for someone to save him. His voice is shrill and pierces the room. It makes me want to cut his tongue out just for that alone.

Actually—that's a good idea.

"There's no point in yelling. No one is coming to save you buddy," I drawl, a bored nonchalance to my tone, kicking his chair over. That shocks him into shutting up. If only for a few seconds.

I pick up the pliers from the stainless steel table near us. He continues to snivel while I place my feet on each side of his head and crouch down. Resting the switchblade beside us, I grab him by the cheeks, squeezing them hard and forcing his mouth open. I salivate at the sight of the pure terror in his eyes, eager to burn him with it like a hot brand to the skin.

I shove the pliers into his mouth and after a few slippery attempts I finally snag his tongue between the pincers and yank it out of his mouth. He's full blown sobbing by now. Like I give a fuck. I reach for the knife and without any preamble I begin to cut through the muscle. It's not easy, but I manage, luckily the blade is serrated. His screams grow even louder as he gargles and chokes on his own blood running down his throat.

"Jesus Christ, brother. What are you doing to him?" The voice behind me says. I don't need to turn around to know it's Connor.

Ignoring him, I finally rip through the final piece of this fucker's tongue while he suddenly falls silent and passes out. At least it's nice and quiet now. Then, I shove his tongue back into his mouth and duct tape it shut.

"Damn...that's pretty fucking gruesome even for me," Connor says with a laugh.

"What do you want?" I bark, annoyed as I haul the chair upright, the mugger's sweaty head flopping over his chest.

"Just wanted to see if you wanted some company," he chirps.

I turn to face him, the switchblade still wet and dripping blood onto the plastic tarp under my boots.

"Really?" I answer, staring at him like he's the dumbest person alive. And maybe he is.

He shrugs, bare chested and wearing swim trunks for fuck sakes.

"I was bored," he replies, flashing me a smile. "Want to have a drink poolside?"

I'm about to tell him to fuck right off and let me finish the job but then I look at this guy's lolling head and decide against it. Let him wake up and remember what I just did to him. Let him understand the length I'll go to protect Sunny. Just the thought gives me a sick sense of justice. I wipe the knife with a rag and grin back at Connor, "Sure."

Chapter 37

SUNNY

I'm back in Byzantine's car. And as usual he's driving me home after a long shift at the pub. It must be three in the morning, the night still a dark blue and eerily quiet.

"I feel like swimming," I say softly, more as an afterthought while looking out the window.

"It's the middle of the night."

"And?" I reply, peering over to him.

He lets out a half chuckle, half snort while he changes gears and turns on a street I don't recognize.

"Then let's go swimming," he says, not elaborating where he's taking me. It's clearly not the public beach based on the affluent neighborhood we're in.

Eventually he turns into a driveway that leads to what I can only call a mansion. The house is surrounded by perfectly manicured lawns, lit up with small yard lights lining the walkway and...is that a fucking fountain?

Then the realization hits.

"Don't tell me this is Connor's house," I deadpan.

Byzantine laughs,"Yeah."

"Should have known," I laugh, taking it all in. "Definitely looks like something he'd own."

"How so?" he asks.

I glance back at him, "Flashy?"

He chuckles and nods. "Come on," he says, opening the car door. "He left for business earlier today and I have a spare key. We can use his pool."

After letting Byzantine open the door for me, as always, I scamper out, eager to snoop around Connor's property. Everything about his place screams modern architecture, with floor to ceiling windows and open spaces. I gawk as Byzantine leads me through the spacious foyer and into the kitchen which leads out to his even more spacious exterior—pool included.

My smile hurts my cheeks as I start pulling off my clothes eager to get in. Skinny dipping is definitely the way to go, especially when Byzantine watches me undress with such hunger.

"You know you also need to take your clothes off if you're going to follow me into the pool," I point out.

"Just let me look at you first," he responds, his voice low and full of want.

I unsuccessfully tamper my reaction to his burning gaze, trying to pull off a casual shrug and walk down the stairs leading into the pool. The damn thing is heated of course. I slowly immerse my body and swim to the deep end, the water feeling amazing against my tired limbs.

I turn on my back and float, looking at the stars. The water trickles nearby, Byzantine having followed me in but I stay in my position, my gaze landing on my favorite constellation ever since I was a child. My eyes seek it without me even thinking. It's the row of three stars that makes Orion's Belt. I peek to my left and see Byzantine has his back against the pool wall, elbows up on the edge watching me.

"Do you have a favorite constellation?" I ask him, curious.

"Never really thought about it, so no," he answers, falling quiet while my eyes rove around the night sky, the expanse of so many stars making me feel small and insignificant. It's comforting—in a larger picture kind of way.

Eventually, I swim over to Byzantine, a half smirk on his face. He squeezes my hand when I reach him while we stay silent and stare at each other.

His face falls suddenly serious, looking conflicted.

"I found the mugger."

My heart drops while I place my hands on his broad shoulders to steady myself in the water.

"Really? That was fast..." I trail off when I notice his expression. It's not the smooth emotionless mask I've grown so used to. Instead, he seems worried, his brows knitted, lips thin.

"I don't want to lie to you, Sunny."

My heart pounds in my chest, a slow dread snaking up my spine as I chase a truth I'm not sure I can even handle.

"Where is he?" I say cautiously.

"Here. In the basement."

"He's here?" I yelp, my voice rising an entire octave. "He's here and we're just *casually* in the pool having a midnight dip? What the fuck Byzantine?" I try to pull away but he wraps his arm around my waist, preventing me from moving. "What are you going to do to him?"

But I already know the answer, don't I? Reality crashes into me, and I chastise myself for having forgotten, even for a second, what this man does for a living.

I can't help but wince when he cradles my cheek with his hand, his eyes desperate as they search mine.

"What did you expect, Sunny? He could have hurt you. He deserves what's coming to him," he says cooly, his jaw hard.

"Which is?" I ask, already knowing damn well what he's going to say but needing to hear it anyway. He doesn't respond, his every intention etched into the scowl he's glaring at me with.

"What happened to killing only the people who deserved it?" I say, a small tremble to my voice.

This time he answers. "He deserves much more than death, little sun. He put you in danger—and I protect what's mine."

A sick thrill zips through me, hearing him speak with such intent, prompting me to question every single one of my morals as I make space for this new reality glaring back at me.

Still I try to stand my ground but I can already feel my morality slipping through my fingers, especially when Byzantine is staring at me with such heat it burns to even look at him.

"So that's it then? I don't want you to kill anyone for me Byzantine. That's fucking insane—"

"He's dying either way, Sunny. Whether you agree with it or not. It's done. No one threatens you and gets to live," he declares, his voice final as he shrugs his shoulders, a movement so goddamn anodyne for what he just said.

I knew this. I've *been* knowing this. But this is the first time he's made me confront the truth since the first night we met. And while I wrestle with my own sense of virtue, I also understand why Byzantine is forcing this on me.

He's forcing me to see him completely. Every ugly piece of him. I needed a reminder of who he is when he's not being the Byzantine I've become so entranced with. Someone who's convinced me and even proven to me that the last thing he would ever do is hurt me.

Fuck—am I okay with this?

What does it make me if I am? What kind of person condones this type of behavior and gets to live a happy life? Are those two things even mutually exclusive? I don't even know if that's how karma even works.

"So you just left him alone in the basement?" I finally say.

"I had more important things to do."

"Which were?" I ask incredulously.

"Driving you home," he says, pulling me into his hard wet body and my legs automatically wrap around his waist. "Having a taste of your sweet fucking cunt," he growls, suddenly flipping us around and plopping me on the edge of the pool.

A million thoughts explode inside me but I can't pinpoint any one of them as my brain melts from Byzantine's thumb on my clit. God, I'm so fucked.

And what does that make him?

Equally fucked.

I peer down at him, his head now cradled between my open thighs.

"What do you think you're doing?" I ask, my voice breathless.

He smirks as his eyes grow hooded.

"Distracting you," he drawls, seconds before the flat of his tongue licks broad strokes against my pussy and I let out a low whimper, opening my legs even wider, my thighs already shaking with lust. I close my eyes, trying to catch my breath, my head falling between my shoulders, sinking into the sensation he's administrating.

My body is wound so tight that it doesn't take long for me to find myself on the edge of elation. And as his fingers slide into me, I fleetingly promise to feel guilty about the man in the basement later. Byzantine makes me lose all sense of reason. And it's then that I realize I will crave his touch for lifetimes to come.

Chapter 38

Sunny

My mind broods as I sit quietly beside Byzantine in his parked car, the sunrise still a few minutes away. He's been making the detour to the flower fields at least once a week since that first time. Something about the sunrise and the quietness of dawn seems to calm him. Calm me.

Well, usually.

I'm distracted. And it's not even because of the obvious issue of Byzantine killing my attacker last week. Shamefully, I haven't really dwelled much on it since. Something else is taking up all the space in my mind.

The countdown to my sister's death has officially started. Like a dark mark. An ink stain seeping onto the calendar page anytime I catch a glimpse. Even saying the date out loud is like a small death itself. Five years. I should be over it by now. Right? Or halfway healed at least.

But grief is tattooed deep into my skin.

It's not only her absence I'm grieving. I'm also mourning my own death. I was ripped in half when she left me here. Half of me, simply gone.

Not to mention the guilt I still carry with me. Sometimes it becomes unbearable to even cope. So I try to forget. Gin tastes better going down than the shame of not protecting her. The guilt of leaving her to die alone.

Cold and wet.

The twisted irony isn't lost on me. The cruel joke weaved into the very fabric of that day. I was the twin who romanticized death. I was the one who felt too much. Who wrote morose poems about my funeral. But she's the twin who died, like a sick cosmic joke. As if finding her dead would somehow make me want to embrace life. To survive for River in her memory. Instead, it only heightened the feeling. The urge to end it all. She was the lucky one.

And I'm still here. Barely living. Barely holding on.

"I can hear you think from all the way over here," Byzantine remarks.

My head rests on the car seat behind me and I let it fall to the side as I give him a droll look. "I can't help it."

"What's on your mind?" he asks.

"Everything," I answer.

"Right."

His hand falls palm up on my thigh but he says nothing else. He just gives his fingers a small wiggle as if to say *well?* So I lace my fingers into his. He brings my hand up to his mouth and presses his lips to my skin and my heart tugs a thousand million ways.

Jesus, I must be starved for affection.

Or maybe it's him. Don't I already know the answer? It's always him. He places our clasped hands on his thigh, his thumbs tracing a slow pattern on the top of my hand as he looks off into the distance, the first rays finally stretching over the field facing us.

"Come away with me," Byzantine says in a quick hush as if he was nervous to let the words out.

I let out a small laugh. "What do you mean, like on a trip?"

"Yeah. Next week," he replies.

A thrill zips through me but it evaporates quickly. "A whole week?"

"Why not?" He hasn't looked me in the eyes since he asked.

"I mean, I would love to Byzantine, but I can't afford to take time off work like that..." Or what it would mean to spend a whole week with Byzantine, just him and I.

"You don't need to think about that."

I try to take my hand back but he holds on to it.

"What does that even mean?" I ask, my laugh full of nerves and I kick myself for how it sounds.

Finally, he looks at me, his eyes a heady force gluing me to the seat.

"It *means*, Sunny, that's it's covered. I'll take care of it. I'll take care of you," he promises, his eyes continuing to burn me from the inside out as I let his words settle inside the cracks of my insecurities. I'm fighting against my defense mechanism, swallowing the sarcasm back down.

Instead, I slump back into my seat and say, "Fine."

He smiles as he lets go of my hand and finds the back of my neck, pulling me towards him as if claiming his prize. His kiss is quick but intense as he quickly pulls away and starts the car, leaving me in a daze, the taste of him melting slowly on my tongue.

"We leave Monday."

Lenix is lying on my bed, plopped on her stomach, scrolling on her phone, her long legs swinging above her while I riffle through my closet trying to figure out what to pack.

"I wish *I* had a dangerously sexy and mysterious man whisking me away for a whole ass week," she whines.

I throw a pair of pants at her from where I'm standing as she giggles and rolls onto her back, narrowly missing the flying piece of clothing.

"I'm sure you could," I say, looking at her with suspicion, still unsure what the hell is going on with her and Connor.

"Oh please," she huffs, flipping her hair off her shoulder. "Most of the time we're trying to hook up with the same girl." She then looks at me as if realizing what she just said. "*Separately.*"

"Sure you are," I say as I try to jam a pair of sweats into my already stuffed suitcase.

"I'm serious Sunny! I kiss and tell remember? Not like *other* people I know," she glares at me with a smirk and then pouts. "I'll miss you."

"It's only a week, Len."

"I know that," she replies, hanging her head over the side of the bed, watching me upside down. "Won't you miss me?"

"Of course, I will. It's you and me against the world, remember?"

"Good," she says, beaming and winking at me. "Just checking. So where is he bringing you anyway?"

"It's a surprise. All I know is that we're taking a plane to get there."

She swings around back on her stomach, her head cradled into her hand. "Oh you just *know*, he's flying you first class."

"You think?"

"Positive. Oh my god I'm so jealous. Please take loads of pictures and text me all the time. I *must* live vicariously through you."

I laugh and continue packing.

"I will, promise."

Chapter 39

Sunny

Lenix was right. We're flying first class. I can't help but gawk while the flight attendant leads us to our seats. I snap pictures for her and she replies immediately with a slew of emojis including the popped champagne bottle and the grinning devil. Needless to say, she's excited for me. And so am I.

I love flying. But flying when you're not squeezed into your seat while trying to fight for limited elbow space is even better.

I'm soaking it all in while Byzantine watches me with a pleased look, as if he's enjoying experiencing the novelty of first class through my eyes.

It's only an hour and a half flight but after the excitement of take-off, I eventually doze off, snuggled underneath a blanket, my legs pulled up to my chest, my head resting on a small pillow against the window.

A small moan escapes my lips, effectively waking me up and I jerk my head up like a startled bird. It's then I become aware of the pressure between my legs. Deft fingers pressing slow circles against my clit over my leggings. I straighten up and look over at Byzantine. A small grin adorns the corner of his lips.

I slap his hand away from under the blanket and whisper-yell, "What the fuck do you think you're doing? Someone will see." I try to catch my breath, realizing how turned on I am by his subtle ministrations.

"Will they?" He gives me a pointed look and I glance around, finding the only other passenger in first class all the way on the other side, headphones on as he watches the inflight entertainment. Byzantine's fingers find their way back and he whispers in my ear.

"I'm about to make you come, my little sun." He presses his fingers over my clit and I gulp loudly. "Right here, right now."

"And if I don't let you?"

His laugh is low and sultry. "Care to find out?"

Fuck. Why is it so hot when he gives me orders?

"What's in it for you?"

"I get to watch."

My eyes nearly roll into the back of my head as my core squeezes tightly at his words.

Byzantine notices my reaction and takes advantage, carefully slipping his hand into the front of my leggings. His eyebrows rise, pupils dilating when he realizes I'm not wearing any underwear. He licks his lips. The sight of him like this, so damn salacious, I forget how to breathe.

Brain scrambled, I settle back under the blanket, trying not to move or give any tells about what Byzantine is currently doing to me. My head falls onto the pillow and I sigh deeply. His fingers gently graze the sensitive skin, his fingers wet with my arousal when he brings them back up to my clit, massaging it in small quick circles.

Byzantine leans over. "This is what's about to happen." His breath is hot against my ear sending shivers down my arms. "Feel these two fingers stroking your clit? I'm about to slide them into your tight little cunt."

My heart pounds, desire roars inside of me as he continues to play with my hard bud with perfect precision. "Now, you're going to close your eyes like you're taking a sweet little nap and then take your own hand and replace mine with yours. So while I fuck you with my fingers, you'll play with yourself and you won't stop until you come all over my hand. Got it?"

I stifle a whimper and give him a small nod. He leans even closer, his hot tongue running across my pulse point before leaning back in his seat, one hand between my thighs and his cellphone in the other.

My breath stutters as I close my eyes and pretend to nap. As if I fucking could. Meanwhile, my hand finds my way to his as Byzantine's fingers slowly slide inside of me, my pussy eagerly clenching around him.

His arm is at an angle that doesn't give Byzantine much mobility but it's just enough for his fingers to pulse in and out at a mind-meltingly slow pace and it's taking everything in me not to jerk forward and push his fingers deeper inside of me. I'm so turned on, I know this won't take long.

I keep my eyes closed as I strum my clit faster and faster, desperately trying to move as little as possible under the blanket. With my eyes squeezed shut, every other sense is heightened. My entire focus is zeroed in on his fingers pumping in and out of me.

Byzantine then slips his middle finger out and replaces it with another as he slowly strokes up my ass, gently pressing at the entrance there, stimulating but never entering. This sends a slew of new sensations barrelling through my body as I'm finally pushed over the edge.

I breathe out a small moan as my eyes fly open and find Byzantine watching me with such heat that my back arches off the seat, biting my bottom lip hard, my eyes wide.

I try to catch my breath while I fall back into the seat. Slowly, he pulls his hand out of my leggings and wipes his hand on his jeans. Somehow the sight of him doing that, along with the look he's currently giving me is so fucking debauched, I lose all speaking ability.

"You loved that didn't you?" he says.

I nod, my brain still blown to pieces.

"I knew you would." He leans over and whispers, "Next time, it'll be my cock instead of my fingers."

Lust splinters me open as I watch him settle back into his seat, his phone still in hand.

Half an hour later, we land in Midnight Cove and I follow Byzantine off the plane, my legs still weak and boneless from his fingers and filthy words alone.

A private car waits for us outside of the airport and I lift my eyebrow inquisitively at Byzantine. He simply shrugs as if a private car with a driver is no big deal.

From the car window, I watch the scenery roll by, excitement swirling inside of me while he reaches for my hand from across the backseat. As if always seeking some type of touch or contact. My walls continue to slowly crumble anytime he does.

When we arrive at the hotel, I take a moment to reel in my shock at the sight of it. I look over to Byzantine, placing my hand on my chest in mock outrage. "You must be kidding."

Byzantine leans across the seat to kiss my cheek. "Only the best for my little sun."

He leans back over and steps out, leaving me stunned. Byzantine beats the driver to my door, helping me out and towards the hotel, leaving our bags for the driver.

Byzantine checks us in while I take in our surroundings, mesmerized by the ritz and glitz of what feels like the fanciest hotel I've ever stepped foot in. The lobby is huge, made almost entirely out of glass, even the elevators. And the fine dining restaurant to our left with its maître d' and waiters dressed to the nines has me straightening my back just to feel like I belong here.

When we get to our room—no suite—I'm near speechless. The view faces the sprawling ocean and it's breathtaking. "Jesus Byzantine, you really are rich aren't you?" I tease.

He chuckles and takes our bags to the bedroom. "Perks of the trade," he simply says.

"Perks of the fucking trade, I bet," I mutter under my breath as I walk around, barely believing we'll be staying here for a whole week. "Please tell me we can order room service and eat it in bed?"

"If that's what you want, then yes," Byzantines answers as I follow his voice into the bedroom. It's as massive as I expected and my jaw slackens while my feet sink into the lush cream carpet.

Total heaven.

"Why? Do you have the whole week planned out for us or something?" I ask.

"Some."

"Ah yes, Byzantine, man of many words," I say as I fall onto my back sinking into the king size duvet.

"That's how you like me," he replies.

"Do I?"

"What?"

"Like you?" I grin as I watch him change into a clean but identical black shirt.

He looks at me, a cocky glint to his eyes. "You seem to like me a whole lot when I'm making you come."

Heat flushes my cheeks. "Well, I mean, that's when you're at an advantage."

"I'd say more than just that."

"Fine," I say, crossing my arms. "I guess I do like you a little then."

In the next breath, Byzantine is on me, straddling my thighs as he pins me down on the bed. His kiss stokes the fire that was already kindling for him, his hand finding the column of my neck, deft fingers squeezing just hard enough for me to moan into his mouth and melt deeper into the duvet. And just as fast, he's off of me, leaving me breathless on the bed.

"What was that for?"

His eyes are dark when he peers over to me, his grin dimpling his cheek.

"Just proving my point."

The next day, it rains. Unbothered, we spend the day in bed. Byzantine seems more relaxed here. Just us. Under the sheets. But I still can't shake the feeling he's hiding something from me. Especially when I catch him watching me like I'm a puzzle he's trying to crack. He spends most of the morning trailing kisses over every inch of my skin, muttering praise as he goes.

I don't hate it. Not one bit.

We order room service and eat in bed just like how I wanted. Eventually, I fall asleep beside him, the rain pattering against the floor to ceiling windows like the softest lullaby. Byzantine lays beside me, a book in hand and the other nestled in my hair. The simple pleasure of the moment hits me like a ton of bricks. So much that I have the irrational urge to ruin it.

Almost. Self-sabotage has always been a fail-safe that I can press at any moment and eject far away from here.

It's living that scares me the most. Not death.

Living when everything feels like it could actually work out. Truly existing like I believe happiness is an attainable goal. If only I could focus on that instead of the darkness constantly eating me alive. It's unsettling and it terrifies me.

But today beside Byzantine, in the most comfortable bed I've ever been in, I allow myself to believe that maybe I deserve this. That I'm worthy of this. Even if my own worth isn't close to what I see when Byzantine looks at me. Like I'm everything he's ever wanted. And he's simply waiting for me to catch up.

What will happen if I let him in and he doesn't like what he sees? My insides are rotten. They've been rotten for years. Sometimes it feels they always have been.

I settle even deeper into the down pillows, Byzantine's solid body pressed close but yet I feel so far away. I stifle a long sigh and keep it inside instead.

This is why it's better not to feel.

Feeling is messy. Feeling is just not worth the hurt. But if I lock myself up again, I lock Byzantine out in the same breath, and a large part of me doesn't want to keep him at a distance anymore. He might not be the most ethical person I've ever met but the way he makes me feel when I'm around him eclipses all of it. He's never shown me anything but kindness and care.

Well maybe not at the beginning, but I'll let that one slide since he's certainly redeemed himself since. Eventually, I fall asleep with my thoughts still circling the drain, feeling guilty I'm even thinking any of this while Byzantine is doing so much just to see me smile.

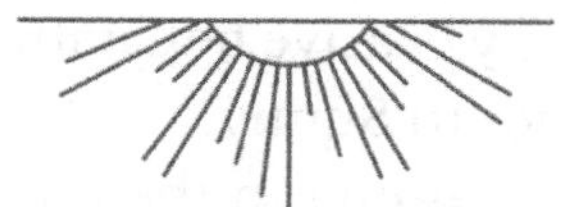

Chapter 40

Byzantine

I've been lying to Sunny. Lying by omission. Still makes me a liar. There's another reason I brought her here. Did I want to help her escape her life for a while? Of course. But I'm also guiding her right to the inevitable.

Well, hopefully.

From all the lives I've remembered spending with her. One has stood out, if only because the memories are that much clearer. Vivid. And because of it, I've also remembered the location. A life spent here, in Midnight Cove centuries ago.

The cliff where Gabriel died still looks the same. I came looking for it five years ago thinking it could give me some answers but it only left me empty.

Didn't stop me from buying a small cottage overlooking that very cliff. Morbid, I know. But it was the only connection I had to her—to him. To whatever soul was linked to mine. Destined to love but also to suffer.

What is more fated than death? I had to die to find Sunny again. And maybe this place is the missing piece for her to remember. Maybe she won't be haunted by the memories of our past lives like I am but at least something.

Guilt throbs against my skin with the thought of keeping this from her. Not telling her the whole truth. And I can tell she's picking up on my evasive behavior, but aren't I always evasive when it comes to Sunny?

I hear the shower running in the en suite and my heart pangs for her. We've been tiptoeing around each other for what feels like forever. Both of us harboring secrets from the other. But mine are so much different than hers. Sunny's are part of her past, secrets she prefers to keep in an effort to protect herself. But mine are about us.

I need to tell her. But I'm a coward and I hope this place will deliver my secrets for me instead.

Sunny strolls into the bedroom, hair still wet and completely naked, the tips of her curls lightly brushing against her dark pink nipples. And I turn fucking feral.

"Sunny," I groan.

She feigns surprise. "What?"

"Come here."

Her shoulders straighten as if proud of her little stunt and saunters up to me, acting oh so casual. I'm sitting on the edge of the bed—fully clothed—widening my legs as she tucks herself inside, her thighs hitting the edge of the bed.

Still standing, she looks down at me with a smirk and once again I'm lost. Lost at the sight of her. I could lose myself in her forever.

She places her hands on each side of my shoulders delicately, slowly leaning even closer and catching my bottom lip with her teeth. I reach around and grab her ass with both hands and dig my fingers into her soft flesh. She lets go of my lip, her perfect mouth opening on a silent gasp. I wrap my hands around her thighs and lift her, making her straddle me.

She giggles and gives me a playful shove. "We can't miss our reservation."

"Like I give a fuck."

I raise my hand up to her face, my fingers cradling her cheek as I slowly push my thumb inside her mouth. She wraps her lips around it, our eyes interlocking. The touch of her hot tongue around my thumb makes my cock throb but I keep my face relaxed. Slowly I drag it out of her mouth and reach down beneath her thighs, finding her clit. This time her gasp is audible.

I would make her come every single hour of the day just to hear that sound. And maybe I fucking will. Right now, it's the only thing on my mind. Her hips grind into me and I just know she's about to give up on our dinner reservation but instead, she pushes me down on the bed. Her hands on my chest, her elbows locked in place as she gives a sly smirk.

"I *said*—we're going to be late," she says as her hips grind against me. "But if you're a good pet you can watch me get dressed." She pats my cheek and leans over, her other hand palming my erection, whispering against my ear. "How does that sound?"

Fuck. She's piqued my curiosity and I can't help but grin as I let her crawl off of me. My eyes never leave her while she strolls back into the bathroom. I hear the hairdryer turn on and for a few minutes, I just sit on the bed, dick hard and fucking paralyzed. My patience is waning when she finally comes back out, her hair now dry but still naked. She heads over to the vanity, her back to me as I watch her in the mirror.

It takes me a second to realize what she's up to. With every small movement she takes, she gives me small peeks of what I'm desperately craving. What I'm dying to taste.

She putters around the bedroom, getting ready—pretending I'm not even here.

A dip of her hips while she bends to grab the earrings off the dresser. The reach for her stockings hanging off the chair. The soft pull of those same stockings on her foot while she steadies herself on the chair. Her angle is just right as I watch her slowly glide it up her smooth leg, clipping it to her garter belt. Then, a slight bend to her hips allows me a peek of her perfect pink cunt.

It's voyeuristic. And I want more and more and more. It's getting harder to swallow and I can tell she's wet as she bends even further, her pussy perfectly angled in front of me.

After the stockings, she slides her bra over her shoulders, clasping it from behind. Then, her hands trace a slow path down her stomach and I nearly launch myself off the bed as I watch her fingers dip between her legs.

Deliciously taunting. My little sun. My windflower.

I can't take it any longer, my willpower faltering. She's making me delirious. As silently as possible, I pop the button of my jeans and unzip. I lean back on the bed on one elbow and pull my dick out, the sight of Sunny getting dressed making me fucking sweat.

She sits, her back to me, her pussy still bare with just the stockings up her thighs and begins to twist her hair into a high ponytail.

She faces the vanity mirror and I watch with unwavering focus as she opens her legs wide, her pussy glistening and so *fucking* inviting as she continues to ignore me. After her hair, it's the makeup. The soft glide of her lipstick on her plump lips, a small spritz of perfume on her neck.

I pump into my fist as I continue to watch her tease me. I can't even wrap my head around why this is so fucking hot but Sunny makes my blood heat, my balls tighten and I know I'm close.

I try to keep my demeanor relaxed—unbothered—as I watch her stand up and reach over to grab the yellow silk dress hanging in the closet. Slowly, with sensual languid movements, she slides it over her body and I let out a low groan.

My head falls back and I close my eyes, the pleasure building at the bottom of my spine. When my eyes pop back open, she's by the side of the bed, bending down close to my ear.

Her voice is breathless as she whispers, "Come for me Byzantine."

"*Fuck,*" I growl through clenched teeth, her voice spiralling through me as I come in my hand in hot spurts, her name on my lips, the orgasm so intense my vision blackens and I'm undone. Utterly destroyed. I look up at her in what can only be fucking shock. I nearly come all over again as I watch the deep satisfaction glow in her hazel eyes. She kisses my lips, hungry, needy. But pulls away, her mouth pouty and pleased.

"Ready?" she asks innocently.

Chapter 41

Sunny

It's our third day in Midnight Cove and I never want to leave. Or more specifically, I don't want to leave Byzantine's side. He's spoiling me and I let myself preen at the attention.

But really, it's his presence I can't get enough of. His grounding touches throughout the days we spend exploring, the look he gives me that feels strangely like adoration. Although, could I even tell what that would look like when it's staring right in front of me? Have I ever experienced this before?

Even saying I'm *dating* Byzantine sounds ridiculous to me. As much as I'm trying to avoid all the right words to describe what I feel for Byzantine, this feels much more than just dating.

Maybe I'm wrong. Maybe it's all in my head. Is it that what I seek in his actions is what I'm most desperate for? Someone who won't hurt me. Someone who won't abandon me. Someone who will love me unconditionally. I wince at the thought. *Gross. Get a grip.*

Deep down, I know it's not love that scares me. It's what it would mean to love and be loved. I would have to choose life. To truly commit to this place.

I always held the belief that I'd never reach my thirties. I'm turning twenty-eight this year. Maybe it's time for me to let go of old beliefs when Byzantine seems so adamant to change my way of thinking.

I look over to him, his face relaxed as he watches the sun dip low on the horizon. We've been sitting on the hotel balcony for over an hour, the conversation waning and waxing into easy silence. These are the moments I collect inside of me like a treasure worth protecting. The easy moments. The moments where it feels like it's just us—only us.

"It's the anniversary of my sister's passing on Friday." I pause, biting my lip nervously. "Did you know?"

"I did, yeah."

I don't bother asking how he knows, Byzantine has a tendency to just know these things. His stalker tendencies are still alive and well.

"Is that why you brought me here?"

That flash of guilt again, so quick I'm starting to believe I'm imagining it. But then his face relaxes and he smiles as he looks at me.

"One of the reasons."

He reaches over and grabs my hand, interlocking our fingers together as they hang between our two chairs.

"What are the other reasons?"

"You'll see."

A flare of frustration spikes in my chest but I try not to let it take over. Why am I so surprised he's evading my questions yet again? A kernel of doubt lodges itself in my mind and I wonder if any of this is real. Do I even know him? At the rate he opens up, it will take me years.

Meanwhile, he keeps digging, urging me to tell him things I've never told anyone else. For now, I choose to let it go and not ruin the moment. I go back to watching the sunset before speaking again.

"Tell me how it feels to die."

Byzantine looks over to me, a soft smile across his beautiful face as if he's not even surprised I've asked him that question.

"What?" I ask.

He chuckles and squeezes my hand in his. "Nothing." He looks back at the sunset, still smiling.

"So?" I scooch my chair closer to his. "How does it feel?"

"Cold."

"Could you tell you were dying?

"I wasn't really lucid but yeah I could tell I wasn't going to survive."

"Did it hurt?"

"You mean this?" He rubs his scars distractedly and I nod.

"I think I was in shock—I don't remember the pain."

I swallow hard. "Do you think my sister suffered?" My voice cracks and I hate how broken I sound.

Byzantine peers over to me, sadness pulling his eyebrows downwards.

"Come here." His voice barely perceptible over the sound of my own thoughts.

This time I don't resist and I stand and curl up into his lap, my head finding the crook of his neck as I feel him sigh deeply. He strokes my back in a long slow motion as we sit in silence, gathering my hair and pushing it off my shoulder so he can kiss my neck.

"No," he finally says. "I don't think she did, my little sun."

I stay silent, deep in contemplation before asking my next question. "What was the rest like?" I can feel Byzantine shift in the chair as if my question makes him uncomfortable.

"It's hard to explain. What I saw...it's beyond words. I don't think I'll ever be able to explain it and do it justice. What I do know is that it changed my perspectives on a few things."

I sit up to properly look at him.

"Like what?"

Byzantine stares into my eyes as if evaluating how to answer or how much to say.

"Reincarnation," he finally says.

"Oh?"

He clears his throat. "I saw myself in other bodies, living completely different lives than I am now." I can feel a slight tremor in his hands clasped behind my back. "I can't tell you how I knew it was me." He leans close for a kiss as if chasing the comfort of my lips. "But I just knew."

The need to kiss him back overwhelms me and I welcome it. I lick the seam of his lips, eager to dive deeper, *dig* deeper and he lets me in, his arms squeezing me tighter. I wish I could just melt inside of him. Close never seems to be close enough. The way I feel for Byzantine scares me but right now I embrace it, let it fuel our kiss like our first and last and all of them in between.

Finally, I pull away. My lips hum with the taste and touch of him. I try to catch my breath as I search his light green eyes for more answers. More. Always more. His gaze is hollow as if lost somewhere else. Haunted by memories he's unwilling to part with or speak out loud.

I could ruin this moment, and I almost do. The twinge in my heart asking for Byzantine to acknowledge how much shutting me out makes me feel but instead, I simply say, "I believe you."

His smile is heavy with relief. It's enough to quell my insecurities for now as I lean back in for another time-warping kiss, the sun finally finding its rest behind us.

Chapter 42

Sunny

On Thursday morning, Byzantine curls behind me in bed and gently presses himself against me. I burn for him, even in this semi-lucid state. I hum my satisfaction and sigh heavily as he explores my body with his hands, his mouth, his touch.

No words are spoken as he pulls my leg over his thigh. There's no rush to his movements while he pushes my underwear aside and slides a finger inside of me, his cock hard against my back.

He breaks the silence just to murmur into my ear, "Always so wet for me."

I moan in response as he drags his hand up my stomach, palming my breast, and pushing himself inside of me. His breath catches in his throat as he slowly pulls out and then back in again.

The sex is slow, unhurried, my limbs soft and pliable under his touch. Like being wrapped in cotton wool, a daydream filled with desire. Even my climax is quiet but powerful as Byzantine follows shortly after, throbbing inside of me and whispering praise like a morning prayer on his tongue.

Fuck. Why was that so intense?

My anxiety carves its way into this perfect moment, ruining it by my constant need to over-analyze. It felt different than the other times. Surely Byzantine felt it too. But by the look of him he's not rattled like I am as I leave him dozing in bed, slinking off to the bathroom to wash off and pee.

When I walk back into the bedroom, he's sitting up, the sheets down near his hips and I take a moment to soak up the view, his chiseled tattooed chest a stark contrast against the white hotel sheets. Fuck me. No wonder I can't keep my hands off him.

He's busy answering emails on his phone—or whatever illegal activity I'm not privy to—when I slide back into bed beside him. Without looking up he says, "You should pack."

"Pack? But we're not leaving until Sunday night."

He gives me one of his classic side grins. "I know."

I blink back at him and raise my arms in irritation.

"Oh my god, why do I even bother." Of course, he's not going to tell me. "I swear you get off on this," I snap as I climb back out of bed and start repatriating all my stuff back into my suitcase.

Byzantine just snickers, clearly very pleased with himself as he continues to type away on his phone.

Byzantine rented a car for the rest of our time here, and so we're back in our familiar places, driving down Highway 1 as he takes us to places I know nothing about. I daydream out the passenger window watching the small coastal towns pass us by.

Still, I wonder where we're headed, knowing full well Byzantine won't tell me even if I ask very, *very* nicely.

The drive reminds me of the time Byzantine drove us to the secluded beach in Noxport and my mind drifts back to that day. Of how wanted I had felt under his dexterous hands, the sound of the ocean lulling me into a dreamy in-between state. Heat drifts low in my stomach and I can't help but to squeeze my thighs together, turned on by the mere thought of Byzantine's tongue.

I lean over and turn the music a little louder just to have something to do and then resume my position. My elbow on the window ledge, my head resting against my closed fist, watching the scenery pass by.

That's when it hits me.

This overwhelming sense of dread so sudden it almost leaves me lightheaded.

But is it dread?

The feeling is evasive as I try to hold on to it but it lingers right at the edge of my consciousness. I jerk my head up, trying to find the reason why I'm feeling like this, awareness pricking my skin.

Byzantine notices and reaches over to turn the volume down. "You okay?"

"Uh, yeah," I say distractedly, still looking around. "Just suddenly started feeling weird...like a strange sense of déjà vu or something."

I notice Byzantine's shoulders tighten, his brows furrowed as he keeps his eyes on the road, his thumb tapping on the steering wheel.

"Hmm," he mutters and then falls silent as if lost in thought. "Anyway, we're almost there."

I sink back in my seat, wondering if I'm reading into Byzantine's subtle shift in mood. I'm probably being paranoid, maybe it's just my own fear rubbing off on him.

Ten minutes later, Byzantine turns off the main road and onto a small trail that leads to a quaint cottage near the water. When he finally parks the car, I don't wait for him to open the door and jump out, eager to see the house up close.

"You rented this place?" I ask him, my smile wide as I head for the wrap-around porch. "This is so cute."

But when I glance back to Byzantine, he almost looks uncomfortable, his hand reaching up to the back of his neck as if to self-soothe. "I own it actually."

"You own it?" I repeat back, confused. I walk back towards him as he pops the trunk and reaches for our bags. "So why didn't we just come straight here?" I ask.

His smile is sincere when he looks over to me. "I thought you would enjoy the hotel life too."

Touched, I don't know what to say so instead I give him a quick kiss on the lips and return the smile.

"Thank you."

Sadness drifts through his eyes, then disappears, shaking it off quickly. "Come. Let me show you around," he says.

Our bags loaded in his arms, I follow him inside the house, but before I step on the porch my attention catches on the looming cliff far off in the distance and the same sense of dread trickles down my throat, the taste bitter. This time, I don't stop to read into it and join Byzantine inside.

Chapter 43

SUNNY

The cottage is a snug little house with most rooms located on the main floor, a large fireplace in the living room and beautiful wooden stairs that lead to the mezzanine bedroom.

I'm obsessed. I might have loved the luxury of the hotel but this is much more my style, the coziness reaching every corner of the house. I explore the main floor, peeking inside cupboards and doors just for the hell of it.

"How is the fridge already fully stocked?"

Byzantine has been watching me explore with an amused look when he answers, "I have someone take care of the house when I'm away."

"How often do you come here?"

"Not often as I would like."

"Always with the vague answers," I sniff.

Byzantine falls serious—preoccupied even.

"I try to come once a year, twice if I can get away," he finally says, after a beat adding, "You're the first person I've brought here actually."

I try to hide the pride that swells in my chest, and simply give him a quick wink. "Is that so? Lucky, lucky," I tut while I make my way towards him. He immediately envelops his arms around me when I reach him. "Why don't you ever bring anyone here?" My curiosity over-powering my coyness.

Byzantine just shrugs. "I like my privacy," he mutters, leaning over for a kiss. Soft and slow, making my spine tingle in response.

After he drops our bags up on the mezzanine, he strolls back down in a simple fitted black t-shirt, sweats and bare feet. I look at him up and down from one of the kitchen barstools.

"Hot."

"What?" he says as he heads to the kitchen.

"Hot. You're hot," I repeat.

Byzantine pauses mid-way into opening a cupboard and looks back at me, a charmed look on his face.

I laugh, "Why are you looking at me like that?"

"Nothing." He turns back around to reach for two glasses. "It's just you've never been very direct with your compliments," he says while reaching for the alcohol bottles lining the kitchen counter. "Gin?"

"Yes, please. Wait, you're saying this is the first time I've told you I find you attractive? I mean, I thought it was pretty obvious," I reply.

Ice clinks in the glasses. "Oh it is. It's just nice to hear it from those pretty little lips of yours for a change," he says with his back turned to me, amusement lacing his tone. My body's reaction is instant as I cross my legs to quell the ache that's beginning to build between my thighs.

He turns and hands me a cold glass full of gin and a twist of lemon. I reach for it, raising it to my lips, tension hanging heavy as we stare at each other, taking small sips of our respective drinks.

It's Byzantine who finally breaks the silence. "Come. Let's go sit outside."

I give a small nod of the head and follow him out.

Outside, I notice a huge circular chair with very comfortable looking cushions.

"Dibs," I call out as I skip excitedly towards it and plop myself into the massive chair with a pleased sigh. I curl my legs under me and Byzantine chuckles softly, settling into a deck chair close to me.

We fall into silence as the hypnotic lull of the ocean waves pulls us in. The water is rougher here, not as calm as back in Noxport, but the cottage is perched on a small hill, raised up and safe from the rocky terrain below. I listen to the waves crash, my chest releasing some of its tension until my attention falls back to the jutting cliff in the distance.

My breath slows, my heart skipping a beat and I can't stop glancing back at it. A small distant part of me notices my body's response, accompanied by a lingering eerie feeling.

Like I've been here before.

That same sense of déjà vu washes over me, and it startles me enough to make me reach for my glass of gin just to feel it burn down my throat.

Of course, Byzantine notices. "You okay?"

I smile at him, knowing the smile doesn't quite reach my eyes. "Yeah." I wave him off. "Just that weird feeling again. It's nothing." I point to the cliff. "How far is it from here? The view is probably pretty cool from up there."

Byzantine grows suddenly very still and if I didn't know any better I would even say he looks terrified. But then, he seems to realize it and I watch him morph his initial reaction into a forced casualness before he answers, "About a twenty minute walk on foot."

His face falls blank as he goes back to staring at the ocean. I'm not an idiot, I can tell he's been acting a little off since we got here. But is it worth bringing it up? He'd probably give me another one of his incredibly vague answers anyway. So I let it go and fall back into the ease of an evening spent with Byzantine, a shared bottle of wine and an oddly competitive game of Go Fish.

Chapter 44

Sunny

My toes sink into the soft grass underneath my feet, every step taking me closer to the edge of the cliff. The one I've visited countless times in my dreams. Or what had felt like a dream. This feels more like walking through the sludge of an echoing memory.

The skies are angry, the clouds dark and looming as the wind howls in my ears. My hair flies into my eyes, as I try to see past the edge, down to the crashing waves. Suddenly, I feel myself tip forward, a hard tug as if gravity has become a sentient force, beckoning me to it.

Fear slashes through my senses, but no sound bursts out of my lungs as I fall down and down and down. The cold wall of water I plummet into does nothing but worsen my fall, making me sink further into the depth. I thrash, filled with suffocating terror, my clothes heavy and pulling me even further down. I gulp in water, my lungs burning with the lack of oxygen and the sea water replacing it.

Then, unexpectedly, my feet find purchase at the bottom and I pump my knees up, my head popping out from the surf as I gasp and retch loudly. I spin around, confused and disoriented, until dread replaces the fear flowing through my veins. I know this place...

I grow eerily still, standing breathless in the middle of the same pool River drowned in. I can barely make sense of it when I hear her voice behind me, "Sunny."

My heart explodes in my chest, swiveling around in near paralyzing shock.

Ever since her death, I've wished to see her again. I didn't care if it was real, or an apparition or even just my imagination—I was just desperate to see her. Her familiar face, smile, eyes. If only I could see her one last time.

And now she's here, a warm smile on her face when nothing else about her radiates the same feeling. Her hair wet, her skin ghostly white, the clothes she wears the same worn the night she drowned.

My heart lurches at the sight. "River," I croak out, my body moving towards her despite it all. My twin. My best friend.

Her smile widens and she opens her arms inviting me into her embrace. I slip into her, my tears falling in a steady flow. "I've missed you so much," I sob into her arms and she holds me, a steady force holding me up.

"I know," she soothes. "I know."

I hiccup, begrudgingly pulling away so I can look at her. She hasn't aged. Her face still holds the youth I've lost. But I've lost a lot more than just our baby face since she died.

I've lost myself.

Her eyes are pure warmth as I continue to study her.

"Why did you have to die?" I ask, my voice cracking with the weight of my heartache. "Why did you have to leave me here alone?" I cry even harder, my tears flowing heavy and merging with the chlorine water we're standing in.

"We'll meet again, Sunny. I promise."

She peers at me, her eyes full of wisdom as if holding the answers to questions she couldn't even fathom when she was alive.

I study her expression trying to understand further.

"When? How?" I finally ask.

"It's not your time. You need to wait. You have so much left to learn here. So many people your path still needs to cross—some you've already met," she says and I'm just left with even more bubbling questions.

"Like who?"

"Byzantine, for one," she responds. Confused, my eyes narrow but she speaks before I have time to formulate a thought. "It's time to remember where you've been, Sunny. He's been waiting lifetimes for this moment."

I blink, stunned into silence.

"What does that eve—"

"But this time you must choose differently. Please remember this, if nothing else."

She then presses her hands to my face and all at once I'm left breathless, sucked out of the dream, and ripped away from River all over again.

My eyes snap open and I'm back in bed, Byzantine breathing softly beside me. It takes a moment for the dream to settle into my bones and when it finally does, I curl onto my side like I've been physically injured. The hole in my chest aches like a knife straight to my heart. The pain is so unbearable, I can barely breathe. It's been years and I still can't believe I'm left here to live a life without River.

Trying to be as silent as possible, I stifle back a sob, and slide off the covers. I wearily climb out of bed and down the stairs without waking Byzantine up. I notice his hoodie on the couch and I pull it over my head. It hangs down to my thighs covering my sleep shorts as I hug myself for warmth and slide the back door open, needing some fresh air.

It's the early morning hours, the birds' chirps promising the upcoming rise of the sun but, for now, it's still dark out. My attention immediately snags on the cliff in the distance and a chill travels down my spine, my subconscious tapping at my mind's door but I'm still too scared to answer.

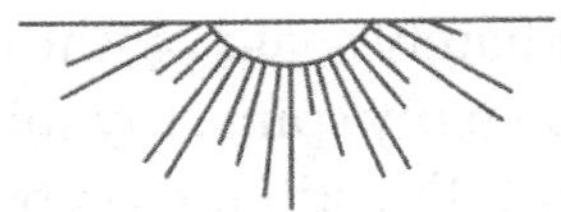

Chapter 45

Byzantine

I roll over in bed, my hand seeking out Sunny's warm body. When I find only rumpled sheets, a slow terror begins at the tip of my fingers and slithers up my arm and into my chest. I fly out of bed, my heart slamming into my ribcage.

Jumping to the worst conclusion, I picture her already at the cliff, yet again too far away to help. I've been here before. The worst case scenario has already happened and nightmares do come true. I trample down the stairs in only boxers, disheveled and panicked.

But then I catch a glimpse of her outside and shudder out an exhale, my heart pumping so fast it feels like I've been running for miles. I take a moment to collect myself before sliding the door open, trying my best to hide the absolute overreaction I just had from finding the bed empty.

Just from my nerves alone, bringing her here was a bad fucking idea. But it's too late now. I can tell she hears me step onto the porch but doesn't stir, her legs pulled under my hoodie she's wearing, curved into a tight ball on the chair, her arms around her knees. It's then I notice the tears staining her cheeks and my heart breaks at the sight.

"Sunny..." I say, my voice hoarse from having just woken up while I kneel in front of her but she evades my gaze.

"It's nothing. I didn't want to wake you," she mutters, her lips trembling as she raises her hand to her face, the sleeve wrapped tightly around her fist, wiping away the wetness found there.

"Talk to me. What happened?"

Her eyes are locked on the cliff and cold dread drips down my throat like bitter medicine.

"Why does that cliff feel so...familiar?" she says, biting at the skin on her bottom lip, tears still flowing down her face. But the question isn't aimed at me, like she just couldn't help but to say it out loud. Finally her gaze finds mine, and for half a second I almost wish it didn't because the grief I find swimming in the depths of her eyes nearly knocks me over.

"It was just a dream," she croaks, her body coiling even tighter around herself. "But it felt so real...River felt so real."

Realization dawns on me and I stand up and pull her into my arms. I'm surprised how easily she lets me. Taking her place, I pull her into me as she curls herself into a ball like before, except this time I can hold her close.

"Do you want to talk about it?" I whisper into her hair.

She stays silent for a moment, sniffling quietly as if lost in the memory of the dream but then says, "We were standing in the pool she drowned in..."

My heart lurches in my chest, but I say nothing, squeezing her tightly while she burrows into my chest.

"She kept telling me all these cryptic things...I barely remember now, I've tried but it's all so vague already. It just left me feeling so sad and empty," she mutters, a small sob spilling out of her lips. "I'm so tired of feeling like this," she adds quietly.

I give her a soft kiss on the forehead. My knuckles trail her spine in a soothing manner, knowing that words don't necessarily matter in this moment, my presence being comfort enough.

"I'm sorry," she says.

"Sorry?"

"I hate it when you see me like this. I'm such a mess."

While her body shakes with her silent cries, I drag her even closer and kiss her soft wet cheek, tasting the salt on my lips.

"There's no part of you I don't want to see, my little sun. Nothing you do can or *will* change my mind about you. Trust me."

A small pained sigh leaves her lips and she sniffles, trying to catch her breath.

"I trust you," she finally whispers.

The sound of those three words guts me, knowing that I've been keeping such a large piece of us hidden from her.

How the fuck am I supposed to tell her now?

There never seems to be the right time.

But it needs to happen. I can't keep lying to her like this.

"I need to show you something," I finally say, my heart clenching with anxiety.

She pops her head up, eyes swollen and cheeks red—vulnerable and so fucking beautiful. I pull her in for a slow, soft kiss, the taste of her tears like a balm to my own heavy emotions. But eventually she pushes away and I crave her immediately. Her eyes search mine with curiosity.

"What do you want to show me?"

My skin pulses as the fear I feel in having to tell her intensifies. I wish I could just play pretend and hold her like this forever.

But she deserves to know
I know it's time.

I park the car near the cliff, my fingers barely willing to pull the keys out of the ignition, stretching the moment as long as I can, having no clue how to even begin.

Sunny unbuckles her seat belt while her head swivels around, taking in her surroundings.

"I know this sounds impossible but I keep thinking I've been here before," she says with a slightly nervous laugh as if the idea is completely crazy and not the cold hard truth.

And then I let it slip. I don't mean to, but maybe deep down I do.

"It's because you have."

I stare at her with all the seriousness I can evoke, my heart beating into my ribcage.

Her eyes are still a little puffy as she glances over to me, surprised. "What do you mean?" Again there's that slightly nervous chuckle, because how else is she supposed to react?

I take a long inhale, taking hold of her hand, dragging my thumb across her knuckles.

"It means we've been here before."

Chapter 46

Sunny

"We?" I say.

Byzantine is being cryptic and something about the way he's looking at me is starting to freak me out. I'm still too rattled from my dream and this, whatever *this* is, feels too serious—too important.

I'm trying not to overthink what he's saying, but the sense tickling at the edge of my mind resembles too closely how I felt before I discovered River had died.

Like a part of me already knows what Byzantine is trying to tell me. Like a subconscious piece of me has unlocked the future but is unwilling to inform the rest of me. Unwilling to face the truth.

It takes a moment for him to answer, but what he says next feels like walking on a landmine, knowing that as soon as I make the decision to step off of it, my whole world will explode.

"Sunny...I don't know how else to tell you but...we've known each other for lifetimes."

I blink rapidly, trying to process what he just said and when it finally sinks in, my first reaction is one of pure disbelief, simply laughing it off.

"Byzantine, stop joking. This isn't funny."

"I'm not."

I unbuckle my seat belt and swivel around in my seat to face him.

"What are you trying to get at?"

"I know this sounds crazy but you need to hear me say this," he clears his throat, seeming uncomfortable sitting here across from me, drumming his fingers on the steering wheel. "We've been here before, at this very cliff...but we weren't *us*, it was...well, it was in another life," he finally says.

His words ring in my ears, my heart squeezing so tightly it feels like I might actually die.

I'm not ready. I'm not ready. I'm not ready.

So instead, I turn irrational.

Like prey trying not to get caught.

Before Byzantine can even react, I yank the door open and escape, heading for the small copse of trees at the bottom of the cliff. I must have surprised him because it takes him longer to catch up than expected.

His hoodie I'm still wearing catches on branches but I just power through, my irrational turning almost obsessive. I don't even know why I'm running, but I can't help myself. Every cell in my body is yelling at me to get as far away from Byzantine as possible, if I know what's good for me. If I don't want my entire world to upheave from just the sound of his voice alone.

"Sunny, wait!" he yells, finally reaching me and dragging my body around to face him, his hand digging into my arm. The fear written clear across his face makes me stop struggling in his grasp and he takes the opportunity to push on. "I told you this already, I saw things when I almost died.

I saw *us*, I know it sounds like I'm making all this up but you have to believe me. We're connected—our souls...this isn't the first time we've met. I knew the second I saw you at Sammies."

My skin sings with the truth of his statement but I refuse to listen, refuse to believe such insane proclamations, so I hold on to the one thing that makes any sense.

"So you've been lying to me this whole time?" I say through gritted teeth.

"Sunny..." His tone full of regret, his fingers loosen on my arm and somehow I manage to push him away. Or maybe he's the one who lets me go, but whatever it is, I take the opportunity given to me, turning away from him and run.

Running feels more metaphorical than literal right now but still, my feet pound into the soft grass, pushing me up the slanting hill and I manage to get close to the edge before Byzantine can stop me.

I try to catch my breath, turning around to find Byzantine frozen behind me as if witnessing something truly horrific. Then suddenly, like a stormy cloud opening up right atop my head, soaking me to the bone, the vision from my recurring dream slams into me.

The cliff.

I glare at him—angry, confused, lost, frightened—the slew of emotions fighting against one another while I grapple with my sudden realization.

"Tell me why this cliff feels so familiar, Byzantine."

He seems to try to find the right words, chewing on them before swallowing them back down as he takes a step forward, arms up in supplication. As soon as he moves, I take a step backwards and he turns to stone, the same fear tattooed into his pupils as if he believes I'm about to jump.

"You died here," he says bluntly, his expression momentarily lost, like he's recalling a painful memory. "Long ago..."

I tilt my head over the edge, staring at the waves crashing on the jagged rocks below while I take in what he just admitted.

"Did I jump?"

"You...fell," he sighs, his arms dropping to his side. "But—initially yes, that had been your intention."

"Why did I want to jump?"

"It's not a simple answer, Sunny...just come back from the edge of the cliff and I'll tell you everything. I promise."

And somehow, with this admission my obsession with death begins to make sense, like an invocation traversing the fabric of time and space.

"This isn't the first time I've wanted to die," I realize. The words stumble out of me as if already formed before I even understand what I'm saying—like a spell I'm trying to conjure with the simple cadence of my speech.

Byzantine looks as pained as before but still responds. "No little sun, you've had lifetimes of this feeling. And..." his voice cracks, almost choking on what he's about to say next, "I've lost you many times because of it."

My throat tightens, making it hard to swallow but I push through.

"Tell me," I rasp.

He looks defeated when he glances at me but finally speaks, "There was a lifetime you overdosed on barbiturates because we couldn't have a baby, another where you jumped from our balcony, one where you drank yourself to death..." His eyes are brimming with tears, his throat bobbing with emotion and now I wish I never heard any of this.

To know the truth, is to drag a blade in an already open and bleeding wound.

"There's a lifetime where you slit your wrist but somehow survived—" he hedges and I can't take anymore of it.

"Stop," I croak as the world begins to close in on me. I can't even tell what emotions barrel into me as I hear him speak his last words but it suffocates me nonetheless as I struggle to breathe, my lips trembling while I try to make sense of it all.

If I had to put a name to the feeling currently clawing its way inside of me—it would be despair.

Immediate and complete desolation. Suddenly, the urge to jump off this cliff is the only thing that makes any real sense.

But that's the irony isn't it?

No matter what I do, I can't evade this. No matter how many lives I cut short by my own hand, I'm sentenced to this feeling. Destined to feel like this forever.

And that—*that* makes me want to fucking die.

For at least I would have some respite before having to do it all over again. The hole inside me grows deeper and darker the more the realization breaks over me, like a wave—I'm drowning.

How can I find the strength to even continue on like this? To stomach the pain, the grief, the sadness.

When will this end?

My vision blurs, my feet so close to the edge, it would be so easy to just let go. I continue to stare at Byzantine through the tears welling up, unwilling to admit how much this hurts. How much simply existing hurts. And how I haven't stopped hurting. Not knowing if it will ever stop. And all I've ever wanted was for it to *stop*.

Instead of voicing any of it, I turn my attention back to him and ask something I should have asked much earlier.

"How do you even know it was me?"

He studies my expression for a few seconds, his gaze so open, the mask he usually hides underneath cracked and discarded, and what I see behind it almost takes my breath away.

"Because I've loved you for lifetimes, Sunny. No matter what happens—whatever you do, I always find you."

The wind whips at my hair, the waves still crashing in a powerful cadence below and my heart follows along with it. I stare at Byzantine, his words echoing softly in my head while I let it all sink in. That's when my subconscious slips in and reminds me of what River told me in my dream last night.

He's been waiting lifetimes for this moment.

And this only makes me want to cry even harder, but somehow I find my voice, my lips quivering as I part them to speak, "Do you? Love me?"

His fearful expression falls and morphs into something much more tender, but his body stays wound tight.

"I can't remember a time I didn't love you, little sun," he confesses.

My body quakes alongside the shock of what Byzantine just admitted—it's all too much. My mind can't fully process all the conflicting thoughts and emotions warring inside of me. I can feel myself slowly spiral, the edge of my vision darkening with the anxiety eating me alive.

But then movement in my periphery catches my attention, making me turn my head towards the open ocean. The sun has just begun to peak above the horizon, turning the darkened skies into a splatter of reds, pinks and oranges and reflecting it back on the surface of the water.

At first, I'm not sure what I think I've seen—until I hear it. It's a peculiar sound, almost like the gas burst in a hot air balloon. Then I see it.

It's a humpback whale.

It breaches the waves, the air entwined with water shooting out of its spout traveling several feet up in the sky, fins jutting out of the water almost like it's waving at me, the large stomach full of barnacles as it rolls back into the water with a splash.

I inhale a surprised breath at the sight.

I've never seen a whale before.

And my heart tugs with a small swell of awe at witnessing such a massive mammal exist in nature. Then my eyes catch on a smaller form close to the whale and realize it's her baby following her. It breaches the water, in quick short succession as if still trying to learn how to do so properly while the mother swims near, the sun stretching into existence and illuminating the ripples of waves their bodies create while they swim.

The sob that rips through me knocks me onto my knees, my body sinking into the grass while Byzantine quickly appears beside me, his arms encircling my shoulders, his breath warm on my neck.

I can taste the grief like a bitter chalky pill I'm trying to swallow. The nostalgia follows close behind, reminding me of the many conversations I had with River when we were young, and the hope that one day we'd see whales in real life.

How can so much beauty exist while I'm in so much pain? How can both exist simultaneously in the same exact time?

A moment so full of hope and sorrow.

Is this what it means to live? To accept the dichotomy of life and death—coming to terms that these bursts of light only exists because darkness exists too.

Through my endless tears, I continue to watch the mother and calf swim and roll, their splashes almost playful. I pray that River is somehow with me, that somehow she's *here*, witness to this just as I am.

Byzantine tucks me closer to him and I let him, but I can't stop crying. I can't stop feeling. My knees are digging in the soft dirt, Byzantine holding me so tightly I can hardly breathe. His heart beats wildly as I turn to cling to him, my mind still not able to make sense of anything that just happened.

"I don't want to feel like this anymore," I whisper, my words wavering with the sob caught in my throat. This darkness that has seemingly followed me for lifetimes. And yet it's such a familiar feeling that it scares me to imagine a life without it, like the tender embrace of a toxic lover.

Who am I without the swords piercing my heart straight through? Who am I without all these gaping wounds I call home?

"Please don't leave Byzantine," I rasp, the words I don't utter out loud hanging heavy between us.

Please don't leave me like River did.

"I'm not leaving," he finally whispers into my hair, kissing my head softly. "I'm here. You're not alone."

His words crack something hardened inside of me and suddenly all I want is him burning on top of me. But we stay silent, our eyes studying each other as if we're both seeking solace in what we're hoping to find reflected back.

Until his lips crash into mine, toppling me over. His warm hard body pins me to the ground, hips rolling over mine and my thighs fall open, inviting him in.

His movements are desperate, touching me with urgency, pushing, pulling, squeezing as if proving to himself that I'm not just a figment of his imagination. His warm breath fans across my throat, his mouth nipping at my ear, harried hands reaching under the hoodie to palm my breasts. My fingers travel down his back, grabbing on to his ass and pulling him even closer to me.

He groans into my neck and suddenly my shorts are yanked down my legs, nearly ripping them off me, his actions becoming even more persistent than before and lust resuscitates me.

"Byzantine," I choke out, feeling him tugging his sweatpants down his strong thighs, freeing his already hard cock. I become desperate in turn, needing to remember what it's like to feel alive. He finds my lips again for another bruising kiss, his fingers finding me wet and so fucking needy I can't keep the small mewl from escaping my lips.

"You scared the shit out of me, Sunny," he says, his voice pained against my mouth, the sound so raw that I'm suddenly fighting back even more tears.

His fingers push harshly into me, making me gasp, my back arching off the wet grass.

I wrap my palm around his jutting length and give it a hard tug while I catch my breath, his charged gaze finding mine and one single tear falls down my face.

"I'm sorry," I breathe out, lost in all the sensations surrounding us.

There's a flash of pain in Byzantine's expression as the thick head of his cock drags against my slit. He doesn't take his time as he pushes into me with a low groan and I moan right along with him. I feel fucking feverish. I'm desperate with need, feeling him pulse inside of me, already feeling so close. And with one powerful thrust, he bottoms out. I'm breathless, the fullness of him so deep, it overtakes me.

"I don't want you to be sorry, little sun," he finally says, thrusting into me fast and hard. "I need you to be mine." His voice is deep, laced with what sounds like anger but also brimming with burning desire. He slams even deeper. "*All* mine."

He's still pinning me down, his fingers digging into my hips, I can feel his lungs swell, full of breath. Full of life. And it centers me. The pleasure builds within every inch of me, pulling me higher and higher into a state of pure elation.

I no longer exist as just one body, I extend into the furthest reach of the universe and back. Time slows to a crawl and then speeds up. It warps and bends and does everything time is known to do and not do.

The veil thins and the past bleeds into the present and the future is nothing but a memory like any other. And it's just like this—with Byzantine hot and burning and hard on top of me, eager and feral and almost violent but so good, so fucking good, my sharp moans piercing the air—that I see it.

Like a bright, burning light amongst the rain inside my soul. A memory or a vision or *something* skating across my eyes. Of Byzantine and I. Of us laughing, of me kissing him, and smiling—*truly* smiling. I'm hit with such joy that I don't even recognize the feeling at first. It's pure and so much more vivid than I've ever experienced it.

And with this I ignite. My orgasm slamming me back into my body, shattering the vision along with it but still I hold on to the feeling while I dig my nails into Byzantine's back.

I feel him spill into me, limbs shaking, heavy breaths and sticky chests. And I'm sated, remembering the feeling of a few moments ago and I hold on to him just like he's been holding onto me. The early morning rays stretch behind us while we catch our breath, Byzantine still nestled inside me.

Finally, he pushes himself on his elbows and gazes down at me. I can tell he wants to say more but stays silent. Instead, he slowly pulls out and gathers me off the ground and into a long embrace.

I love him, I know I do but the words stay dormant, smoldering in my chest. He kisses me slowly, sensually.

"You don't have to say it," he whispers, reading my mind. He pulls me even closer. "I'll be here when you're ready."

My eyes burn with unshed tears, leaning into our kiss, seeking the warmth of his lips against mine. The pesky little voice in my head tells me I don't deserve him, don't deserve his love, and it makes me second guess every single feeling I have for him.

Do I even know what love feels like?

Then, his words from earlier echo back to me as I slip my tongue into Byzantine's mouth, his hands so soft against my back, my hips, my thighs.

I've loved you for lifetimes, Sunny.

I have so many questions to ask him. But the question I'm burning to know as I sigh deeply against him is—what if I've also loved Byzantine before this?

What if I don't need to learn how to love him?

I just need to somehow remember all the times I've loved him before.

Chapter 47

SUNNY

Adulthood has always been unfathomable to me. My future was not darkness, it simply did not exist. But maybe, after all, I did feel River's death. It was her death I rehearsed in my head. Her death I romanticized. The psychic mirror of our two souls. I heard death's requiem before it was sung, it just wasn't mine. It was River's all along.

And now I'm fated to stay here without her, the karmic tie between Byzantine and I keeping me tethered to this life. To this place.

Whatever that means.

We spend the day in bed, Byzantine holding me tight in his arms like he's still terrified I'm about to run. Or jump. Or both. But even in his arms, I'm distant. I can't help but to still resent Byzantine a little for keeping all this a secret.

This whole time he knew so much and yet said so little. Yet, I guess I can't really blame him. How could he know I would even believe him?

Hi, I just killed your boss and oh by the way I know you from a past life and I love you.

The rational part of me thinks this can't be real. He's making this all up. But then I look in his eyes and the familiarity I find there is overwhelming. It overpowers every single rational thought I try to muster up.

It also explains the relentless magnetic pull I've had towards him since the very beginning. Except he had the answer as to why while I was kept in the dark.

I can tell he's relieved that it's finally out in the open. Every question I ask, he answers in as much detail as he can. At least I can find comfort in that and take full advantage of it.

I also can't pretend that things are just magically fixed because of what happened on the cliff. Everything isn't suddenly better. The ache is still there, like an amputated limb that still hurts. That's not how mental illness works. You can't just *decide* to get better. If that was the reality, no one would ever suffer from depression.

I roll on my back and stretch my entire body like a cat. Byzantine watches, his face impassive, like he's calculating every move I make and tabulating the odds against him. I let out a deep sigh and turn onto my side to face him.

"Don't you think it was pretty fucked up for you to bring me to like, the scene of my own death?"

He presses his lips together, and takes a moment to answer. "I mean, yeah, I guess," he finally says, reaching over and tucking a strand of loose hair behind my ear, his hand then falling to my arm, his thumb caressing my skin distractedly. "I just didn't know what else to do. I thought that maybe it would help you remember. Well, maybe not remember like me but help somehow?"

I scoff in disbelief. "Yeah, maybe it worked a little too well." I fall silent, chewing the inside of my cheek. "Why would you buy this cottage? That's pretty morbid—even for me," I say, a small grin pulling at my lips.

Byzantine laughs but then falls sullen. "It was the only connection I had to us, before...I found you again."

"Did we ever have a life where we were just, I don't know, happy?"

He shrugs. "Maybe? But those aren't the ones I saw or remembered." His eyes peer up at the ceiling as if mulling it over. "Maybe those weren't the ones important to what feels unresolved between us."

I can't help but feel a twinge of guilt. Of him stuck remembering all these other lives where I've died tragically, usually by my own hand or close. As if it's my fault we're here. My fault we're stuck in this vicious karmic loop.

But Byzantine manages to pull my thoughts right out of my head. "I'm as much to blame you know. I wasn't perfect either, I hurt you as much as you hurt me."

"I know," I say as I let his words sit beside my guilt. "Just feels very on the nose for me to, yet again, have these same thoughts. I'm so predictable..." I let out a sad laugh. Me wanting to die isn't even original. Very basic of me.

"We just need to make better choices this time," he says, leaning for a quick kiss. "All I want to do now is support you. And be there for you, how I couldn't be there for you before. You already know how I feel about you Sunny, but if you need me to, I will remind you every second of every day."

He kisses me again, this time lazy and unhurried, showing me exactly how he feels, not just with words but with his actions, his mouth promising me all the things I'm still too scared to hear.

The right words stay locked inside of me, connected to the shame of still yearning for the feeling of not being alive—of still yearning for my sister's presence. Even if he deserves for me to profess my love...I'm not even close.

So I let my own lips trace a path to his heart hoping he understands what it feels like to live when all I've ever wanted until now was to die.

My eyes snag on the blue windflower on his chest. My fingers trailing over it again. Byzantine looks down as I gently press on the tattoo over his heart.

"Tell me," I say, gazing inquisitively into his eyes. The same sadness I've found before swimming in his jade irises. "Tell me why you called me windflower."

He wraps his hand over mine, holding our clasped hands against his chest. I can feel the wild beat of his heart, and the sadness pouring out of him, the intensity overwhelming.

"It was your favorite flower when you were Gabriel."

His words are still so strange to hear.

When I was someone else.

But his words somehow ring true. Then, in a hushed almost reverent tone, he recounts the story of the book I once gave to him. And how he wasn't able to tell me how much he loved me then. How a part of him was ashamed of our secret relationship and how his actions slowly poisoned us—especially me. How it eventually led me to that very cliff.

"I never forgave myself," he whispers, his eyes glassy like he's struggling against the emotions he's releasing between us.

Forgive me.

The words Byzantine whispered in my tousled hair the first time we kissed.

How it felt so much more than just forgiveness but repentance. His remorse thick in the air from all the lives spent together. Before us now.

Could it be?

That a subconscious part of myself remembers all the times he failed to love me like he promised? And all the times I promised to embrace life and then didn't?

Could that be what's holding me back?

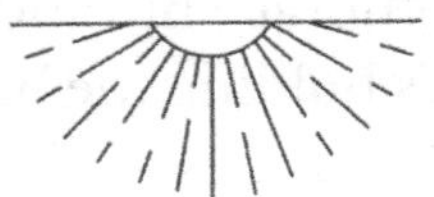

Chapter 48

Byzantine

A long wavy strand of Sunny's hair whips in her face, her cheeks rosy from the wind, eyes bright like the sun. The waves crash below as we sit snug on a blanket, a picnic basket resting close to the large rock beside us. There was no changing her mind this afternoon when she demanded we have lunch on the cliff.

The very cliff I watched her die from. The one where it feels like I nearly lost her again.

But it's hard not to find hope when I look at her as I do now. Hard not to find hope in the sun's rays peeking out from the clouds above as if even the sky itself is hopeful in this very moment.

The way she pops a cherry tomato into her mouth and then another. The way she can still find some peace in the sun warming her cheeks, her closed eyes seeking it while she chews. A simple moment to enjoy when I know her heart still aches for the ghost of her twin.

Sunny deserves a happier life. She deserved better *lives*. A better husband. A better lover. A better friend.

I want to be all of those things for her. But what if I fuck it up again? I've never pretended to be a good person. I've killed, tortured. And a sick part of me enjoys it, finds purpose in it. There's no question I'll kill again. And now I've dragged Sunny into this world, only because—what? I love her? Because of this unhinged belief that we're star-crossed lovers meant to be together?

Dread trickles down my throat as I realize that maybe us being together is actually our demise. Maybe that's the change in the script of life needed for us to finally move on. What if I was shown all of this as a warning? A warning of what could be if we ever end up together again.

But I'm selfish. Does it matter? When simply being in her presence feels like rapture. How could such a feeling be wrong? How could loving her be one step closer to her death? One step closer to me losing her all over again.

I notice Sunny suddenly seems lost in thought.

"You okay?" I ask.

Sunny's eyes heat my skin when her gaze lands on me.

"River died five years ago today," she says, seriousness etched in her brows. "Did you remember?"

My throat constricts with the final secret I need to tell her. "I did," I say, taking her hand in mine. "Actually, there's one last thing I haven't told you."

I feel the fear spike in the air between us.

"It's not bad," I add quickly to reassure her, raising her shaky hand to my lips. "Just interesting...for lack of a better word, I guess." She doesn't say anything as I clear my throat while she continues to sear me with her gaze. I don't know how to say it so I choose just to be blunt. "The time I almost died, my near-death experience..." I stroke my scar absentmindedly. "Well, it also happened five years ago today."

I don't know why I'm fighting off guilt that I shouldn't even harbor in the first place. It's not as if it's my fucking fault. Any of it. But I still brace myself for Sunny's reaction.

She blinks back at me, her soft lips parted in surprise. And then laughs. Bright and effervescent. And all I want is to find a way to bottle it up so I can keep that sound forever.

Sunny laughs and laughs and with it I start laughing too. Because it *is* absurd. Of course we share that date. Of course we are linked yet again by forces so much bigger than the two of us. I've never been a spiritual person but how can I not believe in something beyond this when life continues to shove me into situations like these?

How much of this is freewill when these moments feel so fated? Destiny is pulling at our invisible strings like puppets. The same strings that attach me so firmly to Sunny. The ones I pull on when she drifts away, the very same that led me to her when I myself was drifting.

Then, I tell her something I've asked myself ever since I learned of this coincidence. "Makes me wonder, if maybe our paths crossed, you know? Who knows... Maybe I met River on the other side, before I came back and found you," I admit.

Slowly Sunny's laugh stutters to a stop, her eyes welling with tears. "I like that," she croaks.

My heart swells watching her take in what I just said.

"Come here," I tell her, dragging her into my arms. She curls into me and sighs deeply.

"Don't you dare die on me Byzantine," she mutters, her words laced with fear.

I'm not sure if they're meant to sound so final but I just hug her harder. I breathe in all the emotions crackling on the surface of her skin that she never says out loud, trying as desperately as I can to swallow them down into my own body. But I know it's useless. Useless, because there's no such thing as the ability to save someone from their own emotions.

But I still try.

I still let myself believe I can help as I kiss her hard and urgently. Her soft moan travels down my spine as I kiss her even harder. As if pushing her against my body will somehow make her stay here with me. Forever.

"I promise, my little sun," I finally say.

It's such a callous lie—to promise her I won't die. Because it's inevitable. It's the one thing I can't promise her, but I still pledge it to her because she needs to hear it and I so desperately need for her to believe it.

I promise. I promise. I promise.

Chapter 49

Sunny

"Get the fuck out of here!" Lenix squawks.

It's the middle of the afternoon and we're the only ones sitting at the bar in a neighborhood restaurant we often frequent.

I can't help but to laugh. "I'm dead serious Lenix, I swear to god."

Byzantine and I came back from Midnight Cove on Sunday night. I could tell he wanted me to stay over but I needed a breather. I needed time away. Not away from him particularly but just—away. A little distance, if only for a couple of days.

I needed to find comfort in my own room, with my own things and my own mess. I can never tell how clearly I'm thinking when I'm around Byzantine, when my feelings for him always feel so heightened. Like holding onto a live wire.

It's now Wednesday and Byzantine has given me the distance I've needed. And I'm grateful. But I miss him. Of course I miss him. But I also missed Lenix. And after everything that happened when I was away, I knew she deserved the truth. Especially about my sister. She gave me a long hug when I told her.

She didn't try to fill the silence with pleasantries either, like some people would, as if trying to comfort themselves more than me. And that's why I love her. For those moments where she understands me, just like River did.

Then I moved on to what happened over the weekend. And that's when Lenix couldn't hold it back any longer.

"So you mean to say," Lenix pushes on. "That this dude was looking for you for five fucking years? Not only that but he believes you guys have been together before? Like in another life? And you *believe* him!?"

"It sounds insane, I know," I reply, trying to quell that nagging part of me that feels protective, wanting to defend something so outlandish. It doesn't change the fact that I believe Byzantine. Even if his methods to reveal it to me were shoddy at best. But I also know Lenix will believe it too—eventually.

"I don't know how to explain it other than I could feel it too, Lenix. I might not be able to remember like he does but in a strange way it's like my body remembers what my mind doesn't. And how can you explain my dream about that same cliff? Even you have to admit that that's pretty fucking freaky," I continue.

Lenix just stares at me, a million counter-debate points flashing behind her eyes but she doesn't utter a single one. Instead she leans her elbow on the bar and signals for another round of shots. The bartender has been lingering on the opposite side trying to give us some privacy while I tell Lenix about the boyfriend I knew from a past life.

I cringe at the word boyfriend. Is this even a relationship? It just doesn't sound right for what I feel for him. And it's also not because of some patriarchal belief that calling him my husband would somehow make it better.

Nothing like that.

It just feels like there's no one word that properly defines what we are. What's the term for two souls forever destined to meet, fall in love, fuck up and then meet all over again? Yeah, that.

The bartender slides the shots towards us with a grin and a wink, then slinks back away.

"He told me he loved me," I tell her as we clink and raise the shots to our lips.

"Oh I'm sure he did," Lenix says after swallowing the alcohol down.

I shove her and she pretends I pushed her much harder and almost falls off her stool. Rolling my eyes, I fight the grin pulling at my lips. "Can you be serious for one second please?"

She laughs, "Okay sorry, sorry. But I mean of course he loves you. Have you heard the story you just told me?" She eyes me, suddenly serious. "Well? Do you?"

"Love him?" My knee bounces as I start to sweat. *Fuck*. Am I really getting a visceral reaction to even admitting it? "I think so," I end up muttering.

"You *think* so?" Lenix scoffs. "How romantic."

I fight the urge to pinch her and drum my fingers on the bar top instead. "It's just...I guess I'm scared okay?"

"Scared of what? Loving him or telling him?"

"Both?" I answer while staring at the ground, hoping the wobble in my voice isn't that obvious.

"Well you're just going to have to get over it," she sniffs.

"Gee, thanks," I mutter.

"I mean it babes, let's say all of this *is* true, and you two have been basically boning for centuries," she quirks a smile while I roll my eyes again. "And you say you do feel that connection with him, then what's holding you back?"

"Everything. Literally all of it."

How can I explain that the fear leeched onto me like a fucking parasite stems from the belief that maybe loving him is just opening myself up to more pain? How can I not automatically think of the worst case scenario when I've already lived it? What would happen if I let Byzantine in? Truly let him in and then he just fucking—*dies*. How could I not think of that?

Lenix picks up on all the unsaid words floating between us and leans over to squeeze my hand in hers.

"You can't live your life like that, Sunny. You can't just go around thinking everyone you love will eventually leave you. River's death isn't the blueprint of the rest of your life. It was tragic, of course it was tragic. But it doesn't mean you're destined to suffer tragedy after tragedy. That would be nuts babes."

"But is it that crazy? How can you know it won't happen again?"

"I don't. And you won't know either but you just have to live being okay not knowing. You deserve to be happy too Sunny."

My laugh is weak as I look up at her. "I'm not even sure I know what that feels like..."

Her smile is sad but warm. "So let's figure it out together okay?"

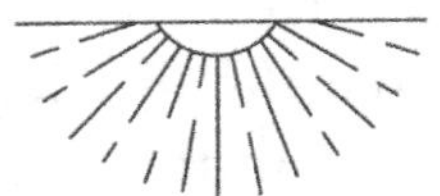

Chapter 50

Byzantine

I walk into Sammies with Connor and Bastian in tow. The place is busy but my eyes still land on Sunny behind the bar as soon as I walk through the door. She's wearing her signature short shorts, and a loose tank top that shows off the tattoo on her arm. I can tell she's not wearing a bra—is she ever—and I hold back the groan at the back of my throat.

She's a fucking vision. A pang rips through me as her gaze finally finds mine and I just stand there, struck dumb. She winks and then turns around, busy serving a waiting customer.

Fuck. I miss her. It's only been a week and I fucking miss her. I miss her body, her mind, those sour moods she gets, I miss her secrets and fears and cute laughs and hazel eyes so deep I could drown in them.

But I'm giving her space, only because she asked.

But as previously mentioned, I've never pretended to be a moral man. I resorted back to stalking her. Forced back into the shadows. An old habit coming in quite handy while I let her *think* I'm giving her space.

I still miss her all the same. I felt like a schoolboy with a crush knowing she was working tonight. Knowing she would let me drive her home at the very least, and I'd be able to smell the subtle hints of her grapefruit lip balm while I steal a kiss from the driver's seat.

Bastian gives me a small shove between the shoulder blades and I realize I've stopped walking entirely. Coming back to life like a wind-up toy, I lead us to our usual table on shaky legs.

Shit, I really need to get it together.

Connor slides into our booth followed by Bastian. They know to leave me the seat on the far left. The one that gives me direct access to Sunny behind the bar. Free to stare and stalk at my leisure. A few seconds later, Lenix struts up with our usual order.

"Hiya boys!" she winks at Bastian, leaning down to hand over our drinks while giving Connor an eyeful of her cleavage. I notice she's avoiding my gaze which confirms my suspicion that Sunny finally told her everything.

I don't especially care either way. The only thing that matters is that Sunny now knows and believes me. Doesn't keep me from wondering what exactly Sunny told Lenix. Especially about what happened on the cliff.

"Let me know if you need anything else," Lenix chirps, popping her hand on her hips.

"Thanks darling, we will," Connor answers, winking and handing her a hundred dollar bill as tip. She flashes him a toothy grin, snatching the bill from his hand and shoving it into her money pouch.

"Always a pleasure, Connor," she sing-songs, walking away.

The table falls silent while Bastian turns to Connor.

"You have to be lying."

"About what?" he asks, pretending he has no clue what Bastian is insinuating.

"You two *must* be fucking."

Connor only grins over his rock glass, the ice clinking as he takes a slow sip watching Lenix from afar. "She wouldn't be acting that way if we were."

"And why is that?" I say, humoring him.

"Because she would hate me by now," he simply states.

I can't tell if he's joking or being serious. It's probably both.

"*Anyway*, it's not really why we're here is it?" Connor turns to me and I wish I could punch his pompous look clean off his face. Even if he is right. There's no denying it. I needed to see Sunny. And Connor knows it. I'm sure everyone in this place knows it.

Shit, I'm *aching* for her. And it's only been a fucking week. And judging by the look of the guys leaning against the bar, I'm not the only one having that same thought. I grind my teeth, jaw tight as I fight the urge to slam someone's teeth on the bar. Then, Sunny turns and stares straight at me. Like fucking Moses parting the Red Sea, the crowd thins and it's only her and I.

I suddenly feel sedated. Then she smiles, and the room becomes ten times brighter. Her eyes hold the type of heat that only means one thing, as if she knows exactly what I'm thinking too.

She keeps watching me as she pulls Julie, the other bartender, by the elbow, leaning close to her ear. I see her lips move and watch Julie nod her head. Then Sunny's moving. The rag she was holding finds its place near the sink. Walking out of the bar, she disappears into the back without giving me a second glance. My vision tunnels as I shoot up from the table, not bothering telling the boys where I'm heading.

Only one thing matters right now. And it's her.

I'm already painfully hard while I push people out of my way, frantic to get to her. To touch her, feel her, smell her. I'm fucking starved by the time I get to the staff room. I find her near her locker and she acts shocked when she sees me.

I lock the door behind me, before stalking right to her. I don't say a word, my eyes glued to hers while I unbutton her shorts and slide my hand inside, finding her wet and wanting.

I groan deeply. "You're a greedy little girl aren't you? Couldn't even finish your shift without needing my cock inside you."

"Yes," she whimpers, catching my lip with her teeth as she fumbles with my belt.

"Eager thing, you couldn't wait for me to fill you up. Is that it? Is that what my sweet little slut needs?" I find her clit already swollen and needy and squeeze it just to hear her high pitched gasp.

"Byzantine," she begs. "I need you to fuck me...please."

I flip her around and press her hard into the locker door. My hands are rough and urgent as I pull her shorts down, kicking her legs as wide as they can go with her shorts still around her thighs. I'm fumbling with my jeans like a teenager seeing pussy for the first time. Hopeless for a touch, a taste, a fuck.

I finally get my cock out, and it pulses in my hand as I line it up to her dripping cunt. I can't wait any longer. I feel selfish. I want to use her. Manhandle her. Remind Sunny who she belongs to.

"Now," I say leaning into her as I notch the head of my cock to her pussy. "This is what's about to happen. I'm going to fuck you against this locker and you'll be nice and quiet for me, got it?" Her ass pushes into me, nodding gingerly. I reach under her shirt finding her bare tits as expected and palm them hard. "That's my good girl."

I slam into her in one single brutal thrust. I fuck her hard and fast and she lets out a long mewl. I wrap my arm around her shoulders, clasping my hand over her open mouth, effectively silencing her as she continues to moan into my hand, biting into my palm as I bite into her shoulder.

"Did my perfect little whore miss me?"

She whimpers loudly, biting harder into my hand, and my cock grows even harder inside her. I'm crazy with lust and filled with dirty fucking thoughts, her small muffled moans only dragging me even further over the edge. The sound of skin on skin fills the room as I sense her getting close to coming.

Her eyelids flutter as she clenches around my cock and I know she's as desperate for me to come inside of her as I am for her to climax.

"Does my little slut need to be filled up?"

She only moans in response, my hand still clamped over her mouth. I slam into her hot cunt and it feels so good I'm nearly losing my mind, but I continue. "I want you so full of my fucking cum that you can feel it dripping for the rest of the night, got it?"

And with that she shatters and I follow right behind, my balls so tight it almost hurts. The pleasure's blinding as I empty myself inside Sunny, hot and messy and *fucking* necessary.

As if my entire existence depends on this moment. As if my dick buried deep inside her burning core is the only thing worth living for. Finally, I still behind her, breathless and completely spent.

Slowly, I unwrap my hand from her mouth, pulling her face towards me and finding her lips, chasing the high I just crashed from. I slip out of her and watch as she faces me, a small sated smile on her mouth as she wiggles back into her tight shorts. The evidence of what I just did to her dripping down her thighs.

I grin, my hindbrain assuaged now that I've claimed her like this. That she's fucking mine and no one else's. "You're so fucking perfect, my little sun," I say as I kiss her, her body still shuddering from her orgasm.

I kiss her one last time, leaving her behind to get cleaned up and find my way back to the table, probably smelling like sex. Like I care. Not when I can still feel Sunny on me.

Neither Connor nor Bastian bother asking where I disappeared to as I reach for my forgotten drink, the ice long melted, watering down the whiskey in the glass but I shoot it back anyway. It's worth it when I spot Sunny ramble back behind the bar, her cheeks flushed and her eyes glazed as she falls back into the flow of orders, a reminder of who owns her still between her legs.

Chapter 51

Sunny

It's been a few days since Byzantine found me in the employee room. We're on our way back from Vinyl, in the backseat of a taxi—a rare occasion—but he's been drinking. Bastian left with Connor, while Lenix disappeared with one of her regular hookups earlier in the night.

I might have taken a few too many shots myself, accompanied with a shared joint in the alley with Lenix but I'm still coherent—enough. The loud music is still ringing in my ears, a smile on my lips as I fish out my phone, while Byzantine is distracted on his.

I'm not sure why I even open this particular social media app, like my fingers have a mind of their own, choosing for me. I've avoided going on it for months now.

I don't even know why I still have the app on my phone, the feed full of memories from my past. Old friends and family updating each other on their lives when I'd rather disappear from their minds forever. I'm as dead as River according to my non-activity, and I want to keep it that way.

But like an apparition, the feed opens in front of my eyes, and the first thing I see is my mother.

I was having such a good night...

My mood sours immediately, my smile turns to dust. I realize then that the pictures I'm looking at have been taken at River's memorial, the one my mother organized and demanded I attend.

I peek over my screen making sure Byzantine isn't privy to my reaction to all this. I can't help but let the quicksand of my guilt overtake me as I sink into obsessing over what my extended family must think of me. As if River would give two shits about this memorial.

The comments under the photos make my lips curl. They're full of support and love for my mother as if she's the best care-taker to ever exist—and not the neglectful and cold parent we grew up with.

My intoxication is muddying my senses and eradicating all clear reasoning. I begin to boil for all the times I wasn't allowed to express my anger towards her. I rage silently knowing she will never acknowledge how bad she treated River and I.

I did my best, wasn't that enough? I can still hear her say.

No. It wasn't.

My immediate reaction is to hide all this from the man sitting quietly next to me. I don't even know why but it's second nature, the alcohol muddling my thoughts further and I can't help myself. I don't even consider the other option, that maybe Byzantine would want to be there for me right now. Instead, I shut down, like turning a knob on a static radio.

I go quiet, my mind shutting down.

Except for one small seed, planted by years of needing some kind of release for all the suffocating anger that's never had any real outlet. I already know what I'm about to do even before the thought is fully formed in my head.

"You okay?" Byzantine mutters beside me and I quickly plaster on a smile and shove my phone in my purse, leaning over to kiss him—and ultimately distract him.

It works.

When we get to his place, I go through the motions. I watch myself get ready for bed and slide under the covers and wait for Byzantine to find me. We have sex and I'm barely there, but I pretend and he must be drunker than I thought because he doesn't notice and I'm so relieved.

Later, he curls around me and falls asleep, and I wait. I try to force my body to relax, my lip silently trembling, a heavy tear falling down my face while the void quietly folds itself around me. I count the seconds until his breath turns steady and he falls even deeper asleep.

My obsession is itching at the edge of my mind like a leech thirsty for blood.

I'm spiraling.

I know I am.

But this pain I'm feeling is too intense to control. I feel weightless. Barely there and floating—observing the scene from afar.

When enough time has passed and I'm convinced Byzantine won't wake up, I watch myself reach for the covers and slowly pull them aside, gently pushing his arm off me and back onto the bed. Luckily he doesn't stir and I successfully creep into the bathroom.

The obsession is morphing into tunnel vision with every step I take, and I don't risk turning on the light while I silently rummage through the drawers and cabinets trying to find what I'm looking for.

I promised I wouldn't do this again.

And I've kept it for months now. But it's no longer enough.

I need to see it. I need visual proof. Evidence that this pain and this anger that is so *fucking* invisible is real. If I can't direct it at my mother, I'll turn in towards me. Someone needs to be punished for how I feel, and my body is the only semblance of control I seem to have. I lord over it when everything else feels like it's being swept into the chaos of living.

Finally, I find what I'm looking for, picking up the razor with shaky fingers, my heart drumming loudly as if I just won a prize. Quickly, I turn my attention to the bedroom, making sure Byzantine is still asleep.

Satisfied, I glance back to the razor and begin to dismantle it, trying to break the plastic to access the blades, the ritual akin to a drug addict setting up their paraphernalia before taking a hit. It's a promise of release, and the obsession only grows headier with the thought. I'm so close—so fucking close, the release only minutes away. I can already visualize the blade on my skin and that dark voice inside rejoices at the thought.

This is the only way out of this feeling.

I need this, I need this, I need this.

But then, like a bright flame flickering through all this darkness—I wake up. I slam back into my body. My lungs fill up with air as if I'm taking the first full breath after being dragged underwater.

I am no longer weightless. No longer so desperate. The fog dissipates, and I'm left just standing here, in Byzantine's dark bathroom, staring at the razor in my clammy hand. Realizing for the first time tonight the full weight of what I was about to do—and how much I would have ultimately regretted it.

It doesn't prevent the shame from rapidly engulfing me, so thick and heavy I can no longer bear the sight of what I'm holding and promptly chuck it in the garbage.

I slide onto the floor next to the glass shower, a sob piercing the heavy silence of the bathroom.

What the fuck just happened?

The more I regain full consciousness, the more it feels like whatever *this* was felt closer to possession than an obsession. Like my past self somehow slithered under my skin and took over.

The one who needed to bleed to feel alive.

My cries get even louder as I give in to this feeling, my knees tucked up into my chest, holding them with my shaking arms.

I barely register Byzantine finding me and settling beside me. He says nothing, his steady presence is a balm to my aching heart and I let my head fall on his shoulder while the tears continue to fall.

He presses a soft kiss to my forehead and I can't help but feel guilty. Like I'm a constant burden for those who love me. I say nothing, crying beside Byzantine as he just sits with me in silence, not questioning, not trying to fix this, just here—present—and slowly I start to calm down.

"Please don't give up on me," I finally whisper into the dark and he grows still beside me.

At first I think he won't say anything back, but then he pulls me into his lap and I crawl onto him like I'm on the edge of a precipice, terrified of falling.

"Oh my little sun," his voice is hoarse when he finally speaks like some unnamed emotion is clogging up his vocal cords. "I could never."

My arms wrap around his neck, my face burying into him, breathing in his sleep warm scent. I can't seem to stop the tears, the guilt slowly replaced with relief with the sound of his words.

"I love you," he reminds me and I gasp on a sob, the feelings so acute inside of me that I can't control my reactions. Instead, I stay wrapped around him on the bathroom floor for the next hour until I slowly calm myself down. Only then does he carry me to bed, my eyes drooping with sleep when he pulls the duvet over my body.

And maybe if I wasn't so emotionally exhausted, I would recognise that this is what it feels like to be safe.

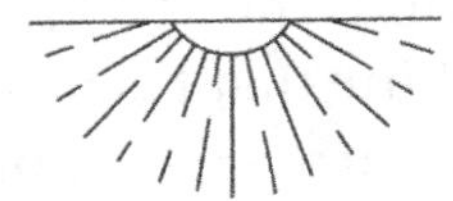

Chapter 52

Byzantine

The afternoon sun is beating down on the windshield while I sit in my idling car outside of Sunny's building complex waiting for her to come out. My mind can't help but to drift while I wait, thinking about everything that has happened between her and I in the past few months since we met.

It's been over a week since I found her crying on my bathroom floor, and although I can't say seeing her like that didn't scare me, I've also felt a small shift in her since. Maybe it's nothing major but it still gives me hope. That somehow we're heading in the right direction together.

The memories of our past lives together are fading. Not enough to forget but enough to begin replacing those haunted memories with better ones. New ones where both our demise is not stitched into the fucking fabric of time. I'm not sure if it's because we're finally doing better but I'm not going to question it. Holding on to all those memories was exhausting.

All I want now is to remember what's in front of me. I want to learn every curve on Sunny's body, every inch of her mind. Hell, I'd tag along in her dreams while she sleeps if she'd let me. Still, the urge to cast a net over her and keep her protected from herself claws at me. But I know I can't crush her like that, she'll fight me every step of the way. And it won't help anything anyway.

She needs the time to heal.

So I continue to do what I've promised her. I remind her that I'm not going anywhere and speak the words she's so terrified of telling me and I act as if it doesn't bother me when she doesn't say it back.

Of course it bothers me. But I'll take this over her disappearing from existence, whether it be mentally or physically. I'll take her charged silence if it means I can have her here—with me.

Does it make me love her any less? Fucking never. She's asked for time and that's what I'm giving her. Even if the memories have faded, I still remember all those centuries waiting, no, *wanting* what I have with Sunny right now. I can give her time, all I have is fucking time for her.

And besides, her body speaks louder than her words ever could. The softness in her gaze when she looks at me. Her fingers fluttering over my skin whenever she's close. Her small thank yous for nothing at all.

We are beyond words her and I. Speaking hasn't really been our speciality anyway has it? I crave her every single fucking day and I will continue to crave her until the very moment I die.

Not even death can keep us apart. We've already proven that. I'll always find her. And maybe next time, this love we ignite between us won't need to be forged through pain. Maybe next time, we'll just find each other and somehow know.

I watch her, then, bound out of the building, heading towards the car as she beams at me and I grin back.

She's perfect.

And for now, I'll cross these burning coals with her, I'll give her the strength to fight her own demons, and protect her when she asks it of me. I want to be right beside her when she rises from the ashes and into her own power. Into the magic of who she is behind the walls, behind the fear and doubt. Because I see her. And she's fucking mesmerizing.

Hopefully one day she sees what I see.

Hopefully one day she burns as bright as the fucking sun. And I'll turn into Icarus if only to have a taste of her fire before I burn and burn and burn.

Chapter 53

Sunny

"So where are we heading?" I ask Byzantine, a few minutes after he's picked me up.

The adorable lopsided smile he gives me while changing gears, tells me that I probably won't know until we get to our destination. He's lucky that today I don't care, happy to just be here with him, feeling closer to him—if that's even possible—since what happened last week.

That night scared me.

I could have really hurt myself and it's frightening to think how little control I had over my actions. It left me weary, and also questioning if maybe I should stop drinking—or at the very least cut back considerably—until I get my mental health in check. I don't want those types of spirals to ever happen again if I can avoid it.

The following morning, wrapped inside Byzantine's strong arms in bed, I was able to give voice to some of the reasons behind what triggered me into plummeting into such a dark space.

One being River, the other my mother.

But it was still hard to explain out loud, when these feelings were so visceral and almost illogical when it came to describing them. He asked me a few questions but didn't pry, simply taking what I was able to offer and I was grateful for it.

When he finally parks the car, I notice that we're just a few minutes walk away from the public beach I always frequent. The terrain is rockier here than the designated swimming area and I look over to Byzantine with a curious look on my face, but he just smiles warmly.

"Come on, I want to show you something," he says casually.

My eyebrows shoot up. "The last time you told me that, the cliff happened," I tease.

"Nothing like that," he says chuckling while climbing out of the car and I wait eagerly until he opens the passenger door.

"Is it a surprise?" I ask, taking his offered hand as he pulls me out of the car.

"Of some sort."

"Classic Byzantine," I huff, "always so allergic to answering questions directly."

He laughs but says nothing more, leading me to a narrow trail slanting up a small hill that eventually turns into a small grassy plain near the ocean. It doesn't seem to be a popular spot to visit according to the wild foliage around, and the lack of place to sit or lay down. I peer around, wondering why he's brought me all the way up here. Until he stops in front of a flat rock and simply points at it.

"What is it?" I say, still not understanding what he's showing me.

"I thought you'd want a place to visit," he adds, looking almost uncomfortable like he doesn't know how to say what he's trying to tell me.

Intrigued, I lean closer to the rock, curious as to what he's referring to. Until I see it.

In memory is carved into the rock and beneath it are two whale engravings. It looks fresh like the markings have been done recently and my breath catches in my throat when I realize what Byzantine was implying—he's made me a memorial.

"It's not much—" he begins to say, but I cut him off.

"It's perfect," I whisper, squeezing his hand before kneeling closer to the flat rock, my fingers softly tracing the grooves, my vision blurring with all the emotions this moment is making bubble up to the surface.

Byzantine stands stoically behind me while I close my eyes, the warm ocean breeze playing with my hair as I let the tears fall. The grief, a never-ending well I keep digging deeper into. But today, I somehow know it will eventually wane, I'll learn to live with it without it consuming me. The thought gives me a small sense of peace while I stand back up, wipe the wetness from my cheeks and smile up at Byzantine.

My heart is so full I find it hard to understand how this person even exists, how he can *see* me in such vivid detail that he can read my needs before I even understand them myself. And it's in these quiet moments that my soul sings, and it becomes that much easier to believe we've spent lifetimes like this.

But this time, we're figuring it out.

This time we're letting the pain fade

"Thank you," I say softly before catching his lips with mine, his hand circling my waist. When we pull away to catch our breath, he smiles.

"There's nothing I wouldn't do for you, my little sun...in this life and the next."

Chapter 54

Sunny

One month later

The bell clangs over the coffee shop door, prompting me to look up from the book I'm reading. Lenix in all her glory strolls in like the vision she is. Effortlessly gorgeous in a summer dress, wedge sandals, and soft pink lipstick. Her long black hair is pulled into a high ponytail as if I hadn't just woken her up less than half an hour ago to ask her to meet me here.

She winks at me from across the coffee shop, stopping at the counter to place her order first. When she reaches our table, she leans down and gives me a quick peck on the cheek before sitting down in front of me.

"Morning gloomy baby," she says with a smirk, crossing one long leg over the other.

"Are you ever going to stop calling me that?" I ask with exasperation.

She shrugs, her smile big and bright. "We'll see," she sing-songs but then falls silent as the barista comes over with her order. She keeps her eyes on me as if she's sizing me up and I squirm in my seat.

When the waiter walks away she finally asks, "How are you?"

"Good."

She quirks an eyebrow. "Are you really? Or are you just saying that."

I roll my eyes. "I swear Lenix, I'm doing better. Not perfect, but better." I chew on my bottom lip. "I'm going back to therapy."

Lenix's face brightens and my heart swells. "Are you really?" she says, her voice all fucking hopeful and I can't help but to smile.

"Yeah, I have my first appointment next week," I reply nervously.

Rationally, I know this is a good thing, I know I need help. Help that's bigger than just the love and support of Lenix and Byzantine. But emotionally, I still feel like a gremlin hissing at anyone who tries to get too close to the thoughts and feelings I'd rather keep secret.

I'll probably hate every second of it. But it's better than the alternative. I tried that and it sucks. The only way out is through—as they say.

"My baby's all grown up," Lenix jokes, pretending to wipe the corner of her eyes.

"Omg I hate you, stop. You're so embarrassing."

She laughs and takes a tentative sip of her latte.

"Anyway, you're one to talk. You sure you don't wanna come with? Discuss your, oh I don't know, commitment issues?" I volley back.

Lenix acts shocked and tongues her cheek, a mischievous glint in her eyes.

"First of all, how dare you, I'm perfect. Second of all, I'm curious..." She taps her finger as if deep in thought trying to decipher something, and I already know where this is going before the words come out of her mouth. "Have you told Byzantine you love him yet?"

I don't even bother defending myself. "Did I mention I hate you?"

Lenix lets out an evil cackle, a smug little pout on her face and settles into her chair like she won a prize.

"Okay but seriously," she says, staring me down with her big brown eyes. "What are you even waiting for? You guys are practically married at this point. It's kind of gross to be honest."

"Okay wow, chill. That's not even *close* to the truth." I mean, we do spend all our time together and I basically stay over every night but that's it really.

Lenix laughs, tonguing her cheek, satisfied with making me sweat.

"It's not like I don't want to...and I'm so close to saying it but it's been so long now that it feels almost awkward to just blurt it out," I say, somewhat morosely.

"You're being an idiot. Just say it for fuck's sake."

"God, you're so annoying. Leave me alone would you?" I bite back

"Never. You're stuck with me."

She winks and I smile, but I'm still peeved that she's right. I just need to blurt it out. I just need to say it. Before he tires of me. I hope he doesn't tire of me. I just can't continue pretending not to see the small dip in his shoulders when he tells me he loves me and I can't say it back.

"Anyway," I say, circling back to the subject at hand. "I'll tell him soon. Promise."

"You fucking better," Lenix shoots back as she takes another sip of her hot drink.

I settle into my seat, at a loss for words because she's right. I have no more excuses.

Chapter 55

Sunny

Byzantine's car winds around the curve when the familiar inlet appears. The small secluded beach he brought me to all those months ago. This time I'm the one who asked for him to bring me here. He looked at me like he was remembering exactly what he did to me on that beach. Then he fucked me right there on the kitchen counter while the coffee was still brewing before agreeing to drive us up here.

Win-win in my opinion.

There's not a cloud in sight as I look up to the blue sky while Byzantine opens my car door and I jump out, eager to spend the afternoon doing absolutely nothing. I throw my arms around his neck, my lips landing on his as I lick my way inside his mouth and he groans into me. His hands trail under my loose top, his fingers grazing up my spine and I shiver. I pull away with a smile and the wide grin he offers back almost knocks the breath out of me.

I follow behind him down the small beaten path and help him set up the blanket and chairs. Stripping down to my bikini as soon as we're done, I settle into one of the chairs and let out a small pleased sigh, my eyes falling closed.

Things have been easy lately between Byzantine and I. It's scary and I'm constantly waiting for the other shoe to drop. Like it's impossible for my life to be going this good and something is bound to happen.

Thank fuck for therapy.

Although, begrudgingly, I'm spending most of my time talking about my mommy issues. It's super fun. And not at all annoying. But I guess it's working, even if I still have a hard time admitting it out loud.

After an hour of dozing in and out of sleep while Byzantine reads beside me, I peel myself off the chair and stand up.

"I'm going in, come with?"

He gazes up at me, one of his eyes closed trying to shield himself from the sun.

"Always."

I lean down to where he's still sitting and give him a slow kiss, tasting the sun-soaked salt on his lips.

He follows me into the surf and we stay near the shore, just deep enough for our bodies to cool off. I lean back and dip my head into the water, my hair sticking to my neck and shoulders. Byzantine finds my hips and I wrap my legs around his, his lop-sided smile bright as he looks at me.

I notice the sun has brought out a few freckles on his face, even a few on his lips and I catch his mouth with my own. His lips taste like the sea and I want to lose myself in them. Pulling away, he buries his face in the crook of my shoulder.

"My beautiful windflower," he whispers slowly into my neck and his voice sends shivers down my arms as the waves rock us gently this way and that. It's so quiet here and my heart soars, laying witness to all of it.

Then it hits me.

The feeling of déjà vu so intense, tears spring to my eyes. This is the moment I saw all those weeks ago. That simple moment in time where I felt...happy.

"I love you," I say softly.

It's suddenly hard to swallow, my tongue still echoing the shape of the words I just uttered out loud. I spoke them so low I'm half convinced the sound of the waves dragged the words away from Byzantine's ear. But then his whole body stills under me and I know he heard me. My heart sinks, scared and hopeful and terrified.

Utterly and painfully in love.

Byzantine's hand moves up my neck and cradles the back of my head as his green eyes find mine. I could spend the rest of my life trying to explain what I see in his gaze at that very moment.

Relief. Devotion. Adoration.

"Sunny..." he says, staring into me with so much depth—searching, seeking and I let him. I let him reach inside and find peace in knowing that my soul is his to keep. It's always been his. "Say it again."

He pulls me even tighter into him, our skin slippery against one another, the water cooling our heated skin as I beam back at him.

"I love you Byzantine. I fucking love you okay?" I say while giggling.

His smile is so bright and wide that he's almost glowing and I suddenly wish I had said it sooner just to watch him like this.

"There's no backing out now," he declares and I giggle into another kiss, barely recognizing the person whose laugh seems so carefree.

I can't say I've ever met this version of myself. But by the way Byzantine looks at me, he recognizes this Sunny. As if he's been waiting all this time for her. But I was too busy romanticizing melancholy to notice I could even become her.

The familiar was always loneliness. Chaos. Even if it hurt, it was comfortable. It's what I knew.

But now I'm at the edge of another cliff. On the precipice of something so much better. A rebirth instead of a death. I don't know what's ahead of me. But somehow the unknown feels familiar too. Like a piece of me always knew I would be led to this very moment.

Happy, safe and alive.

EPILOGUE

Sunny

It's my 30th birthday today.

A milestone I never thought I'd hit, let alone be excited about. Healing is...interesting. And also not at all linear. A lesson that took me a long time to learn.

Happiness doesn't mean happy all the time. Bad days find you no matter what, it's part of being human.

And boy am I human.

Those bad days used to scare me. It always felt like I was falling back into the familiar haunts of depression. But those were just fears. I had to remind myself that having a bad day was normal and that it would pass. And it always would.

Byzantine and Lenix's steady presence through it all also helped me in ways I can't even define.

The concept of happiness itself is also a funny thing. The more I heal the more I reach new heights of this effervescent feeling, and just bask in wonder that some people have been feeling like this their entire life. While I was just surviving.

And finally, there was the sudden realization that I didn't actually know what I wanted to do with my life. I never planned ahead. Never thought I would make it this far. I was left bewildered, feeling lost when I realized how many of my peers actually had their shit together.

What did I even want to do with my life?

A million dollar question that stumped me for at least a solid year while I continued to work at Sammies alongside Lenix. Although Byzantine was relentless about telling me I didn't need to work. But I wanted to. The routine centered me. And what else was I supposed to do?

Eventually, I did figure it out and of course it involved Lenix. We started our own party planning business last year and have been growing it ever since. She's the face of the company, while I take care of business behind the scenes. I wouldn't want to do this with anyone else but her.

"Hiya babes," Lenix says, smiling wide as she walks into the kitchen, heading towards me as I grin back at her.

Byzantine had wanted to move in together immediately. But, as always, I needed time. Finally, a year into dating, I conceded and we found a house near Connor. It's nowhere near the size of his but it's still the biggest house I've ever lived in. And it made it all the more special that I shared it with Byzantine.

"Happy birthday my love. I'm so proud of you," Lenix says, circling me into a long hug. My throat grows thick as I blink back the emotion she brought up with just those five simple words.

"Thanks Len, I'm so happy you're here," I reply, hugging her even harder.

"Of course, babes"

When we finally let go, she glances around.

"So where's your other half?"

"Out back with the guys."

Lenix's face turns sour. "Oh," she sneers.

Connor and Lenix's weird little friendship didn't last long. Almost overnight they went from fun and flirty to ice cold.

They both swear nothing happened and Byzantine doesn't care enough to hound Connor about it. As for me, I've kept so many secrets from Lenix over the years, that she's allowed hers even if I'm dying of curiosity.

The animosity comes mostly from her, she can barely stand being in the same room as him. As for Connor, he simply pretends nothing's the matter.

"Lenix," I sigh. "Don't start, you knew he'd be here."

"I know," she huffs, flipping her long black hair off her shoulder. "Doesn't mean I have to like it." But then she turns to me and smiles. "Besides, today isn't about me now is it?" she says as she kisses my cheek and strolls out the back door while I follow her out.

I watch as Connor notices Lenix and I glare at him from behind her shoulder, warning him to behave—or else. He just grins and turns his attention back to Bastian.

Byzantine watches as I walk up to him, a slight curl to his lips, and my stomach flips even now. My love for him has only grown exponentially over the years, if that's even possible.

His throat bobs and my eyes fall to his neck. You can barely see the scar anymore. It's now replaced by a large hawk tattoo, its wings open and spanning the entirety of his neck. As if he could get any sexier.

"How are you feeling, little sun?" he asks, wrapping his arms around my waist and pulling me into a heated kiss.

"Better now," I answer, a little breathless.

"Need a quick bathroom break?" he murmurs in my ear as his hand grabs a handful of my ass.

I laugh and nip at his bottom lip. "Behave. We have company you weirdo," I tease, pulling myself out of his embrace and towards the patio table where the rest of the group is sitting. Byzantine follows me over, his hand still firmly holding onto my ass.

Bastian sits between Connor and Lenix, looking slightly uncomfortable. The conversation has died out since both guilty parties are glued to their phones, pretending the other one doesn't exist. Lenix brightens up as soon as Byzantine and I sit down, looking desperate for someone to talk to who isn't Bastian. The guy barely ever makes an effort even with us.

My heart squeezes at the sight of the faces sitting around the table. I know we're far from perfect—and most likely a little dysfunctional—but these four have become my family. The people I can depend on. The people I've come to love the most. And with it, my everlasting need to run away or escape disappeared.

I never thought I'd feel like this again after losing River. And a peaceful part of me knows she's here with us now. Rooting for me as I grow into the life I was always meant to live. She was right.

I was always meant to be *here*.

Coming Soon

Lenix and Connor's story is next!

If you don't want to miss out on any announcements make sure to follow me on social media.

You can also join my newsletter to receive updates, teasers, giveaways and special deals.

ACKNOWLEDGMENTS

First, I would like to thank every single one of you who've read this book. I don't think I'll ever be able to convey how much this means to me and how much this amazing community has changed my life for the better. So, a million times—thank you.

Secondly, I would like to thank my husband, Aldo. Without your unwavering support and sacrifice as well as your belief in my own big bold dreams, this book would literally not exist. I wouldn't be where I am in life without you, and I will forever be eternally grateful—love you Taco Taquito.

Thank you to my sister Joëlle, the dedication was always meant to be yours because nothing I've proudly accomplished in my life hasn't been influenced in some way or other by your mentorship, guidance and unconditional love. I am so incredibly lucky and blessed to have you as a sister.

Thank you to my awesome alpha readers, Natalie, Breanna and Elissa. You were there at the very beginning when I needed people who believed in this story as much as me so thank you, thank you, thank you. And a special extra thank you to Elissa, for taking the time to answer all my questions these past months with such patience and even made that amazing publishing document to help me navigate the ins and outs, you have no idea how touched I was by that, so thank you!

Thank you to my beta readers, Mallory, Jessa, Leigh, Summer, Isabella and Lucy. Ya'll made this book what it is today and as much as those were probably some of the most stressful weeks of my life, I literally wouldn't have it any other way. I am so so so grateful for everyone's feedback and suggestions. The biggest hugs all around.

Special thanks to Hailey, who technically was a beta reader for Was I Ever Here but was also SO MUCH MORE. Thank you for bullying me into becoming a better writer (lmao) and letting me VM you on a daily basis with every thought and question that popped into my head. Your help through this has been invaluable and I still can't believe how lucky I've been to have people like you helping me along the way. So thank you from the bottom of my heart.

Thank you to my editor, Louise. You've been such an amazing help, and thank you for just rolling with the punches like when I surprised you with an entirely new third act mid-editing. You're the best!

Last but not least, thank you to my cover designer, Mallory. You quite literally saved my ass and came up with the best book cover a girlie could ask for. It felt like you were in my head. I can't thank you enough for stepping up at the last minute like that. You rock fellow Leo!

About The Author

Naomi Loud is an author of angsty dark romance. While her first love are words; spirituality and magic are the lenses through which she experiences the world and this heavily influences her writing. She lives in Montreal, Canada with her husband and three cats but secretly wishes she could live underwater.

Made in the USA
Monee, IL
28 July 2024